Angel Time

Angel Time

THE SONGS OF THE SERAPHIM

A novel

Anne Rice

ALFRED A. KNOPF
New York • Toronto
2009

This Is a Borzoi Book
Published by Alfred A. Knopf
and Alfred A. Knopf Canada

Copyright © 2009 by Anne O'Brien Rice
All rights reserved. Published in the United States by Alfred A. Knopf,
a division of Random House, Inc., New York, and
in Canada by Alfred A. Knopf Canada, a division of Random House of
Canada Limited, Toronto.
www.aaknopf.com   www.randomhouse.ca

Knopf, Borzoi Books, and the colophon are registered trademarks
of Random House, Inc.
Knopf Canada and colophon are registered trademarks.

Library of Congress Cataloging-in-Publication Data
Rice, Anne, [date]
Angel time : a novel / by Anne Rice. —1st ed.
p.   cm. —(The songs of the seraphim ; 1)
"This is a Borzoi book."
ISBN 978-1-4000-4353-8 (alk. paper)
1. Angels—Fiction.   2. Assassins—Fiction. I. Title.
PS3568.I265A84 2009
813'.54—dc22   2009015470

Library and Archives Canada Cataloguing in Publication
Rice, Anne
Angel time / Anne Rice.
(The songs of the seraphim)
ISBN 978-0-676-97808-7
I. Title.   II. Series: Rice, Anne. Songs of the seraphim.
PS3568.I22A84 2009   813'.54   C2009-902612-0

Manufactured in the United States of America
First Edition

This novel is dedicated to

Christopher Rice, Karen O'Brien, Sue Tebbe,

and

Becket Ghioto

and to the memory of my sister

Alice O'Brien Borchardt

Take heed that ye despise not one of these little ones;
for I say unto you,
That in heaven their angels do always behold
the face of my Father which is in heaven.

—Matthew 18:10
King James Version

Likewise, I say unto you,
there is joy in the presence of the angels
of God over one sinner that repenteth.

—Luke 15:10
King James Version

For he shall give his angels charge over thee,
to keep thee in all thy ways.

They shall bear thee up in their hands,
lest thou dash thy foot against a stone.

—Psalm 91:11–12
King James Version

Angel Time

Shades of Despair

THERE WERE OMENS FROM THE BEGINNING.

First off, I didn't want to do a job at the Mission Inn. Anywhere in the country, I would have been willing, but not the Mission Inn. And in the bridal suite, that very room, my room. Bad luck and beyond, I thought to myself.

Of course my boss, The Right Man, had no way of knowing when he gave me this assignment that the Mission Inn was where I went when I didn't want to be Lucky the Fox, when I didn't want to be his assassin.

The Mission Inn was part of that very small world in which I wore no disguise. I was simply me when I went there, six foot four, short blond hair, gray eyes—a person who looked like so many other people that he didn't look like any special person at all. I didn't even bother to wear braces to disguise my voice when I went there. I didn't even bother with the de rigueur sunglasses that shielded my identity in every other place, except the apartment and neighborhood where I lived.

I was just who I am when I went there, though who I am was nobody except the man who wore all those elaborate disguises when he did what he was told to do by The Right Man.

So the Mission Inn was mine, cipher that I was, and so was

the bridal suite, called the Amistad Suite, under the dome. And now I was being told to systematically pollute it. Not for anyone else but myself, of course. I would never have done anything to harm the Mission Inn.

A giant confection and confabulation of a building in Riverside, California, it was where I often took refuge, an extravagant and engulfing place sprawling over two city blocks, and where I could pretend, for a day or two or three, that I wasn't wanted by the FBI, Interpol, or The Right Man, a place where I could lose myself and my conscience.

Europe had long ago become unsafe for me, due to the increased security at every checkpoint, and the fact that the law enforcement agencies that dreamed of trapping me had decided I was behind every single unsolved murder they had on the books.

If I wanted the atmosphere I'd loved so much in Siena or Assisi, or Vienna or Prague and all the other places I could no longer visit, I sought out the Mission Inn. It couldn't be all those places, no. Yet it gave me a unique haven and sent me back out into my sterile world a renewed spirit.

It wasn't the only place where I wasn't anybody at all, but it was the best place, and the place to which I went the most.

The Mission Inn was not far from where I "lived," if one could call it that. And I went there on impulse generally, and at any time that they could give me my suite. I liked the other rooms all right, especially the Innkeeper's Suite, but I was patient in waiting for the Amistad. And sometimes they called me on one of the many special cell phones I carried, to let me know the suite could be mine.

Sometimes I stayed as long as a week in the Mission Inn. I'd bring my lute with me, and maybe play it a little. And I always had a stack of books to read, almost always history, books on medieval times or the Dark Ages, or the Renaissance, or

Ancient Rome. I'd read for hours in the Amistad, feeling uncommonly safe and secure.

There were special places I went from the Inn.

Often, undisguised, I drove over to nearby Costa Mesa to hear the Pacific Symphony. I liked it, the contrast, moving from the stucco arches and rusted bells of the Inn to the immense Plexiglas miracle of the Segerstrom Concert Hall, with the pretty Cafe Rouge on the first floor.

Behind those high clear undulating windows, the restaurant appeared to float in space. I felt, when I dined in it, that I was indeed floating in space, and in time, detached from all things ugly and evil, and sweetly alone.

I had just recently heard Stravinsky's *Rite of Spring* in that concert hall. Loved it. Loved the pounding madness of it. It had brought back a memory of the very first time I'd ever heard it, ten years before—on the night when I'd met The Right Man. It had made me think of my own life, and all that had happened since then, as I'd drifted through the world waiting for those cell phone calls that always meant somebody was marked, and I had to get him.

I never killed women, but that's not to say that I hadn't before I became The Right Man's vassal or serf, or knight, depending on how one chose to view it. He called me his knight. I thought of it in far more sinister terms, and nothing during these ten years had ever accustomed me to my function.

Often I even drove from the Mission Inn to the Mission of San Juan Capistrano, south and closer to the coast, another secret place, where I felt unknown and sometimes even happy.

Now the Mission of San Juan Capistrano is a real mission. The Mission Inn is not. The Mission Inn is a tribute to the architecture and heritage of the Missions. But San Juan Capistrano is the real thing.

At Capistrano, I roamed the immense square garden, the

open cloisters, and visited the narrow dim Serra Chapel—the oldest consecrated Catholic chapel in the state of California.

I loved the chapel. I loved that it was the only known sanctuary on the whole coast in which Blessed Junípero Serra, the great Franciscan, had actually said Mass. He might have said Mass in many another Mission chapel. In fact surely he had. But this was the only one about which everyone was certain.

There had been times in the past when I'd driven north to visit the Mission at Carmel, and look into the little cell there that they'd re-created and ascribed to Junípero Serra, and meditated on the simplicity of it: the chair, the narrow bed, the cross on the wall. All a saint needed.

And then there was San Juan Bautista, too, with its refectory and museum—and all the other Missions that had been so painstakingly restored.

I'd wanted to be a priest for a while when I was a boy, a Dominican, in fact, and the Dominicans and the Franciscans of the California missions were mixed in my mind because they were both mendicant orders. I respected them equally, and there was a part of me that belonged to that old dream.

I still read history books about the Franciscans and the Dominicans. I had an old biography of Thomas Aquinas saved from my school days, full of old notes. Reading history always soothed me. Reading history let me sink into ages safely gone by. Same with the Missions. They were islands not of our time.

It was the Serra Chapel in San Juan Capistrano that I visited most often.

I went there not to remember the devotion I'd known as a boy. That was gone forever. Fact was, I simply wanted the blueprint of the paths that I'd traveled in those early years. Maybe I just wanted to walk the sacred ground, walk through places of pilgrimage and sanctity because I couldn't actually think about them too much.

I liked the beamed ceiling of the Serra Chapel, and its darkly painted walls. I felt calm in the quality of gloom inside it, the glimmer of the gold retablo at the far end of it—the golden framework that was behind the altar and fitted with statues and saints.

I loved the red sanctuary light burning to the left of the tabernacle. Sometimes I knelt right up there before the altar on one of the prie-dieux obviously intended for a bride and a groom.

Of course the golden retablo, or reredos, as it's often called, hadn't been there in the days of the early Franciscans. It had come later, during the restoration, but the chapel itself seemed to me to be very real. The Blessed Sacrament was in it. And the Blessed Sacrament, no matter what I believed, meant "real."

How can I explain this?

I always knelt in the semidarkness for a very long time, and I'd always light a candle before I left, though for whom or what I couldn't have said. Maybe I whispered, "This is in memory of you, Jacob, and you, Emily." But it wasn't a prayer. I didn't believe in prayer any more than I believed in actual memory.

I craved rituals and monuments, and maps of meaning. I craved history in book and building and paint—and I *believed* in danger, and I *believed* in killing people whenever and wherever I was instructed to do it by my boss, whom in my heart of hearts I called simply The Right Man.

Last time I'd been to the Mission—scarcely a month ago— I'd spent an unusually long time walking about the enormous garden.

Never have I seen so many kinds of flowers in one place. There were modern roses, exquisitely shaped, and older ones, open like camellias, there were trumpet flower vines, and morning glory, lantana, and the biggest bushes of blue plumbago that I'd ever seen in my life. There were sunflowers and orange trees, and daisies, and you could walk right through the heart of this on any of the many broad and comfortable newly paved paths.

I'd taken my time in the enclosing cloisters, loving the ancient and uneven stone floors. I'd enjoyed looking out at the world from under the arches. Round arches had always filled me with a sense of peace. Round arches defined the Mission, and round arches defined the Mission Inn.

It gave me special pleasure at Capistrano that the layout of the Mission was an ancient monastic design to be found in monasteries all over the world, and that Thomas Aquinas, my saintly hero when I was a boy, had probably spent many an hour roaming just such a square with its arches and its neatly laid out paths, and its inevitable flowers.

Throughout history monks had laid out this plan again and again as if the very bricks and mortar could somehow stave off an evil world, and keep them and the books they wrote safe forever.

I stood for a long time in the hulking shell of the great ruined church of Capistrano.

An earthquake in 1812 had destroyed it, and what remained was a high gaping and roofless sanctuary of empty niches and daunting size. I'd stared at the random chunks of brick and cement wall scattered here and there, as if they had some meaning for me, some meaning, like the music of *The Rite of Spring,* something to do with my own wretched wreck of a life.

I was a man shaken by an earthquake, a man paralyzed by dissonance. I knew that much. I thought about that all the time, though I tried to detach it from any continuity. I tried to accept what seemed my fate. But if you don't believe in fate, well, that is not easy.

On my most recent visit, I'd been talking to God in the Serra Chapel, and telling Him how much I hated Him that He didn't exist. I'd told Him how vicious it was, the illusion that He existed, how unfair it was to do that to mortal men, and especially to children, and how I detested Him for it.

I know, I know, this doesn't make sense. I did a lot of things that didn't make sense. Being an assassin and nothing else didn't make sense. And that was probably why I was circling these same places more and more often, free of my many disguises.

I knew I read history books all the time as though I believed a God had acted in history more than once to save us from ourselves, but I didn't believe this at all, and my mind was full of random facts about many an age and many a famous personage. Why would a killer do that?

One can't be a killer every moment of one's life. Some humanity is going to show itself now and then, some hunger for normality, no matter what you do.

And so I had my history books, and the visits to these few places that took me to the times of which I read with such numb enthusiasm, filling my mind with narrative so that it wouldn't be empty and turn in on itself.

And I had to shake my fist at God for the meaninglessness of it all. And to me, it felt good. He didn't really exist, but I could have Him that way, in anger, and I'd liked those moments of conversation with the illusions that had once meant so much, and now only inspired rage.

Maybe when you're brought up Catholic, you hold to rituals all your life. You live in a theater of the mind because you can't get out of it. You're gripped all your life by a span of two thousand years because you grew up being conscious of belonging to that span.

Most Americans think the world was created the day they were born, but Catholics take it back to Bethlehem and beyond, and so do Jews, even the most secular of them, remembering the Exodus, and the promises to Abraham before that. Never ever did I look at the nighttime stars or the sands of a beach without thinking of God's promises to Abraham about his progeny, and no matter what else I did or didn't believe, Abraham was the father of the tribe to which I still belonged through no fault or virtue of my own.

I will multiply thy seed as the stars of the heaven, and as the sand which is upon the sea shore.

So that's how we go on acting dramas in our theater of the mind even when we don't believe anymore in the audience or the director or the play.

I'd laughed thinking about that, as I'd meditated in the Serra Chapel, laughed out loud like a crazy man as I knelt there, murmuring in the sweet and delicious gloom and shaking my head.

What had maddened me on that last visit was that it was just past ten years to the day that I'd been working for The Right Man.

The Right Man had remembered the anniversary, talking about anniversaries for the first time ever and presenting me with a huge monetary gift that had already been wired to the bank account in Switzerland through which I most often received my money.

He'd said to me over the phone the evening before, "If I knew anything about you, Lucky, I'd give you something more than cold cash. All I know is you like to play the lute, and when you were a kid you played it all the time. They told me that, about your playing. If you hadn't loved the lute so much, maybe we never would have met. Realize how long it's been since I've seen you? And I always hope you're going to drop in, and bring your precious lute with you. When you do that, I'll get you to play for me, Lucky. Hell, Lucky, I don't even know where you really live."

Now that was something he brought up all the time, that he didn't know where I lived, because I think he feared, in his heart of hearts, that I didn't trust him, that my work had slowly eroded the love for him which I felt.

But I did trust him. And I did love him. I didn't love anyone in the world but him. I just didn't want anyone to know where I lived.

No place I lived was home, and I changed where I lived often. Nothing traveled with me from home to home, except my lute, and all my books. And of course my few clothes.

In this age of cell phones and the Internet, it was so easy to be untraceable. And so easy to be reached by an intimate voice in a perfect teletronic silence.

"Look, you can reach me anytime, day or night," I'd reminded him. "Doesn't matter where I live. Doesn't matter to me, so why should it matter to you? And someday, maybe I'll send you a recording of me playing the lute. You'll be surprised. I'm still good at it."

He'd chuckled. Okay with him, as long as I always answered the phone.

"Have I ever let you down?" I'd asked.

"No, and I'll never let you down either," he'd replied. "Just wish I could see you more often. Hell, you could be in Paris right now, or Amsterdam."

"I'm not," I'd answered. "You know that. The checkpoints are too hot. I'm in the States as I've been since Nine-Eleven. I'm closer than you think, and I'll come see you one of these days, just not right now, and maybe I'll take you to dinner. We'll sit in a restaurant like human beings. But these days, I'm not up to the meeting. I like being alone."

There had been no assignment on that anniversary, so I was able to stay in the Mission Inn, and I'd driven over to San Juan Capistrano the following morning.

No need at all to tell him I had an apartment in Beverly Hills right now, in a quiet and leafy place, and maybe next year it would be Palm Springs out in the desert. No need to tell him that I didn't bother with disguises in this apartment, either, or in the surrounding neighborhood from which the Mission Inn was only an hour away.

In the past, I'd never gone out without some sort of disguise, and I noted this change in myself with a cold equanimity. I wondered sometimes if they would let me have my books if I ever went to jail.

The Mission Inn in Riverside, California, was my only constant. I'd fly across the country to make the drive to Riverside. The Inn was where I most wanted to be.

The Right Man had gone on talking that evening. "Years ago, I bought you every recording in the world of lute music and the best instrument money can buy. I bought you all those books you wanted. Hell, I pulled some down off these shelves. Are you still reading all the time, Lucky? You know you should have a chance to get more education, Lucky. Maybe I should have looked out for you a little more than I did."

"Boss, you're worrying yourself about nothing. I have more books now than I know what to do with. Twice a month, I drop a box at some library. I'm perfectly fine."

"What about a penthouse somewhere, Lucky? What about some rare books? There must be something I can get for you more than just money. A penthouse would be nice, safe. You're always safe when you're higher up."

"Safe up in the sky?" I'd asked. The fact was my Beverly Hills apartment was a penthouse, but the building was only five stories high. "Penthouses are usually reached by two methods, Boss," I said, "and I don't like being bottled up. No thanks."

I felt secure in my Beverly Hills penthouse and it was walled with books on just about every epoch that had preceded the twentieth century.

I'd known for a long time why I loved history. It was because the historians made it sound so coherent, so purposeful, so complete. They'd take an entire century and impose a meaning on it, a personality, a destiny—and this was, of course, a lie.

But it soothed me in my solitude to read that sort of writing, to think that the fourteenth century was a "distant mirror," to paraphrase a famous title, to believe that we could learn from whole eras as if they had existed with marvelous continuity simply for us.

It was good reading in my apartment. It was good reading at the Mission Inn.

I liked my apartment for more reasons than one. As my undisguised self, I liked to walk in the soft, quiet neighborhood around it, and to stop in the Four Seasons Hotel for breakfast or lunch.

There were times when I checked into the Four Seasons just to be someplace completely different, and I had a favorite suite there with a long granite dining table and a black grand piano. I would play the piano in that suite, and sometimes even sing, with the ghost of the voice I'd once had.

Years ago, I'd thought I'd be singing all my life. It was music that had taken me away from wanting to be a Dominican priest—that and growing up, I suppose, and wanting to be with "girls" and wanting to be a man of the world. But mostly it was the music that had ravaged my twelve-year-old soul, and the total charm of the lute. I think I felt superior to the garage band kids when I played that beautiful lute.

All that was over, and had been over for ten years—the lute was a relic now—and the anniversary had come around and I wasn't telling The Right Man my address.

"What can I get you?" he still pleaded. "You know I was in a rare-book shop the other day, just by chance actually. I was roaming in Manhattan. You know me and roaming. And I saw this beautiful old medieval book."

"Boss, the answer is nothing," I said. And I hung up.

The next day, after that phone call, I'd talked about that to the Non-existent God in the Serra Chapel, in the flicker of the red sanctuary light, and told Him what a monster I was being, a soldier without a war, and a needle sniper without a cause, a singer who never really sang. As if He cared.

And then I'd lit a candle "To the Nothingness" that had become my life. "Here's a candle . . . for me." I think I'd said that. I'm not sure. I know I was talking way too loud by that time because people noticed me. And that surprised me because people seldom notice me at all.

Even my disguises were for the nondescript and the pale.

There was a consistency, though I doubt anyone ever caught on. Grease-slicked black hair, heavy dark glasses, a bill cap, leather pilot's jacket, the usual dragging foot, but never the same foot.

That was plenty enough to make me a man nobody saw. Before I'd ever gone as myself, I'd run three or four disguises by the desk of the Mission Inn, and three or four different names to go with them. It went perfectly fine. When the real Lucky the Fox walked in with the alias Tommy Crane, no one showed a flicker of recognition. I was too good at the disguises. For the agents that hunted me, I was a modus operandi, not a man with a face.

That last time, I'd walked out of the Serra Chapel, angry, and confused, and miserable, and was only comforted by spending the day in the picturesque little town of San Juan Capistrano, and buying a statue of the Virgin in the Mission gift shop before it closed.

It wasn't just an ordinary little Virgin. It was a figure with the Christ Child and the whole made not only with plaster but plastered cloth. It looked dressed and soft, though it wasn't. It was dressed and stiff. And it was sweet. The little Baby Jesus had a lot of character, with His tiny head tilted to one side, and the Virgin herself was just a teardrop face and two hands emerging from the fancy robes of gold and white. I threw the box in my car at the time and didn't give it much of a thought.

Whenever I went to Capistrano, however—and last time had been no exception—I heard Mass in the new Basilica, the grand re-creation of the big church broken to pieces in 1812.

I was very impressed and quieted by the Grand Basilica. It was vast, expensive, Romanesque, and, like so many Romanesque churches, filled with light. Round arches again everywhere. Exquisitely painted walls.

Behind the altar there was another golden retablo, one that made the one in the Serra Chapel look small. This too was ancient and shipped from the Old Country, just as the other had been, and covering the entire back wall of the sanctuary to a momentous height. It was overwhelming in its dazzling gold.

Nobody knew it, but I sent money now and then to the Basilica, though rarely under the same name. I'd buy postal money orders and make up joke names to put on them. The money got there, that was the point.

Four saints had their appropriate niches in the retablo—St. Joseph with his inevitable lily, the great St. Francis of Assisi, Blessed Junípero Serra holding a small model of the mission in his right hand, and then a newcomer as far as I was concerned, Blessed Kateri Tekakwitha, an Indian saint.

But it was the center of the retablo that most completely absorbed me as I sat through Mass. There was the Crucified Christ in high gloss with bloodied hands and feet, and above Him a bearded figure of God the Father who was under the golden rays descending from a white dove. This was the Holy Trinity, actually, though maybe a Protestant wouldn't have known it—with the three figures rendered in literal form.

When you think that only Jesus became Man to save us, well, the figure of God the Father and the Holy Spirit as a dove can be puzzling, and touching. The Son of God, after all, has the body.

Whatever the case, I marveled at it, and enjoyed it. I didn't care whether it was literal or sophisticated, mystical or pedestrian. It was gorgeous, it was gleaming, and it comforted me to see it, even when I was steaming with hate. It comforted me that other people around me were worshipping, that I was somewhere sacred or where people came to be with the sacred. I don't know. I pushed any self-accusations out of my mind and just looked at what was right before me, just the way I do when I'm on the job, and set to take a life.

Maybe when I looked up from the pew at this Crucifix, it was like running into a friend with whom you are angry and saying, "Well, there you are again and I am still in a rage against you."

Underneath the dying Lord was his Blessed Mother, in the form of Our Lady of Guadalupe, whom I'd always admired.

That last visit, I'd spent hours staring at that golden wall.

This wasn't faith. This was art. The art of faith forgotten, the art of faith denied. This was excess, this was egregious and somehow soothing, even if I did keep saying, "I don't believe in you, I'll never forgive you for not being real."

After Mass that last time, I took out the rosary I'd carried since boyhood, and I said it, but I didn't meditate on the old mysteries that meant nothing to me. I merely lost myself in the mantric chant. *Hail Mary, Full of Grace, as if I believe you exist. Now and at the Hour of our Death Amen Like Hell For Them are you ever there?*

Mind you, I was certainly not the only hit man on this planet who went to Mass. But I was one of a very small minority who paid attention, murmuring the responses and sometimes even singing the hymns. Sometimes I even went to Communion, soaked in mortal sin, and defiant. I knelt afterwards with head bowed and I thought: *This is Hell. This is Hell. And Hell will be worse than this.*

There've always been criminals great and small who went to Mass with their families and presided over sacramental occasions. I don't have to tell you about the Italian Mafioso of cinematic legend who goes to his daughter's First Communion. Don't they all?

I had no family. I had no one. I was no one. I went to Mass for myself who was no one. In my files at Interpol and the FBI, they said so: he is no one. No one knows what he looks like, or where he came from, or where he will appear next. They didn't even know if I worked for one man.

As I said, I was a modus operandi to them, and they'd taken years to refine it, listing vaguely disguises poorly glimpsed by video surveillance, never yielding to precise words. Often they detailed the hits with considerable misunderstanding of what had actually taken place. But they did have it almost right: I was nobody. I was a dead man walking around in a live body.

And I did work for only one man, my boss, the one I called, in my heart of hearts, The Right Man. It simply never occurred to me to work for someone else. And nobody else could have sought me out for an assignment, and no one else ever would.

The Right Man might have been the bearded God the Father, of the retablo, and I his bleeding son. The Holy Ghost was the spirit that bound us, because we were bound, that was certain, and I never thought past the commands of The Right Man.

That's blasphemy. So what?

How did I know these things about police files and agency files? My beloved boss always had his connections, and he'd chuckle with me on the phone about the information that came his way.

He knew what I looked like. On the night we met, some ten years back, I'd been myself with him. That he hadn't laid eyes on me in years disturbed him.

But I was always there when he rang, and whenever I dumped the cell phones, I called him with the new numbers. In the beginning, he'd helped me get the phony papers, passports, driver's licenses, and such. But I'd long known how to acquire that sort of material on my own, and how to confuse the people who provided it to me.

The Right Man knew I was loyal. Not a week went by that I didn't call in, whether he called me or not. Sometimes I felt a sudden breathlessness when I heard his voice, just because he was still there, because fate hadn't taken him away from me. After all, if one man is your entire life, your vocation, your quest, well, then, you're going to be afraid of losing him.

"Lucky, I want to sit down with you," he sometimes said. "You know, the way we did that first couple of years. I want to know where you come from." I'd laugh as gently as I could.

"I love the sound of your voice, Boss," I'd say.

"Lucky," he asked me one time, "do you yourself know where you come from?"

That had really made me laugh, but not at him, just at everything.

"You know, Boss," I'd said more than once, "there are questions I'd like to ask you, like who you really are, and who you work for. But I don't ask you, do I?"

"You'd be surprised at the answers," he said. "I told you

once, kid, you're working for The Good Guys." And that's where we left it.

The Good Guys. The good gang or the good organization? How was I to know which? And what did it matter, because I did exactly what he told me to do, so how could I be good?

But I could dream, from time to time, that he was on the good side of things, that government legitimated it, cleaned it up, made me an infantryman, made me okay. That's why I could call him The Right Man, and tell myself, *Well, maybe he is FBI, after all, or maybe he's Interpol working in this country. Maybe we're doing something meaningful.* But in truth, I didn't believe it. I committed murder. I did it for a living. I did it for no reason at all except to go on living. I killed people. I killed them without warning and without an explanation as to why I did it. The Right Man might have been one of The Good Guys, but I certainly was not.

"You're not afraid of me, are you, Boss?" I asked him once. "That I'm just a little bit out of my mind, and someday, I'll bail on you, or come back at you. Because you don't need to be afraid of me, Boss. I'm the last person who'll ever hurt a hair on your head."

"I'm not afraid of you, no, Son," he said. "But I worry about you out there. I worry because you were a kid when I took you up. I worry . . . about how you make it through the night. You're the best I've got, and sometimes it just seems too easy calling you, and your always being there, and things working out perfectly, and me having to say so few words."

"You like to talk, Boss, that's one of your characteristics. I don't. But I'll tell you something. It's not easy. It's thrilling, but it's never easy. And sometimes it takes my breath away."

I don't remember what he'd said to that little confession, except that he'd talked for a long time, saying, among other things, that everybody else who worked for him periodically checked in. He saw them, knew them, visited them.

"It's not going to happen with me, Boss," I'd assured him. "What you hear is what you get."

And now I had to do a job at the Mission Inn.

The call had come last night and woken me up in my Beverly Hills apartment. And I hated it.

CHAPTER TWO

Of Love and Loyalty

As I said before, there never was a real Mission, like San Juan Capistrano, at the hotel in Riverside called the Mission Inn.

It was one man's dream, a giant hotel full of courtyards, arbors, and Mission-style cloisters, with a chapel for weddings and a multitude of charming Gothic elements, including heavy arched wood doors, and statues of St. Francis in niches, and even bell towers, and the oldest-known bell in Christendom. It was a conglomeration of elements that suggested the world of the Missions from one end of California to the other. It was a tribute to them that people found more dizzying and wonderful sometimes than the Missions themselves, fragments that they were. The Mission Inn was also unfailingly lively and warm and inviting, and throbbing with cheerful voices and gaiety and laughter.

From the beginning, I suspect, it was a labyrinth, but it had developed in the hands of new owners so that now it had the conveniences of a top-notch hotel.

Yet you could easily get lost in it, wandering its many verandas, following its innumerable staircases, drifting from patio to patio, or simply trying to find your room.

People create these extravagant habitats because they have vision, love of beauty, hopes, and dreams.

Many an early evening, the Mission Inn swarmed with happy people, brides being photographed on random balconies, families cheerfully wandering the terraces, the many restaurants lighted and filled with lively parties, pianos playing, voices singing, and even a concert, perhaps in the music room. It was dependably festive, and it enfolded me and gave me peace for just a little while.

I had the love of beauty that drove the owners of the place, and a love of excess as well, a love of a vision carried to near divine extremes.

But I had no plans or dreams. I was strictly a messenger, the embodiment of a purpose, *go do this,* not a man at all.

But over and over, the homeless one, the nameless one, the dreamless one, returned to the Mission Inn.

You could say I loved the fact that it was rococo and meaningless. Not only was it a tribute to all the Missions of California, it had set the architectural tone for some of the town. There were bells on the lampposts on the streets around it. There were public buildings done in the same "Mission style." I liked that consciously created continuity. It was all made up, the way I was made up. It was a concoction, the way that I myself was a concoction with the accidental name of Lucky the Fox.

I always felt good when I walked under the arched entrance called the campanario, on account of its many bells. I loved the giant tree ferns and the soaring palm trees, their thin trunks wrapped in twinkling light. I loved the flowerbeds of bright petunias that banked the front walk.

On any given pilgrimage, I spent a good deal of time in the public rooms. I often sought out the vast dark lobby to visit its white marble statue of the Roman boy pulling the thorn from his foot. I was soothed by the shadowy interior. I loved the laughter and gaiety of the families. I sat in one of the big comfortable chairs, breathing the dust, and watching people. I loved the friendliness that the place seemed to induce.

I never failed to venture into the Mission Inn restaurant for lunch. The piazza was beautiful, with its multistory walls of rounded windows and bowed terraces, and I propped up the *New York Times* to read, as I ate under the shade of the dozens of overlapping red umbrellas.

But the interior of the restaurant was no less enticing, with its lower walls of bright blue tile, and the beige arches above artfully painted with twining green vines. The scored ceiling was painted like a blue sky with clouds and even tiny birds. Rounded interior doors with many mullions were paneled in mirrors, and similar doors to the piazza brought the sunshine inside. The pleasing chatter of others was like the sound of water gurgling from a fountain. Nice.

I wandered the dark corridors and the different areas of decorative and dusty carpet.

I stopped in the *atrio* before the St. Francis chapel, my eyes moving over the hugely ornate frame of the doorway, a poured-concrete masterpiece of Churrigueresque style. It warmed my heart to glimpse the inevitable lavish and seemingly eternal wedding preparations, with banquets laid out on draped tables, in silver chafing dishes, and eager people darting about.

I went up to the topmost veranda and, resting against the green iron railing, I looked down upon the restaurant piazza and across it at the immense Nuremberg clock. I often waited for the clock to chime as it does at every quarter of an hour. I wanted to see the large figures in the alcove beneath it slowly progress.

There's something powerful to me about all clocks. When I killed someone, I stopped their clock. And what do clocks do but measure the time we have to make something of ourselves, to discover something inside us that we didn't know was there?

I thought of *Hamlet*'s Ghost often when I killed people. I thought of his tragic complaint to his son.

> *Cut off even in the blossoms of my sin . . .*
> *No reckoning made, but sent to my account*
> *With all my imperfections on my head.*

I thought of things like that whenever I meditated on life and death, or on clocks. There wasn't anything about the Mission Inn—not the music room or the Chinese room, or the smallest nook or cranny—that I didn't perfectly love.

Maybe I cherished it because it was for all its clocks and bells timeless, or so skillfully made up of things from different times that it could drive an orderly person mad.

As for the Amistad Suite, the bridal suite, I chose it for the domed ceiling, painted with an ashen landscape and doves ascending through a bland mist to a blue sky, at the very top of which was an octagonal cupola with stained-glass windows. The rounded arch was even represented in this room—between the dining room and the bedroom, and in the shape of the heavy double doors to the veranda beyond. The three high windows half embracing the bed were arched as well.

The bedroom had a massive gray stone fireplace, cold and empty and black inside, but nevertheless a beautiful frame for imagined flames. I have a fine imagination. That's why I'm such a good killer. I think of so many ways to get it done, and to get away with it.

Heavy draperies covered the three floor-length windows, surrounding the huge half tester antique bed. It had a high heavily carved dark wood headboard, and low thick knobbed posts at the foot. The bed always made me think of New Orleans, of course.

New Orleans was home once, home for the boy in me who died there. And that boy never had the luxury of sleeping in a half tester bed.

> *That was in another country,*
> *And besides, the wench is dead.*

I hadn't been back to New Orleans since I became Lucky the Fox, and I figured I never would go back, and so I'd never sleep in one of its antique tester beds.

New Orleans was where the important bodies were buried, not those of the men I'd dispatched for The Right Man.

When I thought of the important bodies, I thought of my parents and my little brother Jacob and my little sister Emily, all dead back there, and I hadn't the slightest idea where any of those bodies actually might have been placed.

I remembered some talk about a plot in old St. Joseph's Cemetery out Washington Avenue, in the dangerous neighborhood. My grandmother was buried back there. But I never went to the place that I could recall. My father they must have buried near the prison where he was knifed.

My father was a filthy cop, a filthy husband, a filthy father. He got killed two months into his lifetime sentence. No. I didn't know where to find a grave on which I might lay flowers for any of them, and if I did, it wouldn't have been on his grave.

Okay. So you can imagine what it was like, when The Right Man told me the hit had to be in the Mission Inn.

Murder Most Foul was to pollute my consolation, my diversion, my gently guided delirium, my safe place. Maybe it was New Orleans holding me in its arms, just because it was old and creaky and nonsensical and deliberately and accidentally picturesque.

Give me its long vine-shaded arbors, its countless Tuscan pots overflowing with lavender geraniums and orange trees, its long red-tiled porches. Give me its endless iron railings with their pattern of cross and bell. Give me its many fountains, its small gray stone statues of angels above the doorways of the suites, even its empty niches and its whimsical bell towers. Give me the flying buttresses surrounding the three windows of that topmost corner room.

And give me the bells that did ring all the time there. Give me the view from the windows of the distant mountains sometimes visibly covered in gleaming snow.

And give me the dark comfortable steak house with the best meals outside of New York.

Well, it could have been a hit in the Mission of San Juan Capistrano—that might have been worse—but even that wasn't the place where I often lay down to sleep in peace.

The Right Man always spoke to me lovingly and I suppose that's the way I spoke to him.

He said, "The man's Swiss, a banker, money launderer, in thick with the Russians, you wouldn't believe the rackets these guys are into, and it has to be done in his hotel room."

And that was . . . my room.

I gave away nothing.

But without making a sound I said an oath, I said a prayer. *God, help me. Not that place.*

To put it in the simplest terms, a bad feeling came over me, a feeling of falling.

The dumbest prayer of my old repertoire came back to me, the one that made me the angriest:

> *Angel of God, my guardian dear,*
> *to whom God's love commits me here,*

ever this day be at my side,
to light and guard, to rule and guide.

I felt weak listening to The Right Man. I felt fatal. No matter. Turn that into hurt. Turn that into pressure, and you'll be just fine.

After all, I reminded myself, one of your chief assets is you think the world would be better if you died. A good thing for any and every single person I was yet to destroy.

What makes people like me continue day after day? What does Dostoyevsky say about it when the Grand Inquisitor is speaking? *Without a stable conception of the object of life, man would not consent to go on living.*

Like Hell. But then we all know that the Grand Inquisitor is evil and wrong.

People go on under unbearable circumstances, as I well knew.

"This one has to look like a heart attack," said The Boss. "No message—just a little subtraction. So leave the cell phones and the laptops behind. Leave everything as you find it, except be sure the man's dead. Of course the woman can't see you. Blow her away and you blow the cover. The woman's an expensive tramp."

"What's he doing with her in the bridal suite?" I asked. Because that is what the Amistad Suite was, the bridal suite.

"She wants to get married. She tried it in Vegas, failed, now she's pushing for it in the chapel in this crazy place where people go to get married. It's some kind of a landmark, this place. You won't have any trouble finding it or finding the bridal suite. The bridal suite's built under a tiled dome. You can spot it from the street before you take your look around. You know what to do."

You know what to do.

That meant the disguise, the method of approach, the

choice of poison for the syringe, and the departure, under the same circumstances as I'd made my way inside.

"This is what I know already," The Boss said. "The man stays in; the woman shops. That was the Vegas pattern anyway. She leaves about ten o'clock in the morning after screaming at him for an hour and a half. Maybe she lunches. Maybe she drinks, but you can't count on it. Get in as soon as she leaves the room. He'll have two computers going, and maybe even two cell phones. You do it right. Remember. Heart attack. Won't matter if all the equipment goes dead."

"I could download the cells and the computers," I said. I was proud of my abilities at all that, or at least of picking up every scrap of decodable equipment. It had been my calling card with The Right Man ten years ago, that, and a dazzling measure of ruthlessness. But I'd been eighteen years old then. I hadn't really understood how perfectly ruthless I was.

Now I lived with it.

"Too easy for someone to pick up on it," he said. "Then they know it was a hit. I can't have that. Leave it, Lucky. Do as I say. This is a banker. You don't pull this off, and he gets on a plane to Zurich, and we're in a fix."

I didn't say anything.

Sometimes we left a message with these things, and other times we came and went like a cat in an alley, and that was the way this would be.

Perhaps it was a blessing, I thought. There would be no talk of murder among the employees of the one place where I felt solace, and just a little glad to be aboveground.

He laughed his usual laugh. "Well? Aren't you going to ask me?"

And I gave my usual answer. "No."

He was referring to the fact that I didn't care why he wanted me to kill this particular man. I didn't care who the man was. I didn't care to know his name.

What I cared about was that *he* wanted it done.

But he always pushed with that question, and I always pushed back with the no. Russians, bankers, money laundering—that was a common framework, but not a motive. It was a game we'd been playing since the first night I'd met him, or been sold to him, or offered to him, however one might describe that remarkable turn of events.

"No bodyguards, no assistants," he said now. "He's on his own. Even if there is somebody, you know how to handle it. You know what to do."

"Already thinking about it. Worry not."

He clicked off without saying goodbye.

I loathed all this. It felt wrong. Don't laugh. I'm not saying that every other murder I'd ever committed had felt entirely right. I'm saying that something here was dangerous to my equilibrium, and therefore to what might go down.

What if I'd never be able to go back and sleep under that dome again in peace? In fact, that is probably just what would happen. The pale-eyed young man who sometimes carried his lute with him would never appear there again, handing out twenty-dollar tips and smiling so warmly at everyone.

Because another brand of that same young man, heavily disguised, had put murder at the heart of the entire dream.

It seemed foolish suddenly that I'd dared to be myself there, that I'd played the lute softly under that domed ceiling, that I'd lain back on the bed and stared at the upholstered half tester, that I'd gazed up for an hour or more into that blue sky dome.

After all the lute itself was a link to the boy who'd vanished out of New Orleans, and what if some good-hearted cousin was still looking? I had had good-hearted cousins, and I had loved them. And lute players are rare.

Maybe it was time to detonate a bomb before someone else did.

No mistake, no.

It had been worth it to play the lute in that room, to strum it softly and go over the melodies I used to love.

How many people know what a lute is, or what it sounds like? Maybe they've seen lutes in Renaissance paintings, and don't even know such things exist just now. I didn't care. I liked to play it so much in the Amistad Suite, I didn't care if the room service waiters heard or saw me. I liked that very much, the way I liked playing the black piano in the suite at the Four Seasons in Beverly Hills. I don't think I ever played a note in my own apartment. Don't know why. I'd stare at the lute and think of Christmas angels with lutes on richly colored Christmas cards. I'd think of angels hanging from the branches of Christmas trees.

Angel of God, my guardian dear . . .

One time, Hell, maybe just two months back at the Mission Inn, I'd made a melody to that old prayer, very Renaissance, very haunting. Only I was the only one who was haunted.

So now I had to think of a disguise to fool people who had actually seen me many more times than once, and The Boss said this had to be done now. After all, the girl might get him to marry her tomorrow. The Mission did have that brand of charm.

CHAPTER THREE

Mortal Sin and Mortal Mystery

I KEPT A GARAGE IN LOS ANGELES, SIMILAR TO THE one I kept in New York: four panel trucks, one advertising a plumbing company, another a florist, one painted white with a red light on top of it so that it looked like a special ambulance, and one that was simply a beat-up handyman's set of wheels, with rusted junk in the back. These vehicles were as transparent to the public as Wonder Woman's famous invisible plane. A beat-up sedan attracted more attention. And I always drove just a little too fast, with my window rolled down and my bare arm showing, and nobody saw me at all. Sometimes I smoked, just enough to reek of it.

I used the florist truck this time. No doubt it was the very best thing, and especially with a hotel in which tourists and guests mingle freely, and wander freely, in and out and at random and nobody ever asks you where you're headed, or whether or not you've got a room key.

What works in all hotels and hospitals is a resolute attitude, a steady momentum. It would certainly work at the Mission Inn.

No one sees a dark shaggy-headed man with a florist logo stitched to his green shirt pocket, with a soiled canvas bag over one shoulder, carrying only a modest bouquet of lilies in a foil-wrapped earthen pot, and no one cares that he goes in with a quick nod to the doormen, if they even bother to look up. Add to the wig a pair of thick-rimmed glasses that completely distorted the habitual expression on my face. The bite plate between my teeth would give me the perfect lisp.

The garden gloves I wore hid the plastic gloves that were more important. The canvas sack over my shoulder smelled like peat moss. I held the pot of lilies as if it might break. I walked with a weak left knee and a regular swing to my head, something somebody might remember when they didn't remember anything else. I put out a cigarette in a flowerbed on the main path. Someone might make note of that.

I had two syringes for the job, but only one was needed. There was a small gun strapped to my ankle under my trouser, though I dreaded the thought of having to use it, and for what it was worth, I had, in the lapel of my starched company shirt, a long thin blade of plastic, stiff and sharp enough to cut a man's throat, or both his eyes.

The plastic was the weapon I could use most easily when I encountered difficulty, but I never had. I dreaded the blood. I also dreaded the cruelty of it. I detested cruelty in any form whatsoever. I liked things to be perfect. In the files, they call me the Perfectionist, the Invisible Man, and the Thief in the Night.

I counted entirely on the syringe to do this job, obviously, because the heart attack was the desired effect.

It was an over-the-counter syringe of the kind used by diabetics, with a micro needle that some men couldn't even feel. And the poison had a huge fast-acting chaser of another over-the-counter drug that would sink the man almost immediately so that he'd be in a coma when the poison reached his heart. All trace of both drugs would clear his bloodstream in less than an hour. No autopsy would reveal a thing.

Just about every chemical combination I used could be bought in any drugstore nationwide. It's astonishing what you can learn about poison if you really want to hurt people and you do not care what becomes of you, or whether or not you have any heart or soul left. I had at least twenty poisons at my disposal. I bought drugs in suburban drugstores in small amounts. I used the leaf of the oleander now and then, and oleander grew everywhere in California. I knew how to use the poison of the castor bean.

It went as planned.

I was there by nine-thirty. Black hair, black-rimmed glasses. Smell of cigarettes on the soiled gloves.

I took the creaky little elevator up to the top floor along with two people who never glanced at me once, and followed the snaking corridors out into the air and past the herb garden till I came to the green railing over the courtyard. I leaned on the railing and observed the clock.

All this was mine. To the left was the long red-tiled veranda, the long rectangular fountain, with its bubbling urn-shaped jets, with the room at the end, and the iron table and chairs beneath the green umbrella right across from the double doors.

Damn. How I loved to sit in the sun, in the cool California breeze, at that very table. I felt an intense temptation to scrap this job, and sit at that table until my heart stopped racing, and to simply walk off, leaving the pot of flowers there for anyone who might care.

I moved sluggishly up and down the veranda, even making my way around the rotunda, with its plunging circular stairways, as if I were checking the numbers on the doors, or just gaping at things as people do who roam the whole place as I did, on a whim. Who says a delivery boy cannot look around?

Finally the lady came out of the Amistad Suite and slammed the door. Big red patent-leather purse and breakneck high heels full of sequins and gold, skintight skirt, pushed-up sleeves, yellow hair flying. Beautiful and costly no doubt.

She was walking fast as if she was angry and she probably was. I moved closer to the room.

Through the dining area window of the suite, I saw the dim outline of the banker, beyond the white curtains, hunched over his computer on the desk, not even noticing that I was looking in at him, probably oblivious because tourists had been looking in all morning.

He was talking on a tiny phone, with an earpiece, and hammering the keys at the same time.

I made my way to the double doors and knocked.

At first he didn't answer. Then gruffly he came to the door, opened it very wide, stared at me, and said: "What!"

"From the management, sir, with compliments," I said, in the usual hoarse whisper, the bite plate making it hard for me to pronounce the words. I held up the lilies. They were beautiful lilies.

Then I moved right past him towards the bathroom murmuring something about water, they needed water, and with a shrug, the man went back to the desk.

The open bathroom was empty.

There might be someone in the tiny toilet compartment, but I doubted that and heard not a single telltale sound.

Just to be sure, I went in there for the water, and drew it from the spout in the tub.

No, he was the only one here.

The door to the veranda was hanging wide open.

He was talking into the phone and hammering on the computer keyboard. I could see a cascade of numbers flashing by.

Sounded like German, and I could understand only that he was irritated with somebody and mad in general at the whole world.

Sometimes bankers make the easiest targets, I reflected. They think their vast wealth protects them. They rarely use the bodyguards that they need.

I moved towards him, and set the flowers in the center of the dining room table, ignoring the mess of breakfast dishes. He didn't care that I was at his back.

For a moment I turned away from him and looked up at the familiar dome. I looked at the soft beige pine trees painted along the base of it. I looked at the doves ascending through the mist of clouds to the blue sky. I fussed with the flowers. I loved the fragrance of them. I breathed it in and some faint memory came back to me, of some quiet and lovely place where the scent of flowers had been the very air. Where was that? Does it matter?

And all the while the door to the veranda stood gaping and there came the fresh breeze. Anybody walking by could see the bed and the dome, but not him, and not me.

I moved swiftly behind his chair, and I pumped thirty units of the deadly stuff into his neck.

Without looking up, he reached for the spot, as if batting away an insect, which is almost always what they all do, and then I said, slipping the syringe in my pocket:

"Sir, you wouldn't have a tip for a poor delivery boy, would you?"

He turned. I was looming over him, smelling of peat moss and cigarettes.

His ice-cold eyes fixed me with fury. And then suddenly his face began to change. His left hand fell away from the computer keyboard, and with the right he groped for the earpiece. It fell out. He let that hand drop too. The phone slipped off the desk, as his left hand slipped to his leg.

His face was slack and soft and all the belligerence went out of him. He sucked in his breath and tried to steady himself with his right hand but couldn't find the edge of the desk. Then he managed to raise his hand towards me.

Quickly I took off the garden gloves. He didn't notice. He couldn't be noticing much of anything.

He tried to stand but couldn't.

"Help me," he whispered.

"Yes, sir," I said. "You just sit right here till it passes."

Then with my plastic-gloved hands, I shut his computer, and I turned him back in the chair so that he fell silently forward on the desk.

"Yes," he said in English. "Yes."

"You aren't well, sir," I said. "You want me to call for a doctor?"

I looked up and out at the empty veranda. We were right opposite the black iron table, and I noticed for the first time that the Tuscan pots overflowing with lavender geraniums had tall hibiscus trees in them as well. The sun was beautiful there.

He was trying to catch his breath.

As I said, I detest cruelty. I picked up the landline phone beside him, and without punching for a dial tone I spoke to the empty receiver. We needed a doctor right away.

His head was to the side. I saw his eyes close. I think he tried to speak again but he couldn't manage a word.

"They're coming, sir," I told him.

I might have left then, but as I said, I detest cruelty in any form.

By this time, he wasn't seeing anything too clearly. Perhaps he was seeing nothing at all. But I remembered that bit of information they always give you in the hospital that "the hearing is the last thing to go."

They'd told me that when my grandmother was dying, and I'd wanted to watch the television in the room, and my mother had been sobbing.

Finally he closed his eyes. I was surprised he was able to do it. First they were half shut, then shut altogether. His neck was a mass of wrinkles. I couldn't see any breath coming from him, or see the slightest rise or fall to his frame.

I looked beyond him, through the white curtains, at the veranda again. At the black table, among the Tuscan potted flowers, a man had taken his place and appeared to be staring at us.

I knew that he couldn't penetrate the curtains from that distance. All he could see was the whiteness, and perhaps a veiled shape. I didn't care.

I needed only a few more moments, and then I could safely leave with the knowledge that the job was complete.

I didn't touch the phones or the computers, but I made a mental inventory of what was there. Two cell phones on the desk just as The Boss had indicated. One dead phone on the floor. There had been phones in the bathroom. And there was another computer, the lady's perhaps, unopened on the table before the fireplace, between the wing chairs.

I was merely giving the man time to die as I noted this, but the longer I remained in the room, the worse I began to feel. I wasn't shaky, merely miserable.

The stranger on the veranda didn't bother me. Let him stare. Let him stare right into the room.

I made sure the lilies were turned the best way, wiped up a bit of water that had spilled on the table.

By now the man was surely almost dead. I felt a full-fledged despair creeping over me, an utter sense of emptiness, and why not?

I went to feel his pulse. I couldn't find it. But he was still alive. That I knew when I touched his wrist.

I listened to hear his breathing, and to my uncomfortable surprise, I heard the faint sigh of someone else.

Someone else.

Couldn't have been that guy on the veranda, even though he was still staring into the room. A couple passed by. Then a lone man came, gazing up and around himself, and moved on to the rotunda stairs.

I wrote it off to nerves, that sigh. It had sounded close to my ear as if someone were whispering to me. Just this room, I figured, unnerving me because I loved it so much, and the sheer ugliness of the murder was tearing at my soul.

Maybe the room was sighing at the pity of it. I certainly wanted to. I wanted to go.

And then the misery in me darkened as it so often did at these times. Only on this occasion it was stronger, much stronger, and it had language to it in my head which I didn't expect.

Why don't you join him? You know you ought to go where he's going. You ought to take that small gun off your ankle right now and hold the barrel right under your chin. Shoot straight up. Your brains will fly to the ceiling maybe, but you'll be dead finally, and everything will be dark, darker even than it is now, and you'll be separated from all of them forever, all of them, Mama, Emily, Jacob, your father, your unnamable father, and all of these, like him, whom you've personally and mercilessly killed. Do it. Don't wait any longer. Do it.

There was nothing unusual about this crushing depression, I reminded myself, this crushing desire to end it, this crushing and paralyzing obsession with lifting the gun and doing just what the voice said. What was unusual was the clarity of the voice. It felt as if the voice was beside me, instead of inside me, Lucky talking to Lucky, as he so often did.

Outside, the stranger got up from the table, and I found myself watching in cool amazement as he came into the open door. He stood in the room, under the dome, staring at me as I stood behind the dying man.

He was a tall, rather impressive figure, slender, with a mop of soft black wavy hair and blue eyes with an unusually engaging expression.

"This man's ill, sir," I said immediately, pushing my tongue hard against the bite plate. "I think he needs a doctor."

"He's dead, Lucky," said the stranger. "And don't listen to the voice in your head."

This was so utterly unexpected that I didn't know what to do or to say. Yet no sooner had he spoken these words, than the voice in my head kicked in again.

End it. Forget the gun and its inevitable sloppiness. You have another syringe in your pocket. Are you going to let yourself be caught? Your life's Hell now. Think what it will be like in prison. The syringe. Do it now.

"Ignore him, Lucky," said the stranger. An immense generosity seemed to emanate from him. He looked at me with such focus that it was almost devotion, and I had, unaccountably, an instinct that he was feeling love.

The light shifted. A cloud must have unveiled the sun, because the light in the room had brightened, and I saw him with uncommon clarity, even though I was very used to noticing and memorizing people. He was my height, and he was looking at me with obvious tenderness and even concern.

Impossible.

When you know something is clearly impossible, what do you do? What was I to do now?

I put my hand into my pocket and felt for the syringe.

That's right. Don't waste the last precious minutes of your loathsome existence trying to figure this one. Don't you see, The Right Man has worked a double-cross?

"Not so," said the stranger. He stared at the dead man and his face melted in an expression of perfect sorrow, and then he appealed to me again.

"Time to leave here with me, Lucky. Time to listen to what I have to say."

I couldn't form a coherent thought. My heart was thudding in my ears, and with my finger I pushed ever so slightly at the plastic cap on the syringe.

Yes, bow out of their contradictions and their traps and their lies, and their endless capacity to use you. Defeat them. Come now.

"Come now?" I whispered. The words separated themselves from the theme of rage that was common to my mind. Why had I thought that, *Come now?*

"You didn't think it," said the stranger. "Don't you see he's doing his damnedest to defeat both of us? Leave the syringe alone."

He looked young and eager, and almost irresistibly affectionate as he stared at me, but there was nothing young about him, and the sunlight was spilling in on him beautifully, and everything about him was effortlessly attractive. Only now did I notice, a little frantically, that he wore a simple gray suit, and a very beautiful blue silk tie.

Nothing about this was remarkable, but his face and hands were remarkable. And the expression was inviting and forgiving.

Forgiving.

Why would someone, anyone, look that way at me? Yet I had the feeling that he knew me, knew me better than I knew myself. It was as if he knew all about me, and only now did it penetrate that he had three times called me by my name.

Surely that was because The Right Man had sent him. Surely that was because I had been double-crossed. This was the last job for me with The Right Man, and here was the superior assassin who could put an end to an old assassin who was now more of a mystery than he was worth.

Then cheat them, and do it now.

"I do know you," said the stranger. "I've known you all your life. And I'm not from The Right Man." At this he softly laughed. "Well, not The Right Man you hold in such regard, Lucky, but from another who *is* The Right Man, I should say."

"What do you want?"

"For you to come with me out of here. For you to turn a deaf ear to the voice that's plaguing you. You've listened to that voice long enough."

I calculated. What could explain all this? Not merely the stress of being in my room at the Mission Inn, no, that wasn't sufficient. It must have been the poison, that I'd absorbed some of it when preparing it, that in spite of the double gloves, I hadn't done things exactly right.

"You're too clever for that," said the stranger.

And so you devolve into madness? When you have the power to turn your back on them all?

I looked about me. I looked at the tester bed; I looked at the familiar dark brown draperies. I looked at the huge fireplace, now directly behind the stranger. I looked at all the common furnishings and objects of the room that I so well knew. How could madness project itself so sharply? How could it create such a specific illusion? But surely this figure wasn't there, and I wasn't talking to him, and the warm, inviting look on his face was some device of my own wretched mind.

He laughed again very softly. But the other voice was working.

Don't give him a chance to get that syringe away from you. If you won't die in this room, damn you, then step outside. Find some corner of this hotel, and you know all of them, and there put an end to yourself once and for all.

For one precious second, I was certain this figure would vanish if I moved towards him. I did it. He was as solid and palpable as before. He stepped back for me, and gestured that I might go out before him.

And suddenly I found myself standing on the veranda, in

the sunlight, and the colors around me were wondrously vivid and lulling and I felt no urgency whatsoever, no ticking of any clock.

I heard him close the door of the suite and then I looked at him as he stood beside me.

"Don't talk to me," I said crossly. "I don't know who you are or what you want or where you came from."

"You called me," he said in his even and agreeable voice. "You've called me in the past, but never so desperately as you called me now."

Again I had that sensation of love flowing from him, of an infinite knowledge and an unaccountable acceptance of who and what I was.

"Called you?"

"You prayed, Lucky. You prayed to your guardian angel, and your guardian angel relayed the prayer to me."

There was simply no way in the world that I could accept this. But what struck me with full force was that The Right Man couldn't possibly know about my praying, couldn't possibly know what went on in my mind.

"I know what goes on in your mind," said the stranger. His face was as appealing and trusting as before. That was it, trusting, as if he had nothing whatsoever to fear from me, or any weapon I carried, or any desperate thing I might do.

"Wrong," he said gently, drawing closer to me. "There are desperate things that I don't want you to do."

Don't you know the Devil when you see him? Don't you know he's the Father of Lies? Maybe there are special devils for people like you, Lucky, did you ever think of that?

My hand went into my pocket for the syringe again, but instantly I pulled it back.

"Special devils, that's likely," said the stranger, "and special angels as well. You know that from your old studies. Special men have special angels, and I'm your angel, Lucky. I've come to offer you a way out of this, and you must not, you absolutely must not, reach for that syringe."

I was about to speak, when that despair came over me as surely as if someone had wrapped me in a shroud, though I've never seen a shroud. It was simply the image that came to me.

This is how you want to die? Crazy in some little cell with people torturing you to get information out of you? Get out of here. Go. Go where you can put the gun to your chin and pull the trigger. You knew when you came here to this place and this room that you would do that. This was always meant to be your last killing. That's why you brought the extra syringe.

The stranger laughed as if he couldn't help himself. "He's pulling all the stops out," he said quietly. "Don't listen. He wouldn't have raised his voice so stridently if I weren't here."

"I don't want you to talk to me!" I stammered.

A young couple was drifting towards us down the veranda. I wondered what they saw. They avoided us, their eyes scanning the brickwork and the heavy doors. I think they marveled at the flowers.

"It's the lavender geraniums," said the stranger as he looked at them in the pots that surrounded us. "And they want to sit down at this table, so why don't you and I move on?"

"I'm moving on," I said angrily, "but not because you say so. I don't know who you are. But I'll tell you this. If The Right Man sent you, you better be prepared for a little battle, because I'm going to take you down before I go."

I walked off to the right and started down the winding staircase of the huge rotunda. I moved fast, silencing the voice in my head deliberately and certainly, as I crossed one landing after another and came at last to the bottom floor. I found him standing there.

"Angel of God, my guardian dear," he whispered. He had been leaning against the wall, with his arms folded, a collected figure, but now he stood up straight and fell in beside me as I continued to walk on just about as briskly as I could.

"Be straight with me," I said under my breath. "Who are you?"

"I don't think you're ready to believe me," he said, his manner as gentle and solicitous as ever. "I'd rather that we were on the road back to Los Angeles, but if you insist . . ."

I felt the sweat breaking out all over me. I ripped the bite plate out of my mouth, and tore off the plastic gloves too. I shoved them in my pockets.

"Be careful. Uncap that syringe, and I've lost you," he said, drawing close to me. He was moving just as quickly as I was and we were now nearing the front walk of the hotel.

You know madness. You've seen it. Ignore him. You fall for him and you're finished. Get in the truck and drive out of here. Find someplace by the side of the road. And you know what to do.

The feeling of despair was almost blinding. I stopped in my tracks. We were under the campanario. It couldn't have been a more lovely spot. The ivy was trailing over the bells, and people were streaming by us on the pathway, to the left and to the right. I could hear the laughter and chatter from the nearby Mexican restaurant. I could hear the birds in the trees.

He stood close to me, looking at me intently, looking at me the way I'd want a brother to look at me, but I had no brother, because my little brother had died a long, long time ago. *My fault. The original murders.*

The breath went out of me. The breath just left me. I looked directly into his eyes and I saw the love again, the pure unadulterated love, and acceptance, and then very gently, cautiously, he laid his hand on my left arm.

"All right," I whispered. I was shaking. "You've come to kill me because he sent you. He thinks I'm a half-cocked gun out here, and he's dropped the dime on me."

"No, and no, and no."

"Am I the one who's dead? I somehow got that poison into my veins and I don't know it? Is that what's happened?"

"No, and no, and no. You're very much alive and that's why I want you. Now the truck isn't fifty feet away. You told them to keep it at the entrance. Get the ticket out of your pocket. Complete the few gestures required here."

"You're helping me to complete the murder," I said angrily. "You're implying you're an angel, but you're helping a killer."

"The man upstairs is gone, Lucky. He had his angels with him. And I can do no more for him now. I have come for you." There was an indescribable beauty to him when he spoke these words, and again that loving invitation, as if he could somehow make everything in this broken world right.

Rage.

I wasn't going out of my head. And I didn't think The Right Man could come up with this brand of assassin if he searched for a hundred years.

I moved forward with my legs shaking and I handed the ticket to the boy who was waiting, putting a twenty-dollar bill on top of it, and I climbed into my waiting truck.

Of course he climbed in beside me. He appeared to ignore the dust and dirt everywhere, the peat moss and the crumpled newspaper and whatever else I'd added to make it look like a working vehicle rather than a prop.

I pulled out, made a sharp turn, and headed for the freeway.

"I know what's happened," I said over the roar of the warm air in the open windows.

"And what precisely is that?"

"I've made you up. I've concocted you. And this is a form of madness. And all I have to do to end it is ram this truck into the wall. Nobody else will be hurt but me and you, this illusion, this thing I've created because I've come to some sort of end of the line. It was the room, wasn't it, doing it there. I know it was."

He just laughed softly to himself and kept his eyes on the road. After a moment, he said, "You're going a hundred and ten miles an hour. You're going to be stopped."

"Do you or do you not claim to be an angel?" I demanded.

"I am indeed an angel," he responded, still staring forward. "Slow down."

"You know, I read a book about angels recently," I told him. "You know, I like those kind of books."

"Yes, you have quite a library about what you don't believe in and no longer hold sacred. And you were a good Jesuit boy when you were in school."

Again the breath went out of me. "Oh, you are some assassin, throwing all that in my face," I said, "if that's what you are."

"I have never been an assassin and never will be," he said calmly.

"You're an accessory after the fact!"

Again he laughed lightly. "If I had been meant to prevent the murder, I would have done it," he said. "You do remember reading that angels are essentially messengers, the embodiment of their function, so to speak. Those words don't come as any surprise but the surprise is obviously that I've been sent as a messenger to you."

A traffic jam brought us to a slower pace and then to a crawl and a stop. I looked at him intently.

A calm came over me, that made me conscious that I'd sweated through the ugly green shirt I was wearing, and my legs were still unsteady, with a throb in the foot that pressed the brake.

"I'll tell you what I do know from that book on angels," I said. "Three-fourths of the time, they intervene in traffic incidents. Just what exactly did your kind do before there were automobiles? I really left the book wondering about that fact."

He laughed.

Behind me, there came the blast of a horn. The traffic was moving and so were we.

"That's a perfectly legitimate question," he said, "especially after one has read that particular book. It doesn't matter what we've done in the past. What matters now is what you and I can do together."

"And you don't have any name."

We were speeding again, but I was going no faster than the other cars in the far-left lane.

"You can call me Malchiah," he said kindly, "but I assure you, no Seraph under Heaven is ever going to tell you his real name."

"A Seraph? You're telling me you're a Seraph?"

"I want you for a special assignment, and I'm offering you a chance to use every skill you possess to help me, and to help the people who are praying for our intervention right now."

I was stunned. I felt the shock. It was like the coolness of the breeze as we drew closer to Los Angeles and closer to the coast.

You've made him up. Hit the embankment. Don't play the fool for something out of your own diseased mind.

"You did not make me up," he said. "Don't you see what's happening?"

The despair threatened to drown out my own words. *It's a sham. You've killed a man. You deserve death and the oblivion that's waiting for you.*

"Oblivion?" murmured the stranger. He raised his voice over the wind. "You think oblivion is waiting? You think you'll never see Emily and Jacob again?"

Emily and Jacob!

"Don't speak to me about them!" I said. "How dare you mention them to me. I don't know who you are, or what you are, but you don't mention them to me. If you're thriving on my imagination, then shape up!"

This time his laughter had an innocence and a ring to it.

"Why didn't I know it would be this way with you?" he said. He reached out and laid one of his soft hands gently on my shoulder. He looked wistful, sad, and then as if he were lost in thought.

I looked at the road. "I'm losing it," I said. We were driving into the heart of Los Angeles, and within minutes we'd taken the exit that would lead me to the garage where I could leave the truck.

"Losing it," he said, as if he were musing. He seemed to be watching our surroundings, the dipping ivy-covered embankments and the rising glass towers. "That's just the point, my dear Lucky. In believing in me, what do you have to lose?"

"How did you find out about my brother and sister?" I asked him. "How did you learn their names? You made some connections and I want to know how you did it."

"Anything but the obvious explanation? That I am what I say I am." He sighed. It was exactly that sigh I'd heard in the Amistad Suite, right by my ear. When he spoke again, his voice was caressing. "I know your life from the time you were in your mother's womb."

This was beyond anything I could have ever anticipated and suddenly it came clear to me, wondrously clear, that it was beyond anything I could have imagined.

"You are really here, aren't you?"

"I'm here to tell you that everything can change for you. I'm here to tell you that you can stop being Lucky the Fox. I'm here to take you to a place where you can begin to be the person you might have been . . . if certain things had not happened. I'm here to tell you . . ." He broke off.

We had reached the garage, and after hitting the remote for the door, I brought the truck safely and quietly inside.

"What, tell me what?" I said. We were eye to eye and he seemed wrapped in a calm that my fear couldn't penetrate.

The garage was dark, lit only by one grimed skylight, and the single open door through which we'd passed. It was vast and shadowy and filled with coolers and lockers and piles of clothing that I would or could use on future jobs.

It seemed a meaningless place to me suddenly, a place that I could surely and gloriously leave behind.

I knew this sense of elation. It was like the way you feel after you've been sick for a long time and suddenly a clearheaded good feeling comes over you, and life seems worth living again.

He sat perfectly still beside me and I could see the light in two small glints in his eyes.

"The Maker loves you," he said softly, almost dreamily. "I'm here to offer you another way, a way to that love if you'll take it."

I went quiet. I had to go quiet. I wasn't exhausted from the pitch of alarm that had gripped me. Rather I was emptied of that alarm. And the sheer beauty of this possibility arrested me, the way the look of the lavender geraniums could have arrested me, or the ivy trailing from the campanario, or the sway of trees moving in the breeze.

I saw all of these things suddenly, tumbling through my mind from the frantic rush to this dark and shadowy place, reeking of gasoline, and I didn't see the dimness surrounding us. In fact I realized that the garage was now filled with a pale light.

Slowly, I got out of the truck. I moved away from it to the far end of the garage. Out of my pocket, I took the second syringe and laid it there on the workbench nearby.

I slipped off the ugly green shirt and pants, threw them in the deep waste can that was filled with kerosene. I emptied the contents of the syringe into the mess of clothes even as the kerosene was darkening them. I threw in the gloves. And I struck a match and threw it into the can.

The fire exploded dangerously. I threw the work shoes into

it and watched the synthetic material melt. I threw the wig into the blaze too, and ran my hands gratefully over my own short hair. The glasses. I was still staring through the glasses. I took them off, broke them up, and put them into the fire as well. It was burning hot. Every single item was synthetic and it was all melting down to nothing in the blaze. I could smell it. Pretty soon everything was pretty much gone. The poison was most certainly gone.

The stench did not last for long. When there was no fire anymore, I gave the remains another douse of kerosene, and lighted the fire again.

In the uneven flicker of the blaze, I looked at my regular clothes neatly arranged on a hanger on the wall.

Slowly I put them on, the dress shirt, the gray trousers, the black socks and plain brown shoes, and finally the red tie.

The fire died out again.

I put on my jacket, and I turned around and saw him standing there, leaning against the truck. His ankles were crossed and his arms were folded, and the even light showed him to be as appealing as I'd found him earlier, and there was the same affectionate and loving expression on his face.

That deep, appalling despair gripped me again, voiceless, and fathomless, and I almost turned away from him, vowing never to look at him again, no matter where or how he appeared.

"He's fighting hard for you," he said. "He's whispered to you all these years, and now he's raised his voice. He thinks he can take you right out of my hands. He thinks you'll believe his lies, even with me here."

"Who is he?" I demanded.

"You know who he is. He's been talking to you for a long, long time. And you've been listening to him ever more intently. Don't listen anymore. Come with me."

"You're saying there's a battle for my soul?"

"Yes, that's what I'm saying."

I could feel myself shaking again. I wasn't afraid, so my body was getting afraid. I was calm but my legs were wobbly. My mind wouldn't give in to the fear anymore, but my body was weathering the impact and couldn't quite withstand it.

My car was there, a small open Bentley convertible I hadn't bothered to replace for years.

I opened the door and got inside. I closed my eyes. When I opened them, he was beside me, just as I expected. I put the car in reverse, and left the garage behind.

I'd never driven through downtown so quickly before. It was as if the traffic were carrying me swiftly along a river.

Within minutes we were turning off into the streets of Beverly Hills, and then we were on my street lined on both sides by magnificent jacaranda trees in their full bloom. Almost all the green leaves were gone from them now, and their branches were laden with blue blossoms, and the petals carpeted the sidewalks and the tarmac below.

I didn't look at him. I didn't think about him. I was thinking about my life, and fighting that rising despair the way a person fights nausea, and I was wondering, What if this is true, what if he is just what he says he is? What if somehow I, the man who's done all these things, can truly be redeemed?

We had pulled into the garage of my building before I said anything, and as I expected, he climbed out of the car as I did and went with me into the elevator and up to the fifth floor.

I never close the balcony doors to my apartment and I walked out now onto the concrete terrace and looked down at the blue jacarandas.

I was breathing rapidly, my body carrying the weight of all this, but my mind felt wondrously clear.

When I turned around and looked at him, he was as vivid and solid as the jacarandas and their tumbling blue blossoms. He was standing in the doorway merely regarding me, and again there was that promise in his face, that promise of comprehending, and of love.

I felt the urge to cry, to dissolve into a state of weakness, a state of being charmed.

"Why? Why have you come here for *me*?" I asked. "I know I asked you before, but you have to tell me, tell me completely, why me and not someone else? I don't know if you're real. I'm banking on it that you are now. But how can someone like me be redeemed?"

He came up to the concrete railing beside me. He looked down on the blue-blossomed trees. He whispered,

"So perfect, so lovely."

"They're why I live here," I answered, "because every year when they come into bloom—." My voice broke. I turned my back on the trees because I would start crying if I kept looking at them. I looked into my living room and saw its three walls covered with books from floor to ceiling. I saw the bit of hallway visible to me with its bookcases stacked just as high.

"Redemption is something one has to ask for," he said in my ear. "You know that."

"I can't ask!" I said. "I can't."

"Why? Simply because you don't believe?"

"That's an excellent reason," I said.

"Give me a chance to make you believe."

"Then you have to begin by explaining, why me?"

"I've come for you because I've been sent," he said in an even voice, "and because of who you are and what you've done and what you can do. It's no random choice, coming for you. It's for you, and you alone, that I've come. Every decision made by Heaven is like that. *It's particular.* That's how vast Heaven is, and you know how vast is the earth, and you must think of it, for just a moment, as a place existing with all of its centuries, all of its epochs, all of its many times.

"There isn't a soul in the world whom Heaven doesn't regard in particular fashion. There isn't a sigh or a word that Heaven fails to hear."

I heard him. I knew what he meant. I looked down at the spectacle of the trees. I wondered what it was like for a tree to lose its blossoms to the wind, when its blossoms were all that it had. The peculiarity of the thought startled me. I shuddered. The urge to weep was almost overwhelming me. But I fought it. I made myself look at him again.

"I know your whole life," he said. "If you like I'll show it to you. In fact, it seems that's exactly what I'll have to do before you really trust in me. I don't mind. You have to understand. You can't decide if you don't."

"Decide what? What are you talking about?"

"I'm talking about an assignment, I told you." He paused, then continued very kindly. "It's a way to use you and who you are. It's a way to use every detail of who you are. It's an assignment to save life instead of taking it, to answer prayers instead of cutting them off. It's a chance to do something that matters terribly to others while doing only good for yourself. That's what it's like to do good, you know. It's like working for The Right Man except that you believe in it with your whole heart and your whole soul, so much so that it becomes your will and your purpose with love."

"I have a soul, that's what you want me to believe?" I asked.

"Of course you do. You have an immortal soul. You know that. You're twenty-eight years old and that is very young by anyone's count, and you feel immortal, for all your dark thoughts and desires to end your life, but you don't grasp that the immortal part of you is the true part of you, and that all the rest in time will fall away."

"I know these things," I whispered. "I know them." I didn't

mean to sound impatient. I was telling the truth and I was dazed.

I turned, only half realizing what I was about, and went into the living room of my small home. I looked again at the walls lined in books. I looked at the desk where I often read. I looked at the book open on the green blotter. Something obscure, something theological, and the irony of this struck me with full force.

"Oh, yes, you're well prepared," he said beside me. It was as if we'd never moved apart from each other at all.

"And I'm supposed to believe you're The Right Man now?" I asked.

He smiled at that. I saw that much out of the corner of my eye. "The Right Man," he repeated softly. "No. I'm not The Right Man. I'm Malchiah and I'm a Seraph, I told you, and I'm here to give you your choice. It's the answer to your prayer, Lucky, but if you can't accept that, let's say it is the answer to your wildest dreams."

"What dreams?"

"All these years you've always prayed The Right Man was Interpol. He was with the FBI. He was with the good men and everything he told you to do was for the good. That's what you've always dreamed."

"Doesn't matter, and you know it. I killed them. I made the whole thing into a game."

"I know you did, but that was still your dream. You come with me and there will be no doubts, Lucky. You will be on the side of the angels, with me."

We looked at each other. I was trembling. My voice wasn't steady:

"If that were only true," I said, "I would do anything, anything you ask of me, for you, and for God in Heaven. I would suffer anything you demand."

He smiled, but very slowly as if he was looking deep inside

me to find the reservation, and then perhaps he found that there was none. Perhaps I realized there was none.

I sank down into the leather chair beside the couch. He sat opposite me.

"I'm going to show you your life now," he said, "not because I need to do it, but because you need to see it. And only after you see it, will you believe in me."

I nodded. "If you can do that," I said miserably, "well, I'll believe in anything that you say."

"Prepare yourself," he said. "You'll hear my voice and see what I mean to describe, more vividly perhaps than you've ever seen anything, but the order and organization will be mine, and often more difficult for you to bear than a simple chronology. It's the soul of Toby O'Dare we're examining here, not merely a young man's history. And remember, no matter what you see and what you feel, I'm truly here with you. I'll never abandon you."

CHAPTER FOUR

Malchiah Reveals My Life to Me

WHEN ANGELS CHOOSE A HELPER, THEY DON'T ALWAYS start at the beginning. In scanning a human being's life, they might begin with the warm present, then move a good third of the way in, and work towards the earliest beginning and back towards the moment at hand, as they collect the data of their emotional attachment and strengthen it. And don't ever believe anyone who tells you that we have no such emotional attachment.

Our emotions are different but we have them. We never cast a cold eye on life or death. Don't misunderstand our seeming serenity. After all, we live in a world of perfect trust in The Maker, and we are keenly aware that humans often do not, and we feel an active sorrow for them.

But I couldn't help but notice, as soon as I began to investigate Toby O'Dare as a boy, anxious and burdened with countless cares, that he liked nothing better than to watch on late-night television the most brutal of detective shows, and they took his mind off the hideous realities of his own crumbling world, and the firing of bullets always produced a catharsis in him just as the producers of those shows wanted to do. He learned to read early, to finish his homework in study hall, and for pleasure he read the books they call "true crime," also, sinking easily into the well-written prose of Thomas Thompson's *Blood and Money* or *Serpentine.*

Books on organized crime, on pathological murderers, on hideous deviants, all these he picked up from the bins of a bookstore on Magazine Street in New Orleans where he lived, though in those days he never dreamed, never for a moment, that he would one day be the subject of just that sort of story.

Loathing the glamour of evil in *Silence of the Lambs,* he'd thrown it in the trash. The nonfiction books weren't written till the killer was caught, and Toby needed that resolution.

When he couldn't sleep in the very small hours, he watched the cops and killers on the small screen, oblivious to the fact that what drove these shows was the committing of the crime, and not the sanctimonious anger and actions of the artificially heroic police lieutenant or genius detective.

But this early taste for crime fiction and fact is just about the least important thing about Toby O'Dare, so let me get back to the story to which I helped myself as soon as I fixed my inalterable gaze on him.

Toby didn't grow up dreaming of being a killer or a cop. Toby dreamed of being a musician and saving everyone in his little family.

And what drew me to him was not the anger churning inside him and devouring him alive in this present time, or in time past. No, on that darkness I find it as hard to look, as a human might find it hard to walk into an icy winter wind that cut at his eyes and his face and froze his fingers.

What drew me to Toby was a bright and shining goodness that nothing could completely efface, a great glowing sense of right and wrong that had never been forfeit to the lie, no matter where his life had taken him.

But let me make it clear: because I choose a mortal for my

purposes, that does not mean that the mortal is going to agree to come with me. Finding such a one as Toby is hard enough; persuading him to come with me is even harder. You'd think it was irresistible but it's not. People swindle themselves out of Salvation with great regularity.

However there were too many aspects of Toby O'Dare for me to back away from him and leave him to the guardianship of lesser angels.

Toby was born in the city of New Orleans. He was of Irish and German descent. He had some Italian blood but he didn't know it, and his great-grandmother on his father's side was Jewish, but he didn't know that either because he came from hardworking people who never kept track. There was some Spanish blood in him also, on his father's side, dating from the time the Spanish Armada crashed along the coast of Ireland. And though there was talk of that as some in the family had jet-black hair and blue eyes, he never thought much about it. No one in his family ever spoke about lineage. They talked about survival.

Genealogy belongs to the rich in human history. The poor rise and fall without leaving a footprint.

Only now in the age of DNA investigation are the common people enamored of knowing their genetic makeup, and they're not sure what to do with the information, but a revolution of sorts is happening as people seek to understand the blood that runs through their veins.

The more Toby O'Dare became the contract killer of underground fame, the less he cared about who he'd been before, or who had come before him. So as he gained the means that might have made possible an investigation into his own past, he drew further and further from the chain of humanity to which he belonged. He had after all destroyed "the past" as far as he saw it. So why should he care about what had happened long before his birth to others struggling with the same pressures and miseries?

Toby grew up in an uptown apartment, just a block away from prestigious streets, and in that dwelling there were no pictures on the walls of ancestors.

He had cherished his grandmothers, stalwart women, parents of eight children each, loving, tender, and with calloused hands. But they died when he was very young, as his parents were their youngest children.

These grandmothers were worn out from the lives they'd led and their deaths came swift, with the smallest amount of drama, in a hospital room.

Yet gigantic funerals followed, filled with cousins and flowers, and people crying because that generation, the generation of the great families, was passing from America.

Toby never forgot all those cousins, most of whom went on to great success without ever committing a crime or a sin. But by the age of nineteen, he was completely disengaged from them.

Yet the hit man now and then secretly investigated thriving marriages, and used his great computer skills to track this or that impressive career of the lawyers, judges, and priests who came from his related families. He'd played a lot with those cousins when he was a very little child, and he could not entirely forget the grandmothers who brought them together.

He'd been rocked by his grandmothers, now and then, in a big wooden chair that was sold long after their deaths to a junk dealer. He'd heard their old songs before they left the world. And now and then he sang to himself bits and pieces of them. *See Saw, Marjory Daw, Catch Behind the Steam Car!* or the soft tormenting melody of *Go tell Aunt Rhodie, Go tell Aunt Rho oh di, the old gray goose is dead, the one she was saving for Fatty's feather bed.*

And then there were the black songs that the whites had always inherited.

Now, honey won't you play in your own backyard, don't mind what the white child say. For you've got a soul as white as snow, that's what the Lord done say.

These were songs of a spiritual garden extant before the grandmothers departed the earth, and by eighteen Toby had turned his back on everything about his past, except the songs, of course, and the music.

Ten years ago, or at age eighteen, he left that world forever.

He simply vanished from the midst of anybody who knew him, and though none of those boys and girls or aunts or uncles blamed him for going away, they were surprised and confused by it.

They imagined him, with reason, to be a lost soul somewhere. They even imagined him mad, a street bum, a gibbering imbecile begging for his supper. That he'd taken with him a suitcase of clothes and his precious lute gave them hope, but they never saw or heard of him again.

Once or twice over the years, a search was made but, as they were searching for Toby O'Dare, a boy with a diploma from Jesuit High School and professional skill with the lute, they didn't have the slightest chance of finding him.

One of his cousins listened quite a lot to a tape he'd made once of Toby playing on a street corner. But Toby didn't know of this; he couldn't possibly have known. So this potential warmth never reached him.

One of his old teachers at Jesuit High School had even searched every musical conservatory in the United States for a Toby O'Dare, but Toby O'Dare had never enrolled in any such institution.

You might say some of this family suffered grief for the loss of the soft peculiar music of Toby O'Dare, and grief for the loss of the boy who so loved his Renaissance instrument that he would stop to explain, to anyone who asked, all about it, and why he preferred to play it on the street corner, rather than the guitar of rock star affection.

I think you see my point: his family was good stock, the O'Dares, the O'Briens, the McNamaras, the McGowens, and all those who had intermarried with them.

But in every family there are bad people, and weak people, and some people who can't or won't withstand the trials of life, and who fail spectacularly. Their guardian angels weep; demons beholding them dance for joy.

But only The Maker decides what ultimately happens to them.

So it was with the mother and father of Toby.

But both lines gave Toby tremendous advantages: talent for music as well as love for it was certainly the most impressive gift. But Toby inherited keen intelligence, as well, and an unusual and irrepressible sense of humor. He had a powerful imagination that enabled him to make plans, to have dreams. And a mystical bent sometimes caught hold of him. His strong desire to be a Dominican priest at the age of twelve did not pass so easily with the coming of worldly ambition, as it might have done with another teenager.

Toby never stopped going to church during the roughest high school years, and even if he'd been tempted to skip the Sunday Mass, he had his brother and sister to consider, and wouldn't fail to set a good example.

If ever he could have only drifted back some five generations and seen his forefathers studying Torah night and day in their synagogues in Central Europe, maybe he would not have become the killer that he was. If he could have gone further back, and seen his ancestors painting pictures in Siena, Italy, perhaps he would have had more courage to pursue his most cherished designs.

But he had no idea such persons ever existed, or that on his mother's side, generations ago, there had been English priests martyred for their faith in the time of Henry VIII, or that his great-grandfather on his father's side, too, had wanted to be a priest but could not make the grades in school for such to be possible.

Almost no mortal on earth knows his lineage before the so-called Dark Ages, and only the great families can penetrate the deep layers of time to extract from them a series of examples that might inspire.

And the word, "inspired," is not one to be wasted in Toby's case, because as a contract killer, he has always been inspired. And he was inspired as a musician before that.

His success as a killer derived in no small part from the fact that tall and graceful as he was, blessed with beauty as he was, he didn't look like anyone in particular.

By the age of twelve, he had the permanent stamp of intelligence on his features, and when he was anxious, there was something cold in his face, a look of well-established distrust. But this passed almost instantly, as it was not something he wanted to reflect, and did not want to abide in himself. He tended towards calm and people almost always found him remarkable and attractive.

He was six foot four before he graduated high school, and his blond hair had faded to an ashen color, and his level gray eyes were full of ready concentration and gentle curiosity, and gave no offense to anyone.

He frowned seldom, and when he went out for a walk, just a walk on his own, to the casual observer he appeared a bit watchful, like one eager for a plane to land on time, or someone waiting a bit anxiously for an important appointment.

If startled, he would flash with resentment and distrust, but snap away from this almost instantly. He did not want to be an unhappy or bitter person, and he had cause over the years to become both, and he resisted it mightily.

He did not drink, ever in all his life. He hated it.

From childhood on, he dressed beautifully, principally because the children in the uptown grade school to which he went dressed this way, and he wanted to be like them, and he was not above taking expensive hand-me-downs from his cousins, which included navy blue blazers and khaki trousers, and pastel polo shirts. There was a look to the boys of uptown New Orleans that was located in these very clothes and he took to discovering and cultivating it. He also tried to talk like these boys, and slowly he eliminated from his speech the strong indicators of poverty and hardness that had always marked his father's taunts and bawling complaints and ugly threats. As for his mother's voice, it was accentless and pleasant, and he spoke much more like her than like anyone else in his family.

He read *The Official Preppy Handbook,* not as a satire, but as something to be obeyed. And he knew how to roam the secondhand stores for the right kind of leather book bag.

In the parish of Holy Name of Jesus School, he walked through gloriously green streets from the St. Charles car line, and the fresh, beautifully painted houses he passed filled him with vague and dreamy longings.

Palmer Avenue uptown was his favorite street and it seemed to him at times that if he could live someday in a white two-story house on that street, he'd know perfect happiness.

He also came into contact with music very early at the Loyola Conservatory. And it was the sound of the lute, at a public Renaissance concert, that drew him away from his ardent desire to enter the priesthood.

He went from altar boy to passionate student as soon as he encountered a kindly teacher who taught him for nothing. He produced a purity of tone on the lute that astonished her. His finger work was fast, and the expression he gave to his playing was excellent, and his teacher marveled at the beautiful airs he could play by ear, and those included the songs I've mentioned above that always haunted him. He heard his grandmothers singing to him when he played. He played for his grandmothers sometimes in his mind. He played popular songs on the lute with great dexterity, giving them a wholly new sound, and an illusion of integrity.

At one point, one of his teachers put the records of the popular singer Roy Orbison into Toby's hands, and he soon found he could play the slower songs of this great musician, and give them tender expression through the lute that Orbison had so accomplished with his voice. He soon knew every "ballad" that Orbison had ever recorded.

And as he rendered all popular music in his own style, he learned a classical composition for every popular song, so that he could switch back and forth between them, bringing up the rapid and contagious beauty of Vivaldi one moment, and the mournful tender suffering of Orbison the next.

His was a busy life, what with after-school study, and then the demands of the Jesuit High School curriculum. So it wasn't so hard to keep at arm's length the rich boys and girls he knew, for though he liked many of them very much, he was determined they were never to enter the slovenly apartment in which he lived, with two drunken parents, either of whom could hopelessly humiliate him.

He was fastidious as a child and, later on, fastidious as a killer. But in truth, he grew up afraid, a keeper of secrets, a child in permanent dread of shabby violence.

Later, as a full-blown hit man, he thrived on danger, remembering at times with amusement the television dramas he'd once loved, with the thought that he was now living something far more darkly glorious than had ever been revealed to him. While never admitting it to himself, he took some pride in his particular brand of evil. Despair might be the tune he sang to himself about what he did, but a deep polished vanity lay beneath it.

He had, in addition to this passion for the hunt, one truly precious trait which separated him completely from lesser killers. It was this: he didn't care whether he lived or died. He didn't believe in Hell because he didn't believe in Heaven. He didn't believe in the Devil because he didn't believe in God. And though he remembered the ardent and sometimes hypnotic faith of his youth, though he respected it far more than anyone would ever have guessed, it didn't warm his soul in the slightest.

To repeat, he had early on wanted to be a priest, and no fall from grace had taken him from that. Even when he played the lute, he prayed constantly to bring beautiful music from it, and he often devised new melodies for prayers that he loved.

It's worth noting here that he had once wanted to be a saint as well. And he had wanted, young as he was, to understand the whole history of his church, and he had delighted in reading about Thomas Aquinas in particular. It seemed his teachers were always mentioning that name, and when a Jesuit priest came from the nearby university to talk to the grade school class, he told a tale of Thomas that lodged itself permanently in Toby's memory.

It was that the great theologian Thomas had been granted a vision in his last years that caused him to turn against his earlier work, the great *Summa Theologica.* "It is so much straw," said the saint to those who asked him, in vain, to continue it.

The tale was something he thought on even to the very day that he came into my relentless gaze. But he didn't know whether it was fact or beautiful fiction. Lots of things said about the saints weren't true. And yet that never seemed to be the point.

Sometimes, in his later ruthless and professional years, when he was tired of playing the lute, he would jot down his thoughts on these remembered things that had once meant so much to him. He conceived of a book that would shock the world: *Diary of a Hit Man*. Oh, he knew that others had written such memoirs but they weren't Toby O'Dare, who still read theology when not taking down bankers in Geneva and Zurich; who, carrying a rosary, had penetrated Moscow and London long enough to commit four strategic murders within sixty-two hours. They weren't Toby O'Dare, who had once wanted to say Mass for the multitudes.

I said he didn't care whether he lived or died. Let me explain: he didn't take suicide missions. He liked being alive too much to do this, though he never admitted it. Also those who worked for him did not want his body to be found at the scene of any attempted hit.

But he didn't care, truly, whether he died today or tomorrow. And he was convinced that the world, though nothing more than the materialistic realm we can see with our own eyes, would be a lot better off without him. Sometimes he positively wanted to be dead. But these periods didn't last long and music, above all, would bring him out of it.

He'd lie in his expensive apartment listening to the old slow songs of Roy Orbison, or to the many recordings of opera singers he had, or listening to the recordings of music written for the lute especially in the time of the Renaissance when the lute had been such a popular instrument.

How had he come to be this thing, this darkling human, banking money for which he had no use, killing people whose names he didn't know, penetrating the finest fortresses his victims might construct, bringing death as a waiter, a doctor in a white coat, the driver of a hired car, or even a bum on the street, drunkenly careening into the man he would puncture with his fatal needle?

The evil in him made me shudder insofar as an angel can shudder, but the good shining forth attracts me utterly.

Let's return to those early years, when he'd been Toby

O'Dare, with a younger brother and sister, Jacob and Emily—
to the time when he'd been struggling to get through the
strictest prep school in New Orleans, on a full scholarship, of
course, as he'd worked as many as sixty hours a week playing
music on the street to keep the children and his mother fed,
and clothed, and manage an apartment which no one but the
family ever entered.

Toby paid the bills. He stocked the refrigerator. He talked
to the landlord when his mother's howling woke the man next
door. He was the one who cleaned up the vomit, and put out
the fire when the grease spilled out of the frying pan into the
gas flame, and she fell back with her hair ablaze, shrieking.

With another spouse, his mother might have been a tender
and loving thing, but her husband had gone to prison when she
was pregnant with the last child, and she'd never gotten over it.
A cop who preyed on prostitutes in the French Quarter streets,
the man was stabbed to death at Angola.

Toby was only ten when that happened.

For years, she drank herself drunk, and lay on the bare
boards murmuring her husband's name, "Dan, Dan, Dan."
And nothing Toby ever did could comfort her. He'd buy her
pretty dresses, and bring home baskets of fruit or candy, and
for a few years there before the toddlers went off to kinder-
garten, she'd been an evening drunk more than anything else,
and had even scrubbed herself and her children well enough to
take them all to Mass on Sundays.

In those days Toby watched TV with her, the two on her
bed, and she shared his love of the police kicking in doors and
catching the most depraved killers.

But once the little ones weren't underfoot, his mother drank
by day and slept by night, and Toby had to become the man of
the house, dressing Jacob and Emily every morning with care,
and taking them to school early so he had time to make it to his

own classes at Jesuit on time, a bus ride away, with perhaps a few moments to go over his homework.

By the age of fifteen, he'd been studying the lute and composition for it every afternoon for two years, and now Jacob and Emily did their homework in a practice room nearby and his teachers still taught him for nothing.

"You have a great gift," his teacher told him, and urged him to move on to other instruments which might have given him a living later on.

But Toby knew he could not give enough time to that, and having trained Emily and Jacob as to how to watch and handle their drunken mother, he was out on the French Quarter streets all Saturday and Sunday, the lute case open at his feet as he played, earning every cent he could to supplement his father's meager pension.

Fact was, there was no pension, though Toby never told anyone that. There were just the silent stipends of the family and the regular handouts of other policemen, who had been no worse and no better than Toby's father.

And Toby had to bring in the money for anything extra or "nice," and for the uniforms his brother and sister required, and any toys they were to have in the miserable apartment that Toby so detested. And though he worried every moment as to the condition of his mother at home, and the abilities of Jacob to keep her quiet should she go into a rage, Toby took great pride in his playing, and in the attitudes of the passersby who never failed to drop large bills in the case if they lingered.

Even though the earnest study of music went slowly for Toby, he still dreamed of entering the Conservatory of Music when he came of age, and of landing a job playing in a restaurant where his income would be steady. Neither plan was beyond possibility by any means, and he lived for the future, while struggling desperately through the present. Nevertheless when he played the lute, when he made enough money easily to pay the rent and buy the food, he knew a joy and a sense of triumph that was solid and beautiful.

He never ceased trying to cheer and comfort his mother and assure her that things would be better than they were now, that her pain would go away, and that they would someday live in a real house in the suburbs, and have a backyard for Emily and Jacob and a real front lawn and all the other things that normal life offered.

Somewhere in the back of his mind, he thought that someday, when Jacob and Emily were grown and married and his mother had been cured by all the money he would make, he would perhaps think again about the seminary. He couldn't forget what it had meant to him once, to serve Mass. He couldn't forget that he had felt called to take the host in his hands and say, "This is My Body," thereby making it the very flesh of the Lord Jesus Christ. And many a time as he played on a Saturday evening, he turned to liturgical music that delighted the ever-shifting crowd as much as the familiar tunes of Johnny Cash and Frank Sinatra that so delighted the audience. He cut a sharp picture as a street musician, hatless and trim in a blue wool jacket and dark wool pants, and even these traits gave him a sublime advantage.

The better he became, playing requests effortlessly and pulling the full range out of the instrument, the more the tourists and the natives grew to love him. He soon came to recognize regulars on certain nights, who never failed to give him the largest bills.

He sang one modern hymn, *"I am the bread of life, he who comes to Me will not hunger . . ."* It was a rousing hymn, one that used his full range, and his full ability to forget everything else as he played, and those who clustered around him always rewarded him for it. In a daze, he'd look down and see the money that could buy him a little peace for a week or even more. And he'd feel like crying.

He also played and sang songs that he made up, variations on themes he'd heard in the records his teacher gave him. He wove together the airs of Bach and Mozart and even Beethoven, and other composers whose names he couldn't remember.

At one point he began to jot down some of his compositions. His teacher would help him to copy them outright. Music for the lute wasn't written like ordinary music. It was written in tabulature, and this he specially loved. But the real theory and practice of written music was hard for him. If only he could learn enough to teach music someday, he thought, even to little children, that would be a workable life.

Soon enough, Jacob and Emily were able to dress themselves, and they too had the grave look of little adults as did he, riding alone on the St. Charles car to school, and never bringing anyone home as their brother had forbidden it. They learned how to do the wash, to iron the shirts and blouses for school, and how to hide the money from their mother, and distract her if she became maddened and started to tear the house to pieces.

"If you have to pour it down her throat, then do it," Toby told them, for in truth there were times when nothing but the drink would stop his mother from raving.

I observed all these things.

I turned the pages of his life and raised the light to read the finer print.

I loved him.

I saw the *Daily Prayer Book* ever on his desk, and beside it another book, which he read from time to time for pure delight, and sometimes read to Jacob and Emily.

This book was *The Angels* by Fr. Pascal Parente. He'd found it in the same Magazine Street shop where he'd found his books on crime and bloody murder, and he bought it, along with a life of St. Thomas Aquinas by G. K. Chesterton, which he struggled from time to time to read to himself though it was difficult.

You might say that he lived a life in which what he read was as important as what he played on the lute, and these things were as important to him as his mother, and Jacob and Emily.

His guardian angel, always desperate to guide him on the right path in the most chaotic of times, seemed perplexed by the combination of loves that gripped Toby's soul, but I didn't come to observe that angel, but only to see Toby, not the angel who labored so hard to keep faith blazing in Toby's heart that Toby would somehow save all of them.

One summer day, as Toby read on his bed, he turned over on his belly, clicked open his pen, and underlined these words:

As of faith we need only hold that the Angels are not endowed with cardiognosis (knowledge of the secrets of the heart) nor with a certain knowledge of future acts of the free will; these being exclusively divine prerogatives.

He had loved that sentence, and he had loved the atmosphere of mystery that enveloped him when he read this book.

In truth, he didn't want to believe that angels were heartless. Somewhere once he'd seen an old painting of the crucifixion in which the angels above had been weeping, and he liked to think that the guardian angel of his mother wept when he saw her drunken and despondent. If angels didn't have hearts or know hearts, he didn't want to know it, yet the concept enthralled him, and angels enthralled him, and he talked to his own angel as often as he could.

He taught Emily and Jacob to kneel down every night and say the age-old prayer:

Angel of God, my guardian dear,
to whom God's love commits me here,
ever this day be at my side,
to light and guard, to rule and guide.

He even bought a picture of a guardian angel for them. It was a common enough picture, and he'd first seen a print of it himself in a grade school classroom. This print he matted and framed with the materials he could buy in the drugstore. And he hung it on the wall in the room the three of them shared, he and Jacob in the bunk bed and Emily against the far wall on her own cot, which could be folded up in the morning.

He had chosen an ornate gold frame for the picture, and he liked the beading on it, the leafy corners and the wide margin it established between the world of the picture and the faded wallpaper of the little room.

The guardian angel was huge and womanly with streaming golden hair and great white blue-tipped wings, and she wore a mantle over her flowing white tunic as she stood above a small boy and girl who made their way together over a treacherous bridge with gaping holes in it.

How many millions of little children have seen that picture?

"Look," Toby would say to Emily and Jacob when they knelt down for night prayers. "You can always talk to your guardian angel." He told them how he talked to his angel, especially on those nights downtown when the tips were slow. "I say, Bring me more people, and sure enough, he does it." He insisted upon it though Jacob and Emily both laughed.

But it was Emily who asked if they could pray to Mother's guardian angel too and stop her from getting so drunk so much.

This shocked Toby, because he had never spoken the word "drunk" under his own roof. He had never used the word "drunk" to anyone, not even his confessor. And he marveled that Emily, who was only seven at this time, knew everything. The word sent a dark shiver through him, and he had told his little brother and sister that life would not always be like this, that he would see to it that things got better and better.

He meant to keep his word.

At Jesuit High, Toby soon rose to the top of his class. He played fifteen hours at a stretch on Saturdays and Sundays to make enough that he didn't have to play after school, and could keep up his musical education.

He was sixteen when a restaurant hired him for Saturday and Sunday nights, and though he made a little less, he knew he could count on it.

When needed, he waited tables and made good tips. But it was his spirited and unusual playing that was wanted of him and he was glad of it.

All this money over the years he hid in various places around the apartment—in gloves in his drawers, beneath a loose board, beneath Emily's mattress, under the bottom of the stove, even in tinfoil in the refrigerator.

On a good weekend, he was making hundreds, and when he passed his seventeenth birthday, the Conservatory gave him a full college scholarship to study music in earnest. He had made it.

That was the happiest day of his life and he came home brimming with the news. "Ma, I did it, I did it," he said. "Everything's going to be good, I'm telling you."

When he would not give his mother money for drink, she took his lute out and smashed it over the edge of the kitchen table.

The breath went out of him. He thought he might die. He wondered if he could make himself die simply by refusing to breathe. He became sick and sat down on the chair with his head down and his hands between his knees, and he listened as his mother went roaming the apartment, sobbing and murmuring and cursing in foul language all those whom she blamed for all that had become of her, arguing with her dead mother in turns, and then blubbering, "Dan, Dan, Dan," over and over again.

"You know what your father gave me?" she screamed. "You know what he gave me from those women downtown? You know what he left me with?"

These words terrified Toby.

The apartment stank of booze. Toby wanted to die. But Emily and Jacob were due to get off the St. Charles car a block away at any minute. He went to the corner store, bought a flask of bourbon, though he was underage, and brought it home and forced it down her throat, swallow after swallow, until she passed out cold on the mattress.

After that, her cursing increased. As the children dressed for school, she'd call them the worst names imaginable. It was like a demon lived inside her. But it wasn't a demon. The booze was eating her brain, and he knew it.

His latest teacher gave him a new lute, a cherished lute, one far more expensive than the one that had been broken.

"I love you for this," he said to her and he kissed her on her powdered cheek, and she told him again that someday he'd make a name for himself with his lute and a string of recordings of his own.

"God forgive me," he prayed as he knelt in Holy Name Church, looking up the long shadowy nave to the high altar, "I wish my mother would die. But I can't wish it."

The three children cleaned the place from top to bottom that weekend as they always did. And she, the mother, lay drunk like an enchanted princess under a spell, her mouth open, her face smooth and youthful, her drunken breath almost sweet, like sherry.

Under his breath, Jacob whispered, "Poor drunk Mommy."

This shocked Toby as much as the time Emily had said something like it.

When he was halfway through his senior year, Toby fell in love. It was with a Jewish girl from Newman School, the co-educational prep school in New Orleans that was as good as Jesuit. Her name was Liona and she came to Jesuit, an all-boys' school, to sing the lead in a musical that Toby made time to attend, and when he asked her to go with him to the prom, she said yes immediately. He was overwhelmed. Here was a lovely dark-haired beauty with a marvelous soprano voice, and she took to him completely.

In the hours after the prom they sat in her backyard uptown, outside of her beautiful home on Nashville Avenue. In the warm, fragrant garden, he broke down and told her about his mother. She had nothing but sympathy and understanding for him. Before morning they had slipped into her family guesthouse and been intimate together. He didn't want her to know that it was his first time, but when she confessed it was hers, he admitted it.

He told her that he loved her. This made her cry, and she told him that she had never known anyone like him.

With her long black hair and dark eyes, her soft soothing voice, and her immediate understanding, she seemed everything that he could ever desire. She had a strength he greatly admired, and something of a searing intelligence. He felt dreadful fear of losing her.

Liona came down to be with him in the heat of spring as he played on Bourbon Street; she brought him cold Cokes from the grocery store, and stood only a few paces away listening to him. Only her studies kept her away from him. She was clever and had a great sense of humor. She loved the sound of the lute, and she understood why he cherished this instrument for its unique tone and its beautiful shape. He loved her voice (which was much better than his), and soon they attempted duets. Her songs were Broadway songs and this brought a whole new songbook to his repertoire, and when time would allow, they played and sang together.

One afternoon—after his mother had been all right for a little while—he brought Liona home, and try as she might, she couldn't conceal her shock at the small overcrowded apartment, and at his mother's drunken slatternly manner as she sat smoking and playing solitaire at the kitchen table. He could tell that Emily and Jacob were ashamed. Jacob had asked him afterwards, "Toby, why did you ever bring her here with Mom like that? How could you do that?" Both his sister and brother looked at him as if he'd been a traitor.

That night, after Toby finished playing on Royal Street, Liona came down to meet him and they talked for hours once more, and crept again into her parents' darkened guesthouse.

But Toby felt increasing shame that he had confided his deepest secrets to anyone. And he felt in his heart of hearts that he wasn't worthy of Liona. Her tenderness and warmth confused him. Also he believed it was a sin to make love to her when there was no chance that they could ever be married. He had so many worries that normal courtship through their college years seemed an utter impossibility. He was deeply afraid that Liona pitied him.

As the period of final exams came on, neither of them had time to see each other.

The night of his high school graduation, Toby's mother began to drink at four o'clock, and finally he ordered her to stay home. He couldn't bear the thought of her coming downtown, with her slip showing beneath her hem, and her lipstick smeared and her cheeks too rouged, and her hair a mass of tangles. He tried for a time to brush her hair, but she slapped him repeatedly until, gritting his teeth, he grabbed her wrists and yelled, "Stop it, Mama." He burst into sobs like a child. Emily and Jacob were terrified.

His mother wept on her folded arms at the kitchen table as he took off his good clothes. He wasn't going downtown to his graduation either. The Jesuits could mail him the diploma.

But he was angry, angrier than he'd ever been in his life, and for the first time in his life, he called her a drunk and a slut. He shivered and cried.

Emily and Jacob sobbed in the other room.

His mother began to bawl. She said she wanted to kill herself. They struggled together over a kitchen knife. "Stop it, stop it," he said between his clenched teeth. "All right, I'll get the damn booze," he said, and he went out for a six-pack and a bottle of wine, and a flask of bourbon. Now she had the seemingly endless supply that she wanted.

After she drank a beer, she begged him to lie down on the bed beside her. She drank the wine in gulps. She cried and asked him to say the rosary with her. "It's a craving in the blood," she said. He didn't answer. He'd taken her to meetings of Alcoholics Anonymous many a time. She'd never stay even for fifteen minutes.

Finally he settled next to her. And they said the rosary together. In a low voice, devoid of drama or complaint, she told him how her father had died of the drink, a man he never knew, and his father before him. She told him about all those uncles who had gone before who'd been drunkards. "It's a craving in the blood," she said again. "A positive craving in the blood. You have to stay with me, Toby. You have to say the rosary with me again. Dear God, help me, help me, help me."

"Listen, Ma," he said to her. "I'm going to make more and

more money playing music. This summer I have a full-time job playing at the restaurant. All summer I'll be making money every night seven nights a week. Don't you see what that means? I'll be making more than ever."

He went on as her eyes glazed over and the wine made her stuporous.

"Ma, I'm going to get a degree from the Conservatory. I'll be able to teach music. Maybe I'll even be able to make a record sometime, you know. But I'll get my degree in music, Ma. I'll be able to teach. You have to hang on. You have to believe in me."

She stared at him with eyes like marbles.

"Look, after this coming week, I'll have enough to get a woman to come in, to do the laundry and all and help Emily and Jacob with their homework. I'll work all the time. I'll play outside before the restaurant opens." He put his hands on her shoulders and her mouth worked itself into a skewed smile. "I'm a man now, Ma. I'm going to do it!"

She slowly slipped into sleep. It was past nine o'clock.

Do angels really lack knowledge of the heart? I wept as I listened to him and watched him.

He went on and on talking to her as she slept, about how they'd move out of this crummy little apartment. Emily and Jacob would still go to Holy Name School, he'd drive them in the car he was going to buy. He already had his eye on it. "Ma, when I perform at the Conservatory for the first time, I want you to be there. I want you and Emily and Jacob to be in the balcony. That won't be long at all. My teacher's helping me now. I'll get the tickets for us all to come. Ma, I'm going to make things all right, you understand? Ma, I'll get you a doctor, a doctor who knows what to do."

In her drunken sleep, she murmured. "Yes dear, yes dear, yes dear."

Around eleven o'clock, he gave her another beer and she went dead asleep. He left the wine beside her. He saw to it Emily and Jacob were in their pajamas and tucked in, and then he put on the fine black tuxedo and boiled shirt he'd bought for graduation. They were, of course, the finest of the garments he had. And he'd bought them outright because he knew that he could use them on the street to good effect, and maybe even in the better restaurants.

He went downtown to play for money.

There were parties all over the city that night for the Jesuit graduates. They were not for Toby.

He parked himself very near to the most famous bars on Bourbon Street, and there he opened his case, and began to play. He sank his heart and soul into the saddest litanies of woe ever penned by Roy Orbison. And soon the twenty-dollar bills came flying at him.

What a spectacle he was, already at his full height, and so finely dressed compared to the ragged street musicians seated here or there, or the mumblers simply begging for coins, or the ragged but brilliant little tap dancers.

He played "Danny Boy" at least six times that night for one couple alone, and they gave him a hundred-dollar bill that he slipped into his wallet. He played all the ripping crowd-pleasers he knew, and if they clapped for the bluegrass then off he went, the country fiddler with the lute, and they jigged around him. He put everything out of his mind, except his music.

When early morning came, he went into the St. Louis Cathedral. He prayed the psalm he had so loved from his grandmother's Catholic Bible:

Save me, O God, for the waters have come up to my neck. I am stuck fast in the mire of the deep, and there is nowhere to set my foot. I am come into deep waters, and the waves overwhelm me. I have grown weary from crying, my throat has become hoarse; my eyes have failed while I await my God.

Finally, he whispered, "Dear God, will you not end this pain!"

He had over six hundred dollars now to pay the bills. He was way ahead. But what did it matter if he couldn't save her?

"Dear God," he prayed. "I don't want for her to die. I'm sorry I prayed for her to die. Dear Lord, save her."

A beggar came up to him as he left the cathedral. She was poorly dressed and murmured under her breath of her need for medicine to save a dying child. He knew she was lying. He'd seen her many a time, and heard her tell the same story. He stared at her for a long time, then silenced her with a wave of his hand and a smile, and he gave her twenty dollars.

Tired as he was, he walked through the Quarter rather than spend the few bucks for a cab, and he rode the St. Charles car up home, staring dumbly out the window.

He wanted desperately to see Liona. He knew that she had come last night to see him graduate—she and her parents, in fact—and he wanted to explain to her why he had not been there.

He remembered that they had had plans afterwards, but now it seemed remote and he was too tired to think of what he would say to her when he finally spoke to her. He thought of her large loving eyes, of the ready wit and sharp intellect she never concealed, and her ringing laugh. He thought of all the wondrous traits she had, and he knew that as the college years passed, he would surely lose her. She had a scholarship at the Conservatory too, but how could he compete with the young men who would inevitably surround her?

She had a glorious voice, and in the production at Jesuit, she had seemed a natural star, loving the stage, and graciously but confidently accepting applause and flowers and compliments.

He didn't understand why she had bothered with him at all. And he felt he had to draw back, let her go, and yet he almost cried thinking about her.

As the rattling clanking streetcar moved uptown, he hugged his lute and even went to sleep against it for a little while. But he woke with a start at his stop, and got off and dragged his feet as he went down the pavement.

As soon as he entered the apartment he knew something was wrong.

He found Jacob and Emily drowned in the bathtub. And she, with her wrists slit, lay dead on the bed, the blood soaking the spread and half of the pillow.

For a long time, he stared at the bodies of his brother and sister. The water had drained out but their pajamas were in moist wrinkles. He could see the bruises all over Jacob. What a fight he had put up. But the face of Emily at the other end of the tub was smooth and perfect, with eyes closed. Maybe she hadn't been awake when their mother had drowned her. There was blood in the water. There was blood on the waterspout where Jacob must have cracked his head as she pushed him down.

The kitchen knife lay beside his mother. She'd all but chopped off her left hand, so deep was the wound, but she'd bled to death from both wrists.

All this had happened hours ago, he knew it.

The blood was dry or at best sticky.

Yet still he lifted his brother out of the tub and actually tried to breathe life into him. His brother's body was icy cold, or so it seemed. And it was soggy.

He couldn't bear to touch his mother or his sister.

His mother lay with her lids half shut, her mouth open. She looked already dried out, like a husk. A husk, he thought, exactly. He stared at the rosary in the blood. The blood was all over the painted wood floor.

Only the smell of wine hung over all these pitiable visions. Only the smell of the malt in the beer. Outside cars passed. A block away, there came the roar of the passing streetcar.

Toby went into the living room, and sat for a long time with his lute on his lap.

Why hadn't he known such a thing could happen? Why had he left Jacob and Emily alone with her? Dear God, why had he not seen that it would come to this? Jacob was only ten years old. How in the name of Heaven had Toby let this happen to them?

It was all his fault. He had no doubt of it. That she might hurt herself, yes, of this he'd thought, and God forgive him, maybe he had even prayed for that in the cathedral. But this? His brother and sister dead? His breathing stopped again. For a moment he thought he'd never be able to breathe again. He stood up and only then did the breath come out of him in a dry soundless sob.

Listlessly he stared at the mean apartment with its ugly mismatched furnishings, its old oak desk and cheap flowered chairs, and all the world to him seemed filthy and gray and he felt a fear and then a growing terror.

His heart pounded. He stared at the drugstore prints of flowers in their ugly frames—these foolish things he'd bought—ranged around the papered walls of the apartment. He stared at the flimsy curtains he'd bought as well, and the cheap white window shades behind them.

He didn't want to go into the bedroom and see the print of the guardian angel. He felt he would rip it to pieces if he saw it. He would not ever again, ever, raise his eyes to such a thing.

A gloom followed the pain. A gloom came when the pain could not be sustained. It covered every object that he beheld, and concepts such as warmth and love seemed unreal to him, or forever beyond reach, as he sat in the midst of this ugliness and ruin.

Sometime or other during the hours he sat there, he heard the answering machine on the phone. It was Liona calling him. He knew that he could not pick up the phone. He knew that he could never see her again, or speak to her, or tell her about what had happened.

He didn't pray. It didn't even occur to him. It didn't even occur to him to talk to the angel at his side, or the Lord to whom he'd prayed only an hour and a half ago. He'd never see his brother and sister alive again, or his mother, or his father, or anyone he knew. This is what he thought. They were dead, irrevocably dead. He believed in nothing. If someone had come to him at that moment, as his guardian angel sought to do, and told him, *You will see them all again,* he might have spat at that person in a perfect fury.

All day he remained in the apartment with his dead family ranged around him. He kept the bathroom and bedroom doors open, because he didn't want the bodies to be alone. It seemed horribly disrespectful.

Liona called twice more, and the second time he was half dozing and wasn't sure whether or not he had really heard her.

Finally he fell deep asleep on the sofa, and when he first opened his eyes, he forgot what had happened, and he thought they were all alive and things were as usual. At once, the truth came back to him with the force of a hammer.

He changed into his blazer and khakis and packed up all his fine clothes. He got them into the suitcase his mother had taken to the hospital years ago when she'd had her babies. He took all the cash from the hiding places.

He kissed his little brother. Rolling up his sleeve, he reached down into the soiled bathtub to put a kiss with his fingers on his sister's cheek. Then he kissed his mother's shoulder. Again he stared at the rosary. She hadn't been saying it as she died. It was just there, caught in the snarled spread, forgotten.

He picked it up, took it into the bathroom, and ran the basin water over it until it was clean. Then he dried it on a towel and put it in his pocket.

Everybody looked very dead now, very empty. There was no odor yet, but they were very dead. The rigidity of his mother's face absorbed him. The body of Jacob on the floor was dry and wrinkled.

Then, as he turned to go, he went back to his desk. He wanted to take two books with him. He took his prayer book, and he took the book called *The Angels* by Fr. Pascal Parente.

I observed this. I observed it with keen interest.

I noticed the way that he packed these treasured books in the bulging suitcase. He thought about other religious books that he loved, including a *Lives of the Saints,* but he had no room for them.

He took the streetcar downtown and, outside the first hotel he reached, he caught a cab to the airport.

Only once, it crossed his mind to call the police, to report what had happened. But then he felt such rage that he put these thoughts out of his mind forever.

He went to New York. Nobody could find you in New York, he figured.

On the plane, he clutched his lute as if something might happen to it. He stared out the window and he knew a misery so deep that it didn't seem possible life could ever hold a particle of joy again.

Not even murmuring melodies to himself of the songs he

most liked to play meant anything to him. In his ears, he heard a din as if the imps of Hell were making a horrid music to drive him out of his mind. He whispered to himself to silence it. He slipped his hand into his pocket, found his rosary, and prayed the words but he didn't meditate upon the mysteries. "Hail Mary," he whispered under his breath, ". . . now and at the hour of our death. Amen." *These are just words,* he thought. He could not imagine eternity.

When the stewardess asked him if he wanted a soft drink, he answered, "Someone will bury them." She gave him a Coke with ice. He didn't sleep. It was only two and a half hours to New York but the plane circled for more than that before it finally landed.

He thought about his mother. What could he have done? Where could he have put her? He had been looking for places, doctors, some way, any way to buy time until he could save everyone. Maybe he hadn't moved fast enough, been clever enough. Maybe he should have told his teachers at school.

Didn't matter now, he told himself.

It was evening. The dark giant buildings of the East Side of the city seemed infernal. The sheer noise of the city astonished him. It enclosed him in the bouncing taxi, or battered him at the stoplights. Behind a thick window of plastic the driver was a mere ghost to him.

Finally banging on the plastic, he told the man he needed a cheap hotel. He was afraid the man would think he was a child and take him to some policeman. He didn't realize that at six foot four inches of height and with the grim expression on his face, he didn't look like a child at all. The hotel was not as bad as he'd expected.

He thought about bad things as he walked the streets in search of a job. He carried his lute with him.

He thought of the afternoons when he was little and he

would come home and find both of his parents drunk. His father was a bad policeman, and everyone knew it. None of his mother's people could stand him. Only his own mother had pleaded with him over and over to treat his wife and children better.

Even when Toby was small, he knew his father bullied the loose women in the French Quarter, forcing favors out of them before he would "let them off." He'd heard his father brag about that kind of thing with the few other cops who had come over for beer and poker. They'd shared those stories. When the other men said that his father ought to be proud of a boy like Toby, his father had said, "Who, you mean Pretty Face over there? My little girl?"

Now and then when he'd been very drunk, his father had taunted Toby, pushing him, asking to see what Toby had between his legs. Sometimes Toby had gotten a beer or two from the icebox for his father to move him along to the time when he'd pass out and doze with his arms crossed on the table.

Toby had been glad when his father went to prison. His father had always been coarse and cold, and had a shapeless and red face. He was mean and ugly and he looked mean and ugly. The handsome young man he'd been in photographs had turned into an obese and red-faced drunk with jowls and a roughened voice. Toby was glad when his father was stabbed. He couldn't remember any funeral.

Toby's mother had always been pretty. In those days, she'd been sweet. And her favorite words for her son had been "my sweet boy."

Toby resembled her in face and manner, and he'd never ceased to be proud of that, no matter what had happened. He never ceased to be proud of his increasing height, and he took pride in the way he dressed to wring the money from the tourists.

Now as he walked through the streets of New York, trying to ignore the great booming noises that accosted him at every turn, trying to weave amongst the people without being knocked about, he thought over and over again, *I was never enough for her, never enough. Nothing I did was ever enough. Nothing.* Never had anything he had done been enough for anyone, except perhaps his music teacher. He thought of her now and he wished he could call her and tell her how much he loved her. But he knew he wouldn't do this.

The long dreary day of New York suddenly switched dramatically to evening. Cheerful lights went on everywhere. Store awnings sparkled with lights. Couples moved swiftly along to movie theaters or to stage plays. It wasn't hard to realize that he was in the Theater District and he loved looking in the windows of the restaurants. But he wasn't hungry. The thought of food revolted him.

When the theaters let out, Toby took up his lute, set down the green velvet–lined case, and began to play. He shut his eyes. His mouth was half open. He played the darkest most intricate music by Bach that he knew, and he saw every now and then, through a slit of vision, the bills piling in the lute case, and heard even here and there applause from those who stopped to hear him.

Now he had even more money.

He went back to his room and decided he liked it. He didn't care that it looked on rooftops and a shiny wet alley below. He liked the real bedstead and the little table, and the large television that was an infinite improvement on the one he'd watched all those years in the apartment. There were clean white towels in the bathroom.

The next night, on the recommendation of a cabbie, he went to Little Italy. He played on the street between two busy restaurants there. And this time he played all the melodies he knew from the opera. Poignantly he played the songs of Madame Butterfly and Puccini's other heroines. He went through stirring riffs and wove together the songs of Verdi.

A waiter came out of one restaurant and told him to move on. But someone interrupted the waiter. It was a big heavyset man in a white apron.

"You play that again," said the man. He had thick black hair and only a little white at the sides over his ears. He rocked back and forth as Toby played the music from *La Bohème*, and attempted again the most heart-wrenching arias.

Then he moved on into the gay and festive songs of *Carmen*. The old man clapped for him and wiped his hands on his apron and clapped some more.

Toby played every tender song that he knew.

The crowd shifted, paid, and filled out again. The pudgy old man stood listening to all of it.

Over and over the pudgy man reminded him to collect the bills out of his case and hide them. The money kept coming.

When Toby was too tired to play anymore, he started to pack up but the pudgy old man said, "Wait a minute, son." And he asked him to play Neapolitan songs that Toby had never played, but he knew them by ear and it was easy.

"What are you doing here, son?" asked the man.

"Looking for a job," said Toby, "any kind of job, dishwasher, waiter, anything, I don't care, just work, good work."

He looked at the man. The man was wearing decent trousers and a white dress shirt open at the neck with the sleeves rolled just below the elbows. The man had a soft fleshy face, graven with kindliness.

"I'll give you a job," said the man. "Come inside. I'll fix you something to eat. You've been out here all night playing."

By the end of his first week he had a little second-floor hotel apartment downtown, and a fake set of identification papers saying that he was twenty-one (old enough to serve wine) and he had the name Vincenzo Valenti because the name had been suggested to him by the gentle old Italian who had hired him. A real birth certificate had come with the suggestion.

The man's name was Alonso. The restaurant was beautiful. It had huge glass windows facing the street, and very bright lights, and in between their waiting tables, the waiters and waitresses, students all, sang opera. Toby was the lutist beside the piano.

It was good, good for Toby who didn't want to remember that he had ever been Toby.

Never had he heard such fine voices.

On many a night, when the restaurant was crowded with convivial parties, and the opera was sweet, and he could play his lute in a ripping fashion, he felt almost good and didn't want for the doors to close, or the wet pavements to be waiting for him.

Alonso was good-hearted, smiling, and took a special liking to Toby, who was his Vincenzo.

"What I wouldn't give," he said to Toby, "just to see one of my grandchildren."

Alonso gave Toby a little pearl-handled gun and told him how to shoot it. It had a soft trigger. It was just for protection. Alonzo showed him the guns he kept in the kitchen. Toby found himself fascinated with these guns, and when Alonso took him into the alley behind the restaurant and let him shoot with these guns, he liked the feel of them, and the deafening sound that echoed up the high blind walls on both sides of them.

Alonso got work for Toby at weddings and at engagement parties, paid him well, bought him fine Italian suits for the job, and sometimes sent him to serve private dinners in a house only a few blocks from the restaurant. People unfailingly found the lute to be elegant.

This house where he played was a handsome place, but it made Toby uneasy. Though most of the women living there were old, and kind, there were a few young women, and men came to see them. The woman who ran the place was named Violet and she had a deep whiskey voice, and wore heavy makeup, and treated all the other women as her young sisters or children. Alonso loved to sit for hours and talk to Violet. They spoke Italian mostly but sometimes English and they seemed involved in times gone by, and there were hints they had once been lovers.

There were card games there, and sometimes little birthday gatherings, mostly of elderly men and women, but the young women smiled at Toby lovingly and teasingly.

One time, behind a painted dressing screen, he played the lute for a man who made love to a woman, and the man hurt her. She hit the man and the man slapped her.

Alonso waved it away. "She does that all the time," he explained as if the conduct of the man had not been involved in it. Alonso called the girl Elsbeth.

"What kind of name is that?" Toby asked.

Alonso shrugged. "Russian? Bosnian? How do I know?" He smiled. "They have blond hair. The men love them. And she's run away from some Russian, that I can tell you. I'll be lucky if the bastard doesn't come looking for her."

Toby grew to like Elsbeth. She did have an accent that might have been Russian, and once she told him that she had made up her name, and as Toby was now calling himself Vincenzo, he felt a certain sympathy with that. Elsbeth was very young. Toby wasn't sure she was past sixteen. The makeup she wore made her look older and less fresh. With a bit of lipstick only on Sunday morning, she was beautiful. She smoked black cigarettes on the fire escape as they talked together.

Alonso sometimes took Toby home for a plate of spaghetti with him and his mother. This was in Brooklyn. Alonso served Northern Italian food at the restaurant, since that was what the world wanted now, but as for the old man, he liked his meatballs and red gravy. His own sons lived in California. His daughter was dead from drugs when she was fourteen. He pointed to her picture once and that was the last of it.

He would sneer and wave his hand at the mere mention of his sons.

Alonso's mother didn't speak English, and would never sit at the table. She poured the wine, cleaned up the dishes, and stood against the stove, with her arms folded, staring at the men as they ate. She made Toby think of his grandmothers. They had been women like that, who stood while the men ate. Such a dim memory.

Alonso and Toby went to the Metropolitan Opera several times, and Toby concealed what a revelation this was, to be hearing one of the greatest companies in the world, to be sitting in good seats with a man who knew the story and the music perfectly. Toby knew something in those hours that was the perfect imitation of happiness.

Toby had been to operas in New Orleans, with his teacher from the Conservatory. And he had heard the students at Loyola sing opera too, and been moved by these dramatic spectacles. But the Metropolitan Opera was infinitely more impressive.

They went to Carnegie Hall and also to the symphony.

It was a thin emotion, this happiness, drawn like a gossamer sheet over the things he remembered. He wanted to be joyful as he looked around these great auditoriums and listened to the dazzling music, but he didn't dare to trust in anything.

One time he told Alonso he needed a beautiful necklace to send to a woman.

Alonso laughed and shook his head.

"No, my music teacher," said Toby. "She taught me for free. I have two thousand dollars saved up."

Alonso said, "You leave it to me."

The necklace was stunning, "an estate piece." Alonso paid for it. He wouldn't take a dime from Toby.

Toby shipped it to the woman at the Conservatory because that was the only address he had for her. He put no return address on the package.

One afternoon, he went to St. Patrick's Cathedral and sat for an hour staring at the main altar. He believed nothing. He felt nothing. The words of the psalms he had so loved did not come back to him.

As he was leaving, as he was lingering in the foyer of the church, looking back at it as if it were a world he would never behold again, a rough policeman forced a young tourist couple to leave because they had been embracing. Toby stared at the policeman, who gestured for him to get out. But Toby just took his rosary out of his pocket and the policeman nodded and moved away from him.

In his own mind, he was a failure. This world of his in New York wasn't real. He had failed his little brother, his sister, his mother, and he had disappointed his father. *Pretty Face.*

At times, an anger began to blaze in Toby but it wasn't directed at anyone.

This is an anger angels have trouble understanding because what Toby had long ago underlined in the book of Pascal Parente was true.

We angels do in some respects lack cardiognosis. But I knew intelligently what Toby felt; I knew from his face and from his hands, and even from the way that he now played his lute, more darkly and with a forced gaiety. His lute, with its deep roughened tones, took on a melancholy sound. Both sorrow and joy were subjected to it. He couldn't put his own private pain in it.

One night his employer, Alonso, came to Toby's little hotel apartment. He carried a big leather knapsack over his shoulder.

This was a place Alonso had sublet to Toby on the very edge of Little Italy. It was a fine place as far as Toby was concerned, though the windows looked out on walls, and the furniture was fine and even a little fancy.

But Toby was surprised to open the door and see Alonso. Alonso had never come there. Alonso might put him in a cab to go home after the opera, but he'd never come home with him.

Alonso sat down and asked for wine.

Toby had to go out to get it. He never kept liquor in his apartment.

Alonso started to drink. He took out from his coat a large gun and laid it on the kitchen table.

Alonso told Toby he was up against a force that had never threatened him before: Russian mobsters wanted his restaurant and his catering business, and they had taken his "house" away from him.

"They'd want this hotel," he said, "but they don't know I own it."

A small band of them had gone right into the house where Toby had played for the card gamers and the ladies. They had shot the men there, and four of the women and girls, and run off everybody else, and put in their own girls in place of them.

"I've never seen this kind of evil," said Alonso. "My friends won't stand by me. What friends do I have? I think my friends are in this with them. I think my friends have sold me out. Why else would they let this happen to me? I don't know what to do about this. My friends blame me for this."

Toby stared at the gun. Alonso took the clip out of it, then shoved it back in. "Know what this is? This will shoot more rounds than you can imagine."

"Did they kill Elsbeth?" Toby asked.

"Shot her in the head," said Alonso. "Shot her in the head!" Alonso began to shout. Elsbeth was the reason these men had come, and Alonso's friends had told him how foolish it was for him and Violet to have given her shelter.

"Did they shoot Violet?" Toby asked.

Alonso began to sob. "Yes, they shot Violet." He wept uncontrollably. "They shot Violet first, an old girl like that. Why would they do that?"

Toby sat thinking. He wasn't thinking about all the crime dramas he had once watched on television, or the true-crime novels he had read. He was thinking his own thoughts, about those who prevail in this world and those who don't, those who are strong and resourceful, and those who are weak.

He could see Alonso getting drunk. He detested this.

Toby thought for a long time and then he said, "You have to do to them what they are trying to do to you."

Alonso stared at him and then broke into laughter.

"I'm an old man," he said. "And these men, they're going to kill me. I can't go up against them! I've never fired a gun like this one in my life."

He talked on and on as he drank wine, getting drunker and angrier, explaining that he had always cared about "the basic things," a good restaurant, a house or two where men could relax, play a little cards, have a little friendly companionship.

"It's the real estate," Alonso sighed. "If you want to know. That's what they want. I should have gotten the Hell out of Manhattan. And now it's too late. I'm finished."

Toby listened to everything that he said.

These Russian gangsters had moved right into his house, and brought the deeds for the house to the restaurant. They had deeds for the restaurant as well. Alonso, confronted at the crowded dinner hour, and safe amongst witnesses, had refused to sign anything.

They'd bragged about the lawyers who handled their deeds and the men at the bank who worked for them.

Alonso was supposed to sign his businesses away. They promised if he signed the deeds and cleared out, they'd give him a piece of things, and they wouldn't hurt him.

"Give me a piece of my own house?" Alonso bawled. "It's not enough for them, the house. They want the restaurant my grandfather opened. That's what they really want. And they'll move on this hotel soon as they find out about it. They said if I didn't sign the papers, they'd have their lawyer take care of it, and no one would ever find my body. They said they could do to the restaurant the things they'd done in the house. They would make it look to the cops like a robbery. That's what they said to me. 'You're murdering your own people if you don't sign.' These Russians are monsters."

Toby pondered this, what it would mean if these gangsters had moved on the restaurant at night, shut the big blinds to the street, and murdered all the employees. He felt a shiver when he realized that death was coming very close to him.

Without words, he pictured the bodies of Jacob and Emily. Emily with her eyes closed underwater.

Alonso drank another glass of wine. Thank Heaven, Toby thought, that he had bought two fifths of the best Cabernet.

"After I'm dead," Alonso said, "what if they find my mother?"

A sullen silence came over Alonso.

I could see his guardian angel beside him, seemingly impassive yet striving somehow to comfort him. I could see other angels in the room. I could see those that give off no light.

Alonso brooded and so did Toby.

"As soon as I sign these deeds," said Alonso, "as soon as they legally own the restaurant, too, they'll kill me." He reached into his coat and he took out another large gun. He explained that it was an automatic weapon and could shoot even more rounds of ammunition than the first one. "I swear, I will take them with me."

Toby didn't ask, Why not go to the police? He knew the answers to such questions as that and nobody from New Orleans ever trusted the police very much in these sorts of affairs anyway. After all, Toby's father had been a drunken crooked cop. It wasn't in Toby's nature.

"These girls they're bringing in," said Alonso. "They're children, slaves, just children." He continued, "No one's going to help me. My mother will be alone. No one can help me."

Alonso checked the clip of bullets in the second gun. He said he would kill all of them if he could, but he didn't think he could do it. He was very drunk now. "No, I can't do this. I have to get out, but there's no way out. They want the deeds, the legal deeds done. They have their men in the bank, and maybe even in the licensing offices."

He reached into his knapsack and took out all the deeds and spread them on the table. He spread out the two business cards these men had given him. These were the papers that Alonso had yet to sign. They were his death warrant.

Alonso got up, staggered into the bedroom—the only other room in the place—and passed out. He began to snore.

Toby studied all of these items. He knew the house very well, its back door, its fire escapes. He knew the address of the lawyer whose name was on the card, or rather where he could find the building; he knew the location of the bank, though the names of these people meant nothing, obviously.

A glorious vision seized Toby, or I should say Vincenzo. Or should I say Lucky? He had always had a stunning imagination and a great capacity for visual imagery, and now he saw a plan and a great leap forward from the life he led. But it was a leap into pure darkness.

He went into the bedroom. He shook the old man's shoulder.

"They killed Elsbeth?"

"Yeah, they killed her," the old man said with a sigh. "The other girls were hiding under the beds. Two of them got away. They saw those men shoot Elsbeth." He made his hand into a gun, and made the noise of the gun with his lips. "I'm a dead man."

"You really think so?"

"I know so. I want you to care for my mother. If my sons come around, don't talk to them. My mother has all the money I have. Don't talk to them."

"I'll do it," said Toby. But it was not an answer to Alonso's entreaty. It was a simple private confirmation.

Toby went into the other room, gathered up the two guns, and went out the back door of his building. The alley was narrow and the walls went up five stories on either side. The windows appeared, as best he could see, to be covered. He studied each gun. He tested the guns. The bullets flew with such speed it jolted and shocked him.

Somebody opened a window and shouted for him to shut up down there.

He went back into the apartment and put the guns into the knapsack.

The old man was cooking breakfast. He set down a plate of eggs for Toby. And then he sat down himself and began dipping his toast in his egg.

"I can do it," Toby said. "I can kill them."

His employer looked at him. His eyes were dead the way Toby's mother's eyes used to die. The old man drank half a glass of wine and wandered back into the bedroom.

Toby went and looked down at him. The smell made Toby

think of his mother and father. The dead glassy gaze of his employer as he looked up at Toby made him think of his mother.

"I'm safe here," the old man said. "This address, nobody has it. It's not written down anywhere at the restaurant."

"Good," said Toby. He was relieved to hear it, and had been afraid to ask about it.

In the wee hours as the new clock ticked on the sideboard in the little kitchen, Toby studied all the deeds and both the business cards, and then he slipped the cards into his pocket.

He woke up Alonso again and insisted that he describe the men he'd seen, and Alonso tried to do it, but finally Toby realized he was too drunk.

Alonso drank more wine. He ate a dried crust of French bread. He asked for more bread and butter and wine, and Toby gave him these things.

"Stay here, and don't think of anything until I come back," said Toby.

"You're just a boy," said Alonso. "You can't do anything about this. Get word to my mother. That's what I ask. Tell her not to call my boys on the coast. Tell her, the Hell with them."

"You can stay here and do as I say," said Toby. Toby was powerfully exhilarated. He was making plans. He had certain specific dreams. He felt superior to all the forces collected around him and Alonso.

Toby was also furious. He was furious that anyone in the world thought he was a boy who could do nothing about this. He thought of Elsbeth. He thought of Violet with her cigarette on her lip, dealing the cards at the green felt table in the house. He thought of the girls talking together in whispers on the sofa. He thought over and over of Elsbeth.

Alonso stared at him.

"I'm too old to be defeated in this way," he said.

"So am I," said Toby.

"You're eighteen," said Alonso.

"No," said Toby. He shook his head. "That's not true."

Alonso's guardian angel stood beside him, staring at him with an expression of sorrow. This angel was at the limit of what he could do. The angel of Toby was appalled.

Neither angel could do anything. But they didn't give up trying. They suggested to Toby and to Alonso that they should flee, get the mother from Brooklyn and get on a plane for Miami. Let the men of violence have what they wanted.

"You're right that they'll kill you," said Toby, "as soon as you sign these papers."

"I have nowhere to go. How do I tell this to my mother?" asked the old man. "I should shoot my mother, so that she doesn't suffer. I should shoot her and then shoot myself and that would be the end of it."

"No!" said Toby. "Stay here as I told you."

Toby put on a recording of *Tosca,* and Alonso sang along with it and was soon snoring.

Toby walked for blocks before he went to a drugstore, bought a black cosmetic hair rinse, and unflattering but fashionable black-rimmed tinted glasses, and, from a table vendor on West Fifty-sixth Street, an expensive-looking briefcase and, from another vendor, a fake Rolex watch.

He went into another drugstore, and he bought a series of items, little items no one would notice, such as plastic devices people use to place between their teeth when they sleep, and lots of the soft rubber and plastic offered to help people line their shoes. He bought a pair of scissors, and he bought a bottle of clear nail polish and an emery board for trimming his nails. He stopped again at a vendor's table on Fifth Avenue and bought himself several pairs of lightweight leather gloves. Handsome gloves. He also bought a yellow cashmere scarf. It was cold and it felt good to have this around his neck.

He felt powerful as he walked along the street, and he felt invincible.

When he came back to the apartment, Alonso was sitting there anxiously, and the music was Callas singing *Carmen*. "You know," Alonso said, "I'm afraid to leave."

"You should be," said Toby. He began polishing his nails and filing them.

"What on earth are you doing?" Alonso asked him.

"I'm not certain yet," said Toby, "but I notice when there are men in the restaurant who have polished nails, people notice it, especially women."

Alonso shrugged.

Toby went out to get some lunch and several bottles of excellent wine so that they could make it through another day.

"They might be killing people at the restaurant now," said Alonso. "I should have warned everyone to get out." He sighed and put his heavy head in his hands. "I didn't lock up the restaurant. What if they go there and gun down everybody?"

Toby merely nodded.

Then he went out, walked a couple of blocks, and called the restaurant. No one answered. This was a terrible sign. The restaurant should have been crowded for dinner, with people grabbing for the phone and jotting down evening reservations.

Toby reflected that he'd been wise to keep his apartment a secret, to make friends with no one but Alonso, to trust no one just as he had trusted no one when he was growing up.

Early morning came.

Toby showered and put the black tint in his hair.

The employer slept in his clothes on top of Toby's bed.

Toby put on a fine Italian suit that Alonso had bought for him, and then he added the accoutrements so that he didn't look like himself at all.

The plastic bite device changed the shape of his mouth. The heavy frames of the tinted glasses gave his face an expression that was alien to it. The gloves were dove gray and beautiful. He wrapped the yellow scarf around his neck. He put on his only and best black cashmere overcoat.

He'd fitted his shoes with plenty of material to make him look taller than he was, but not by much. He put the two automatic weapons in his briefcase, and the small handgun he put in his pocket.

He looked at his employer's knapsack. It was black leather, very fine. So he slung it over his shoulder.

He went to the house before the sun came up. A woman he'd never seen before opened the front door. She smiled at him and welcomed him in. No one else was in sight.

He took the automatic weapon from his briefcase and shot her, and he shot the men who came running down the hall towards him. He shot the people who thundered down the stairs. He shot the people who seemed to run right into the gunfire as if they did not believe it was happening.

He heard screaming upstairs and he went up, stepping over one body after another, and shot through the doors, breaking big holes in them until everything was silence.

He stood at the very end of the hall and waited. Out came one man cautiously, gun visible before his arm and then his shoulder. Toby shot him immediately.

Twenty minutes passed. Maybe more. Nothing stirred in the house. Slowly, he made his way through every room of it. All dead.

He gathered up every cell phone he could find, and put them in the leather shoulder bag. There was a laptop computer there, and he folded it up and took it too, though it was a little heavier than he wanted it to be. He cut the wires to the computer desk, and to the landline phone.

As he was leaving, he heard the sound of someone crying

and talking in a low pathetic voice. He kicked open the door and found a very young girl there, blond with red lipstick, crouched down on her knees with a cell phone to her ear. She dropped the phone in terror when she saw him. She shook her head, she begged in some language he couldn't understand.

He killed her. She fell down dead instantly and lay there as his mother had lain on her bloody mattress. Dead.

He picked up her phone. A gruff voice demanded of him, "What's happening?"

"Nothing," he said in a whisper. "She was out of her mind." He slammed the phone shut. The blood coursed hot through his veins. He felt powerful.

Now he made his way again very fast through every room. He found one man wounded and moaning and he shot him. He found a woman bleeding to death and he shot her too. He collected more phones. His knapsack was bulging.

Then he went out, walked several blocks, and caught a taxi.

It took him uptown to the office of the lawyer who had handled the transfer of the property.

Affecting a limp as he walked and sighing as if the briefcase weighed too much, and the shoulder bag were dragging him down, he made his way into the office.

The receptionist had just unlocked the door, and smiling, she explained her boss had not come in yet, but would come any minute. She said the yellow scarf around his neck was beautiful.

He slumped down on the leather couch and, carefully removing one glove, he wiped his forehead as though a terrible ache were bothering him. She looked at him tenderly.

"Beautiful hands," she said, "like those of a musician."

He laughed under his breath. In a whisper, he said, "All I want to do is go back to Switzerland." He was very excited. He knew that he was lisping as he whispered because of the plastic bite plate in his mouth. It made him laugh, but only to himself. He had never been so tantalized in all his life. He thought for one split second that he understood the old words, "the glamour of evil."

She offered him coffee. He put back on his glove. He said, "No, it will keep me awake on the plane. I want to sleep over the Atlantic."

"I can't recognize your accent. What is it?"

"Swiss," he whispered, lisping effortlessly because of the device in his mouth. "I'm so eager to go home. I loathe this city."

A sudden noise from the street startled him. It was a pile driver beginning the day's work on a construction site. The noise was repetitive and shook the office fiercely.

He winced in pain, and she told him how sorry she was that he had to endure this.

In came the lawyer.

Toby stood up to his full commanding height and said in the same lisping whisper, "I've come on an important matter."

The man was immediately afraid, as he let Toby into his office.

"Look, I'm moving as fast as I can," said the man, "but that old Italian's a fool. And he's stubborn. Your employer expects miracles." He rummaged through the papers on his desk. "I have found out this. He's sitting on a teardown just a few blocks from the restaurant, and the place is worth millions."

Again, Toby almost laughed, but he didn't. He took the papers from the man, glancing at the address, which was that of his hotel, and shoved them in his briefcase.

The lawyer was petrified.

There were clanging noises from outside, and huge reverberating shocks as if heavy loads of material were being dropped to the street. Toby saw a big white painted crane when he looked out the window.

"Call the bank now," Toby whispered, struggling over the lisp. "And you'll find out what I'm talking about." Again he almost laughed to himself. And it came across as a smile to this man, who instantly punched in a number on his cell phone.

The lawyer cursed. "You guys think I'm some kind of Einstein." His face changed. The man at the bank had answered.

Toby took the cell phone out of the lawyer's hand. He said into the phone, "I want to see you. I want to see you outside the bank. I want you to be waiting for me."

On the other end the man gave his consent immediately. The number in the little digital window on the phone was the same as the number on one of the business cards in Toby's pocket. Toby closed the phone and slipped it in his briefcase.

"What are you doing?" asked the lawyer.

Toby felt total power over the man. He felt invincible. Some vagrant wisp of romance prompted him to say, "You are a liar and a thief."

He took the small gun out of his pocket and shot the man. The sound was swallowed by the booms and clatters from the street.

He looked at the laptop computer on the desk. He couldn't leave it. Awkwardly he jammed it into the shoulder bag with the others.

He was loaded down, but he was very strong with good broad shoulders.

He found himself laughing again under his breath as he stared at the dead man. He felt wonderful. He felt marvelous. He felt as he had felt when he imagined himself playing the lute on a world-famous stage. Only this was better.

He was deliciously giddy, as giddy as he'd been when he'd

first thought of all these things, these bits and pieces of things which he'd garnered from television crime dramas and occasional novels, and he forced himself not to laugh but to move on quickly.

He took all the money in the man's wallet, some fifteen hundred dollars.

In the outer office, he smiled lovingly at the young woman. "Listen to me," he said, leaning over the desk. "He wants you to leave now. He's expecting, well, some people."

"Ah, yes, I know," she said, trying to look very clever and very approving and very calm, "but how long should I be out?"

"The day, take the day," said Toby. "No, believe me, he wants you to." He gave her several of the man's twenty-dollar bills. "Take a taxi home. Enjoy yourself. And call in the morning, you understand? Don't come in before calling."

She was charmed by him.

She went out with him to the elevator, very elated to be with him, such a tall young man, such a mysterious and handsome young man, he knew this, and she told him again that his yellow scarf was gorgeous. She noticed his limp but pretended not to notice.

Before the elevator doors closed, he gazed down at her through the dark glasses, smiling as brightly as she smiled, and said, "Think of me as Lord Byron."

He walked the few blocks to the bank, but stopped a few yards from the entrance. The thickening crowd almost knocked him aside. He moved to the wall, and he punched in the number of the banker on the phone he'd stolen from the lawyer.

"Come outside now," he said in his now practiced lisping whisper, as his eyes moved over the crowd before the bank's entrance.

"I am outside," the man said gruffly and angrily. "Where the Hell are you?"

Toby easily spotted him as the man shoved the phone back into his pocket.

Toby stood looking about himself in amazement at the speed of those moving in both directions. The roar of the traffic was deafening. Bicycles whizzed through the sluggish rumble of trucks and taxis. The noise rolled up the walls as if to Heaven. Horns blared and the air was full of gray smoke.

He looked up at the slice of blue sky which gave no light whatsoever to this crevice of the giant city, and he thought to himself he had never been so alive. Not even in Liona's arms had he felt this vigor.

He punched the number again, this time listening for the ring and watching for the man, almost lost in this ever-shifting glut of people, to answer.

Yes, he had his man, gray haired, heavy, red faced now with fury. The victim stepped to the curb. "How long do you want me to stand out here?" he barked into the phone. He turned and walked back to the granite wall of the bank and stood to the left of the revolving door, looking around coldly.

The man glared at everybody passing him, except the lean bent-over young man who limped as if because of his heavy shoulder bag and briefcase.

This man he didn't notice at all.

As soon as Toby moved behind him, Toby shot the man in the head. Quickly he shoved the gun back in his coat and, with his right hand, helped the man slide down the wall to the pavement, with his legs out in front of him. Toby knelt solicitously right beside him.

He took out the man's linen handkerchief and wiped his face. The man was dead, obviously. Then in plain sight of the unseeing crowd, he took the man's phone, his wallet, and a small notebook from his breast pocket.

Not a single person passing had paused, not even those who were stepping over the banker's outstretched legs.

A flash of memory surprised Toby. He saw his brother and sister, wet and dead in the bathtub.

Emphatically, he rejected this memory. He told himself it was meaningless. He folded the linen handkerchief as best he could with one gloved hand, and laid it across the man's moist forehead.

He walked three blocks before catching a cab, and left the taxi three blocks from his apartment.

Toby went upstairs, his fingers shaking as he held the gun in his pocket. When he knocked on the door, he heard Alonso's voice. "Vincenzo?"

"You're alone in there?" he asked.

Alonso opened the door, and pulled him in. "Where have you been, what's happened to you?" He stared at the darkened hair, the tinted glasses.

Toby searched the apartment.

Then he turned to Alonso and told him, "They're all dead, the people who were bothering you. But this is not finished. There was no time to get to the restaurant and I don't know what's going on there."

"I do," said Alonso. "They fired all my people and closed the place up. What in Hell are you telling me?"

"Ah, well," said Toby, "that's not so bad."

"What in the world do you mean they're all dead?" Alonso asked.

Toby told him everything that had happened. Then he said,

"You have to take me to people who know how to finish this. You have to take me to your friends who wouldn't help you. They'll help you now. They'll want these computers. They'll want these cell phones. They'll want this little notebook. There's data here, tons of data about these criminals and what they want and what they're doing."

Alonso stared at him for a long time without speaking, and then he sank down in the only armchair in the room and ran his fingers through his hair.

Toby bolted the door of the bathroom. He kept the gun with him. He laid the heavy porcelain top of the toilet tank against the door, and he took a shower with the curtain open, washing and washing until all the dark tint was gone from his hair. He smashed the glasses. He wrapped up the gloves, the shattered glasses, and the scarf and put them in a towel.

When he came out, Alonso was talking on the phone. He was deeply absorbed in his conversation. He was talking in Italian or a Sicilian dialect, Toby wasn't sure. He'd picked up some words at the restaurant, but this stream of words was much too fast.

When the man hung up, he said, "You did get them. You got all of them."

"That's what I told you," said Toby. "But others will come. This is only the beginning of something. The information in this lawyer's computer is invaluable."

Alonso stared at him in quiet amazement. His guardian angel stood with his arms folded watching everything sadly—or that is as well as I can describe in human terms his attitude. The angel of Toby was weeping.

"Do you know people who can help me use these computers?" Toby asked. "There were desktops in the house and in the office. I didn't know how to get out the hard drives. I need to know that next time, how to remove the hard drive. All these computers, they have to be loaded with information. There are phone numbers here, hundreds most likely."

Alonso nodded. He was amazed.

"Fifteen minutes," he said.

"Fifteen minutes what?" asked Toby.

"They'll be here, and they'll be very glad to see you and very glad to teach you anything that they can."

"You sure of this?" he asked. "If they wouldn't help you before, why won't they simply kill both of us?"

"Vincenzo," said Alonso. "You're just what they don't have right now. You're just what they need." Tears came to Alonso's eyes. "Son, do you think I would betray you?" he said. "I am in your debt forever. Somewhere there are copies of all these deeds, but you've killed the men who were handling them."

They went downstairs. A black stretch limousine was waiting for them.

Before they got into the car outside, Toby threw the towel with the glasses and the scarf and the gray gloves into a trash can, pushing it deep down into the crackling mess of paper cups and plastic sacks. He hated the smell of it on his left hand. He had his suitcase and his lute, and the briefcase and the leather shoulder bag with the computers and the cell phones.

He didn't like the look of the car and he didn't want to get into it, though he had seen many such cars inching up Fifth Avenue in the evenings, and lumbering past the entrances of Carnegie Hall and the Metropolitan Opera.

Finally, after Alonso, he slipped in and sat facing two young men on the opposite black leather seat.

Both of them were fiercely curious. They were pale, and blond haired, almost certainly Russians.

Toby almost stopped breathing like he had the time his mother had smashed his lute. He kept his hand on the gun in his coat. Neither man had a hand in a pocket. All hands were in plain sight except for Toby's hand.

He turned and looked at Alonso. *You've betrayed me.*

"No, no," said the man opposite, the elder of the two, and Alonso was smiling as if he had just heard a perfect aria. The man spoke like an American, not a Russian.

"How did you do it?" the younger blond-haired man asked. He too was American. He looked at his watch. "It's not even eleven o'clock."

"I'm hungry," Toby said. He held the gun steady in his pocket. "I've always wanted to eat at the Russian Tea Room." Whether he was to die or not, this answer made Toby feel profoundly clever. Also it was true. If he was to have a last meal, he wanted it to be in the Russian Tea Room.

The older man laughed.

"Well, don't shoot either of us, son," he said, gesturing to Toby's pocket. "That would be stupid because we're going to pay you more money now than you've ever seen in your life." He laughed. "We're going to pay you more money than *we've* ever seen in *our* lives. And of course, we'll take you to the Russian Tea Room."

They stopped the car. Alonso got out.

"Why are you leaving?" Toby asked. Again came that breathless fear and his hand tightened on the little gun that was almost tearing his pocket.

Alonso leaned in and kissed him. He grabbed his head and kissed his eyes and kissed him on the lips, then let him go.

"They don't want me," he said. "They want you. I sold you to them but for your sake. You understand? I can't do the things you can do. We can't follow up on this, you and me. I sold you to them for your protection. You're my boy. You'll always be my boy. Now go with them. They want you, not me. You go on. I'm taking my mother down to Miami."

"But you don't have to do this now," Toby protested. "You can have the house back. You can have the restaurant back. I took care of things."

Alonso shook his head. Toby immediately felt stupid.

"Son, with what they paid me, I'm glad to go," Alonso said. "My mother will see Miami and she'll be happy." He grabbed Toby's face with both hands again and kissed him. "You brought me luck. Every time you play those old Napoli songs, you think of me."

The car moved on.

They ate lunch at the Russian Tea Room, and while Toby ate the Chicken Kiev almost greedily, the older man said:

"Do you see those men over there? They're New York policemen. And the man with them is from the FBI."

Toby didn't look. He just stared at the man who was speaking. He still had the gun in easy reach, though he hated the weight of it.

He knew that he could, if he wanted to do it, shoot both of the men with him, and probably shoot one of those other men before the others got him. But he wasn't going to try any such thing yet. Another, better moment would present itself.

"They work for us," said the older man. "They've been following us since we left your place. And they'll follow us now out of town and into the country. So just relax. We're very well protected, I assure you."

And that's how Toby became a hit man. That's how Toby became Lucky the Fox. But there is just a little more to the transition.

That night as he lay in bed, in a large country house, miles from the city, he thought about the girl who had crouched down and put up her hands. He thought about how she had begged in words that needed no translation. Her face had been stained with tears. He thought about how she had doubled over and shaken her head and put out her two hands against him.

He thought about her after he'd shot her, lying there, still, like his brother and sister had lain in the bathtub.

He got up, put on his clothes and his overcoat, keeping the gun in his pocket, and he went down the steps of the big house, past the two men playing cards in the living room. The room was like a great cavern. There were groups of gilded furnishings everywhere. And plenty of dark leather. It was like one of those old elegant private clubs in a black-and-white movie. You expected to see gentlemen peering at you from wing chairs. But there were only the two playing cards under a lamp, though a fire did burn in the grate giving off a cheerful flicker in the darkness.

One of the men got up. "You want something, a drink maybe?"

"I need to walk," Toby said.

No one stopped him.

He went out and he walked around the house.

He noticed the way the leaves looked in the trees that were nearest the lampposts. He noticed how the branches of barren trees were gleaming with ice. He studied the tall steep slate roofs of the house. He looked at the glint of light in the diamond-paned windows. A northern house, built for the heavy snow, built for the long winter, a house he'd only known from pictures, perhaps, if ever he had noticed them.

He listened to the sound of the frozen grass under his feet, and he came to a fountain that was running in spite of the cold, and he watched the water erupt from the jet and fall down in an airy white shower into the basin that boiled under the dim light.

Light came from the lantern in the porte cochere. The black limousine stood there gleaming under this lantern. Light came from the lamps that flanked the many doors of the house. Light came from small fixtures that lined the many garden paths of pea gravel. The air smelled of pine needles and of burning wood. There was a freshness and a cleanness he had not experienced in the city. There was a deliberate beauty.

It made him think of a summer when he'd gone for the holidays to a home across Lake Pontchartrain with two of the richer boys at Jesuit. They were nice boys, twins, and they liked him. They liked to play chess, and they liked classical music. They were good in the plays at school, which were so well done that everybody in the city came to see them. Toby would have been friends with those two boys, but he had had to keep his own life at home a secret. And so he never really became friends with them at all. By senior year, they hardly spoke.

But he had never forgotten their beautiful house near Mandeville, and how handsome the furnishings had been, and how their mother spoke perfect English, and their father had several records of great lutists that he had let Toby play in a room he called his study that was actually lined with books.

This house in the country here was like that house in Mandeville.

I watched him. I watched his face and his eyes, and saw those images in his memory and in his heart.

Angels don't really understand human hearts, no. That's true. We weep at the sight of sin, at the sight of suffering. But human hearts we have not. Yet theologians who write down observations like that do not really take into consideration our full intelligence. We can string together an infinite number of gestures, expressions, changes in respiration, and movements and draw from all this many deeply moving conclusions. We can know sorrow.

I formed my concept of Toby as I did this, and I heard the music he'd heard in that long-ago Mandeville house, an old recording of a Jewish lutist playing themes from Paganini. And

I watched Toby standing under the pine trees until he was near frozen with cold.

Toby made his way back towards the house slowly. He couldn't sleep. The night meant nothing to him.

Then a strange thing occurred as he drew near the ivy-covered stone walls, which was wholly unexpected. From within the house he heard a subtle stirring music. Surely a window was open to the cold for him to hear something of such tenderness, and subtle beauty. He knew it to be a bassoon or a clarinet. He wasn't certain. But there was the window up ahead, tall and made of leaded glass and opened to the cold. From there the music was coming: a long swelling note, and then a cautious melody.

He came closer.

It was like the sound of something waking, but then the melody of the lone horn was joined by other instruments, so raw, they were like the sound of an orchestra tuning up, yet held together by some fierce discipline. Then the music lapsed back to the horns, before once again an urgency began to drive it, the orchestra swelling, the horns soaring, becoming more piercing.

He stood outside the window.

The music went mad suddenly. Violins strummed and the drums beat as if a locomotive were roaring through the night made up of sound. He almost put his hands to his ears, it was so fierce. The instruments squealed. They wailed. It seemed crazed, the crying trumpets, the dizzying torrent of the strings, the pounding of the kettledrums.

He could no longer identify what he was hearing. At last the thunder stopped. A softer melody took over, grounded in peace, in musical transcriptions of solitude and an awakening.

He stood at the very windowsill now, his head bowed, his fingers at his temples, as if to stop anyone who would come between him and this music.

Though soft random melodies began to intertwine, a dark urgency beat under them. Again the music swelled. The brass rose unbearably. The shape of it was threatening.

Suddenly the whole composition seemed full of menace, the prelude and recognition to the life he had lived. You couldn't trust the sudden descents into tenderness and quietude, because the violence would erupt with rolling drums and violins shrieking.

On and on it went, dying to melody or near quiet and then erupting into a surge of industrial violence so fierce and dark it paralyzed him.

Then the strangest transformation took place. The music ceased to be an assault. It *became* the governing orchestration of his own life, his own suffering, his own guilt and terror.

It was as if someone had thrown an all-encompassing net over what he had become and how he had destroyed all things he held to be sacred.

He pressed his forehead to the icy-cold side of the open window.

The guided cacophony became unbearable, and when he thought he could not endure any more, when he almost reached to cover his ears, it stopped altogether.

He opened his eyes. Inside a deep dark firelit room, a man sat in a long leather chair, looking at him. The fire glinted on the edge of the man's square silver-rimmed glasses, and on his short white hair, and on his smiling mouth.

He beckoned with a languid motion of his right hand for Toby to go around to the front and, with his left hand, he motioned *Come in* to me.

The man at the front door said, "The Boss wants to see you now, kid."

Toby walked through a string of rooms that were furnished in gilt and velvet, with heavy draperies. The draperies were tied with golden tasseled ropes. There were two fires going, one in what seemed a vast library, and just beyond it, there was a room of white-painted glass that contained a small steaming pool of ice blue water.

In the library, and it could be nothing else, for all its towering shelves of books, "The Boss" sat as Toby had seen him through the window, in his high-backed chair of oxblood leather.

Everything in the room was fine. The desk was black and heavily carved. There was a special bookcase to the man's left with figures carved on both sides of the doors. The figures intrigued Toby.

It looked German, all this, as if it were furnishings from the German Renaissance in Europe.

The carpet had been woven for the room, an immense sea of dark flowers, banded in gold along the walls and their high polished baseboards. Toby had never seen a rug made for a room, cut away around the half columns that flanked the double doors, or cut away around the protruding edges of the window seats.

"Sit down and talk to me, Son," said the man.

Toby took the leather chair opposite. But he said nothing. Nothing would come out of his mouth. The music still rang in his ears.

"I'm going to tell you exactly what I want you to do," said the man, and then he described it.

Elaborate, yes, but hardly impossible, and elegantly challenging.

"Guns? Guns are crude," said the man. "This is simpler, only you have but one chance." He sighed. "You sink the needle into the back of the neck, or into the hand, and you keep moving. You know how to do that, to keep walking, with your eyes focused ahead as if you never even brushed up against the guy. These people will be eating, drinking, off their guard. They think the men outside are watching for the gunmen whom they have to fear. You hesitate? Well, your chance is gone, and if they catch you with that needle—."

"They won't," Toby said. "I don't look dangerous."

"That's true!" said the man. He opened his hands as he spoke in surprise. "You're a handsome boy. I can't place your voice. I think Boston, no. I think, New York, no. Where did you come from?"

This didn't surprise Toby. Most people of Irish and German descent who lived in New Orleans had accents that no one could place. And Toby had cultivated the uptown accents of the rich and that must have been even more confusing.

"You look English, German, Swiss, American," said the man. "You're tall. And you're young and you've got the coldest eyes I've ever seen."

"You mean I look like you," said Toby.

The man was startled again, but then he smiled. "I suppose so. But I'm sixty-seven and you're not even twenty-one."

Toby nodded.

"Why don't you stop clutching that gun and talk to me?"

"I can do everything you've asked," said Toby. "I'm eager to do it."

"You understand, one chance."

Toby nodded.

"You do it right and he won't notice. He won't die for at least twenty minutes. By that time, you'll be out of the restaurant, normal pace, just keep on walking and we'll pick you up."

Toby was powerfully excited again. But he didn't let on. The music in his head wouldn't stop. He heard the first major drive of strings and kettledrums.

I knew how excited he was as I watched him. I could see it

in his breathing and in the warmth in his eyes, which perhaps the man did not notice. Toby looked like Toby for a moment, innocent, with plans.

"What is it you want for all this, besides money?" asked the man.

Now Toby was the one who was startled. And there was a dramatic change in his face. The man noticed it, the blood in Toby's cheeks, and the flash in his eyes.

"More work," said Toby. "Lots of it. And the finest lute you can buy."

The man studied him.

"How did you come to all this?" the man asked him. He made a little gesture with his open hands again. He shrugged. "How did you manage to do the things you did?"

I knew the answer. I knew all the answers. I knew the exhilaration Toby was feeling; I knew how much he distrusted this man, and how he liked the challenge of carrying out what the man wanted and then trying to stay alive. After all, why shouldn't this man kill him after he did this work for him? Why not indeed?

An errant thought took hold of Toby. It wasn't for the first time that he found himself wishing that he were dead. So what did it matter if this man killed him? This man wouldn't be cruel. It would be fast and over, and then the life of Toby O'Dare would be no more, he figured. He tried to imagine, as countless humans have, what it means to be annihilated. The despair took hold of him as if it were the deepest chord he would strike on his lute, and its reverberation went on unendingly.

The coarse excitement of the job at hand was its only counterweight, and the chord throbbing so steadily in his ears gave him what passes for courage.

This man seemed reachable. But in truth, Toby didn't trust

anybody. Nevertheless, it was worth a try. The man was educated, confident, polished. The man was, in his own way, very
alluring. His calm was alluring. Alonso had never been calm.
Toby pretended to be calm. But he didn't really know the
meaning of it.

"If you never betray me," Toby said, "I'll do anything for
you, absolutely anything. Things other people can't do." He
thought of that girl sobbing, pleading, he thought of her
stretching out her arms, her palms up to push him away. "I
mean I will do absolutely anything. But there's bound to come
a time when you won't want me around."

"Not so," said the man. "You'll outlive me. It's imperative
that you trust me. Do you know what 'imperative' means?"

Toby nodded. "Absolutely," he said. "And for the moment, I
don't think I have too many choices, so yes, I trust you."

The man was thoughtful.

"You could go into New York, do the job, and keep on
going," said the man.

"And how would I be paid?" Toby asked.

"You could take half up front, and just disappear."

"Is that what you want me to do?"

"No," said the man. He pondered.

"I could love you," the man said under his breath. "I mean
it. Oh, not, you know, that I want you to be my bitch, I'm not
saying that. Nothing like that. Though at my age, I don't much
care whether it's a boy or a girl, you know. Not when they're
young and fragrant and tender and beautiful. But I don't mean
that. I mean, I could love you. Because there's something beautiful about you, about the way you look and talk and about the
way you move through a room."

Exactly! That is what I was thinking. And I was understanding now, what they say angels cannot understand, about their
two hearts, both of them.

I was thinking about Toby's father and how he used to call him "Pretty Face" and taunt him. I was thinking of fear and the utter failure to love. I was thinking of the way that beauty on earth survives though thorns and wretchedness try perpetually to choke it. But my thoughts were in the background here. The foreground is what matters.

"I want these Russians pushed back," said the man. He looked off, musing, finger curled for a moment under his lip. "I never planned on these Russians. No one did. I never even dreamed of anything like these Russians. I mean I never thought of them operating on so many levels. You can't imagine the things they do, the scams, the rackets. They work the system in any conceivable way they can. That's what they did in the Soviet Union. That's how they lived. They have no concept that it's wrong.

"And then these crude kids come along, somebody's third cousins, and they want Alonso's house and his restaurant." He made a disgusted sound and shook his head. "Stupid."

He sighed. He looked at the open laptop on the little table to his right. Toby hadn't noticed it before. It was the laptop he'd taken from the lawyer.

"You keep pushing them back for me, over and over again," the man said, "and I'll love you even more than I do now. I'll never betray you. In a few days you'll understand that I just don't betray anybody, and that's why I'm . . . well, who I am."

Toby nodded. "I think I understand already," he said. "What about the lute?"

The man nodded. "I know people, yes, of course. I'll find out what's on the market. I'll get it for you. But it can't be the finest. The finest of lutes would be too ostentatious. Cause talk. Leave a trail."

"I know the meaning of the word," said Toby.

"Fine lutes are on loan to young soloists, never really given to them, I don't think. There are only so many in the entire world."

"I understand," said Toby. "I'm not that good. I just want to play a good one."

"I'll get you the finest that can be bought without any trouble," said the man. "Only you have to promise me one thing."

Toby smiled. "Of course. I'll play it for you. Anytime that you like."

The man laughed. "Tell me where you come from," he said again. "Really. I want to know. I can place people like that," he snapped his fingers, "by the way they talk, no matter how much training they've had, no matter how much polish has been added. But I can't figure your voice at all. Tell me."

"I'll never tell you," Toby said.

"Not even if I tell you that you're working for The Good Guys now, Son?"

"It doesn't matter," said Toby. Murder is murder. He almost smiled. "You can think of me as coming from no place. Just someone who popped up at the right time."

I was astonished. This is just what I was thinking. He is someone who has popped up at the right Time.

"And one more thing," said Toby to the man.

The man smiled and opened his hands. "Ask me."

"The name of that piece of music you just played. I want to buy a copy of it."

The man laughed. "That's easy enough," he said. "*The Rite of Spring* by Igor Stravinsky."

The man was beaming at Toby, as though he'd found someone of priceless mettle. So was I.

By noon, Toby was deep asleep and dreaming of his mother. He was dreaming that he and she were walking through a big beautiful house with coffered ceilings. And he was telling her how grand it was all going to be, and his little sister was going to go to the Sisters of the Sacred Heart. Jacob would go to Jesuit.

Only something was very wrong in this spectacular house. It became labyrinthine, and impossible to comprehend as one wholesome dwelling. Walls rose up like cliffs, floors tilted. There was a giant black grandfather clock in the living room and on the front of it was the figure of the Pope, as if hanging from a gibbet.

Toby woke up, alone, and for a moment frightened and unsure of where he was. And then he began to cry. He tried to hold it in, but it became uncontrollable. He turned over and buried his face in the pillow.

He saw the girl again. He saw her lying dead in her little short silk skirt and ludicrous high-heel shoes, like a child playing dress-up. She had had ribbons in her long blond hair.

His guardian angel laid his hand on Toby's head. His guardian angel let him see something. He let him see the soul of the girl rising upwards, retaining the shape of her body out of habit and out of ignorance that it now knew no such bounds.

Toby opened his eyes. Then his cries became worse, and that deep chord of despair grew louder than ever.

He got up and began to pace. He looked at his open suitcase. He stared at the book about angels.

He lay back down and cried until he fell asleep, the way a child might do it. He was also saying a prayer as he cried. "Angel of God, my guardian dear, let 'The Good Guys' kill me sooner than later."

His guardian angel, hearing the despair in that prayer, hearing the grief and the utter misery, had turned his back and covered his face.

Not me. Not Malchiah.

He's the one, I thought.

Flash forward ten years of your time to the point where I began: He's Toby O'Dare, to me, not Lucky the Fox. And I'm going for him.

CHAPTER FIVE

Songs of the Seraphim

IF EVER I'D BEEN STUNNED IN MY LIFE, IT WAS NOTH-
ing compared to what I felt now. Only gradually did the shapes
and colors of my living room emerge from the haze in which
I'd plummeted as soon as Malchiah had stopped.

I came to myself, seated on the couch and staring forward.
And I saw him, with utter clarity, as he stood against the wall of
books.

I was shattered, broken, unable to speak.

All he'd shown me had been so vivid, so immediate, that I
was still reeling to find myself in the present moment, or
anchored securely in any moment at all.

My sense of sorrow, of deep and terrible remorse, was such
that I looked away from him, and slowly dropped my face in
my hands.

The thinnest hope of salvation sustained me. In my heart of
hearts I whispered, "Lord, forgive me that I ever separated
myself from you." Yet I felt at the same moment that I formed
these words, *You don't believe it. You don't believe it, even though
he's revealed* you *more intimately than you could ever have
revealed yourself. You don't believe. You're afraid to believe.*

I heard him move towards me and then I came to myself
again with him beside me.

"Pray for faith," he whispered in my ear.

And I did.

An old ritual came back to me.

On bitter winter afternoons, when I'd dreaded going home from school, I'd shepherded Emily and Jacob into Holy Name of Jesus Church, and there I'd prayed: *Lord, set my heart afire with faith, because I am losing faith. Lord, touch my heart, and set it afire.*

The old images I'd used returned to me, as fresh as if it were yesterday. I saw the faint design of my heart and the bursting yellow flame. My memory lacked the vibrant inescapable color and motion of all Malchiah had shown to me. But this I prayed with all my being. The old pictures faded suddenly, and I was left with the words of the prayer alone.

It was no ordinary "being alone." I stood before God without moving. I had some instantaneous flash of walking up a hillside on soft grass, and seeing ahead of me a robed figure, and the old ruminations came to me: *That's the glory of it; thousands of years have passed, and yet you can follow Him so close!*

"Oh, my God, I am heartily sorry," I whispered. *For all my sins because of the fear of Hell, but most of all, most of all, most of all, because I have separated myself from You.*

I sat back on the couch, and I felt myself drifting, dangerously close to losing consciousness, as if I'd been beaten by all I'd seen, deservedly so, but my body couldn't sustain the blows. How could I love God so much, and be so utterly sorry for what I had become, and yet not have faith?

I closed my eyes.

"My Toby," Malchiah whispered. "You know the extent of what you've done, but you can't comprehend the extent of what He knows."

I felt Malchiah's arm around my shoulder. I felt the tightness of his fingers. And then I was aware that he'd risen, and softly I heard his footfall as he moved across the room.

I looked up to see him standing opposite me, and once again there was that sense of his vivid coloring, his distinct and beguiling shape. A subtle but certain light emanated from him. I wasn't sure, but I thought I'd seen this incandescent light when he first appeared to me at the Mission Inn. I hadn't had an explanation for it and so rejected it as fancy, out of hand.

Now I didn't reject it. I marveled. His face was stricken. He was happy. He seemed almost joyful. And something came back to me from the gospels, about the joy in Heaven when one penitent soul returns.

"Let's make swift work of it," he said eagerly. And this time no jarring images accompanied his softly spoken words.

"You know well enough how things went afterwards," he said. "You never told The Right Man your real name, no matter how he insisted, and in time, when the agencies named you Lucky, it became The Right Man's name for you as well. You took it to yourself with bitter irony, accomplishing one mission after another, and begging not to be idle when you knew what those words meant."

I said nothing. I realized I was looking at him through a thin veil of tears. How I had gloried in my despair. I had been a young man drowning, and fighting a sea beast as if it mattered, as the waves closed overhead.

"In those first years, you worked in Europe often. No matter what the disguise, your height and your high blond coloring served you well. You penetrated banks and fine restaurants, hospitals and fine hotels. You never used a gun again, because you didn't have to. 'The Needle Sniper,' said the reports that detailed your obvious triumphs, and always well after the fact. They shuffled the dim conflicting video images of you in vain.

"Alone, you went to Rome and wandered St. Peter's Basilica. You traveled north through Assisi and Siena and Perugia, and on to Milan and Prague and Vienna. Once you went to England just to visit the barren landscape where the Brontë sisters had lived and written their great books; alone you watched performances of Shakespeare's plays. You roamed the Tower of London, colorless and lost among the other tourists. You lived a life devoid of witnesses. You lived a life more perfectly alone than anyone could imagine, except perhaps for The Right Man.

"But soon enough you stopped your visits with him. You didn't care for his easy laughter or agreeable observations, or the casual way in which he discussed the things he wanted you to do. Over a phone you could tolerate it; at a dinner table you found it unbearable. The food was tasteless and dry in your mouth.

"And so you drifted far from that last witness who became instead a phantom at the end of a lifeline, and no longer a pretended friend."

He stopped. He turned and ran his fingers over the books on the shelves before him. He looked so solid, so perfect, so unimagined.

I think I heard myself gasp, or perhaps it was a dull choking sound that might have meant tears.

"This became your life," he said in the same muted, unhurried voice, "these books of yours and safe trips within this country because it had become too dangerous for you to risk the borders, and you settled here, not nine months ago, drinking in the southern California light as if you'd lived your earlier days in a darkened room."

He turned around.

"I want you now," he said. "But your redemption lies with The Maker, with your faith in Him. The faith is stirring in you. You know that, don't you? You've already asked for forgiveness. You've already admitted the truth of all I revealed to you, and seventy times more. Do you know that God has forgiven you?"

I couldn't answer. How could anyone forgive the things I'd done?

"We're speaking here," he whispered, "of Almighty God."

"I want it," I whispered. "What can I do?" I asked. "What is it that you want of me that might make up for the smallest part of it?"

"Become my helper," he said. "Become my human instrument to help me do what I must do on Earth." He leaned against the book-lined wall, and brought his hands together, as any man might, to make a steeple of his fingers, just below his lips.

"Leave this empty life you've fashioned for yourself," he said, "and pledge to me your wits, your courage, your cunning, and your uncommon physical grace. You're remarkably brave where others might be timid. You're clever where others might be dull. All that you are, I can use."

I smiled at that. Because I knew what he meant. Actually I understood everything he was saying.

"You hear the speech of other humans with the ears of a musician," he continued. "And you love what is harmonious and what is beautiful. For all your sins, yours is an educated heart. All this I can put to work to answer the prayers that The Maker has told me to answer. I've asked for a human instrument to do His bidding. You are that instrument. Entrust yourself to Him and to me."

I felt the first inkling of true happiness I'd known in years. "I want to believe you," I whispered. "I want to be this instrument, but I think, for the first time in my life perhaps, I am genuinely afraid."

"No, you're not. You haven't accepted His forgiveness. You must *trust* that He can forgive a man like you. And He has."

He didn't wait for me to respond.

"You cannot imagine the universe that surrounds you. You

cannot see it as we see it from Heaven. You cannot hear the prayers rising everywhere, in every century, from every continent, from heart after heart.

"We're needed, you and I, in what for you will be a former era, but not for me, who can see those years as clearly as I see this moment now. From Natural Time to Natural Time you'll go. But I exist in Angel Time, and you'll travel with me through that as well."

"Angel Time," I whispered. What did I envision?

He spoke again. "The glance of The Maker encompasses all time. He knows all that is, was, or will be. He knows all that could be. And He is the Teacher of all the rest of us, insofar as we can comprehend."

Something was changing in me, completely. My mind sought to grasp the sum total of all he'd revealed to me, and as much as I knew of theology and philosophy, I could only do this without words.

There came back to me some phrases of Augustine, quoted by Aquinas, and I murmured them softly under my breath:

"Although we cannot number the infinite, nevertheless it can be comprehended by Him whose knowledge has no bounds."

He was smiling. He was musing.

A great shift in me had now taken place.

I remained quiet.

He went on.

"I can't rock the sensibilities of those who need me as I've rocked yours. I need you to enter their solid world at my guidance, a human being as they are human, a man as some of them are men. I need you to intervene not to bring death, but on the side of life. Say that you're willing, and your life is turned from evil, you confirm it, and you're at once plunged into the danger and heartache of trying to do what is unquestionably good."

Danger and heartache.

"I'll do it," I said. I wanted to repeat the words, but they seemed to linger in the air before us. "Wherever—only show me what you want from me, show me how to do your bidding. Show me! I don't care about danger. I don't care about heartache. You tell me that it's good, and I'll do it. *Dear God, I believe You have forgiven me!* And give me this chance! I'm Yours."

I felt an immediate and unexpected happiness, a lightness, and then joy.

At once the air around me changed.

The colors of the room blurred and brightened. It seemed I was being lifted out of the frame of a picture, and the picture itself grew larger and fainter, and then dissolved around me in a thin and weightless and shimmering mist.

"Malchiah!" I cried out.

"I'm beside you," came his voice.

We were traveling upwards. The day had melted into a fine purple darkness but the darkness was filled with a soft caressing light. Then it shattered into a billion pinpoints of fire.

An inexpressibly beautiful sound caught me. It seemed to hold me as surely as the currents of air were supporting me, as surely as Malchiah's warm presence guided me, though I could see nothing now but the starry heavens, and the sound became a great deep beautiful note, like the after echo of a great bronze gong.

A sharp wind had risen, but the echoing tone rose over it, and there came other notes, melting, vibrant, as if from the throats of so many pure and weightless bells. Slowly, the music dissolved the sound of the wind into itself entirely, as it swelled and quickened, and I felt I was hearing a singing more fluid and rich than anything I had ever heard. It transcended the anthems of the earth so obviously and indescribably that all sense of time left me. I could only imagine listening to these songs forever and I felt no sense of myself at all.

Dear God, that I ever abandoned You, turned my back on You . . . I am Yours.

The stars had so multiplied in number as to seem the sands of the sea. In fact, there was no darkness apart from brilliance, yet each star pulsed with a perfect iridescent light. And all around me, above, below, beside, I saw what seemed like shooting stars, whipping past me without a sound.

I felt bodiless, in the very midst of this, and never wanting to leave this again. Suddenly, as if it had been told to me, I realized these shooting stars were angels. I simply knew it. I knew they were angels traveling up and down and across and diagonally, their swift and inevitable journeys part of the warp and woof of this great universal realm.

As for me, I wasn't traveling with this speed. I was drifting. And yet even that word carries too much the weight of gravity for the state in which I found myself completely at ease.

Very slowly the swelling music yielded to another sound. It came hushed and then ever more urgent, a chorus of whispers rising from below. So many soft and secretive voices joined in this whispering as it blended itself with the music that it seemed all the world beneath us, or around us, was filled with this whispering, and I heard a multitude of syllables, yet all seemed to be sending up one simple plea.

I looked down, amazed that I had any sense of direction. The music continued to fade as the sight of a great solid planet came into view. I ached for the music. I felt I couldn't bear losing it. But we were plunging down towards the planet, and I knew this was just and right, and I didn't resist it in any way.

Everywhere the moving stars still darted to and fro, and there was no doubt in my mind at all now that these were angels answering prayers. These were the active messengers of

God, and I felt utterly privileged to be seeing this, even though the most ethereal music I'd ever heard was now almost gone.

The chorus of whispers was vast and in its own way a perfect yet darker sound. *These are the songs of earth,* I thought, quite consciously, *and they are filled with sadness and need and worship and reverence and awe.*

I saw the dark masses of land appear, spectacled with myriad lights, and the great satin gleam of the seas. Cities were visible to me as great webs of illumination appearing and disappearing beneath the layer upon layer of dim cloud. Then I made out smaller configurations as we moved down.

The music was altogether gone now, and the chorus of prayers was the melody that filled my ears.

For a split second, a multitude of questions came to me, but at once they were answered. We were approaching Earth *but in a different time.*

"Remember," Malchiah said softly against my ear, "that The Maker knows all things, all that is past and present, all that has happened and will happen, and what might happen as well. Remember there is no past or future where The Maker is but only the vast present of all things living."

I was utterly convinced of the truth of this, and absorbed in it, and again an immense gratitude filled me, a gratitude so overwhelming that it dwarfed any emotion I'd ever consciously known. I was traveling with Malchiah through Angel Time and back into Natural Time, and I was safe in his purpose because that was his grasp.

The myriad pinpoints of light, those moving at great speed, were now thinning, or deliberately fading from my view. Just below us, in a well of whispering and frantic praying, I saw a great group of snow-covered rooftops, and chimneys giving to the night air their reddened smoke.

The delicious smell of burning fires rose to my nostrils. The prayers had words and varying intensity, but I couldn't make out what they said.

I felt my entire body take form again, even as the whispering enveloped me, and I became aware too that my old garments were gone. I wore something that felt like heavy wool.

But I didn't care about myself or how I was clothed. I was too entranced by the sight below.

I thought I saw a river moving through the houses, a ribbon of silver in the darkness, and the vague shape of what must have been a very large cathedral with its inevitable cruciform shape. On a great rise, there stood what had to be a castle. And all the rest was the rooftops crowded together, some utterly blanketed in white and others so steep that the snow had somewhat fallen away.

Indeed the snow was falling with a delicious softness that I could hear.

Louder and louder came the great chorus of overlapping whispers.

"They're praying, and they're frightened," I said aloud, and heard my voice very immediate and close to myself, as though I weren't in this vast expanse of sky. A chill came over me. The air enveloped me. I felt the snow on my face and hands. I wanted desperately to hear the lost music one last time, and to my astonishment I did hear it in a great swelling echo, and then it was gone.

I wanted to weep in gratitude just for that, but I had to find out what I was meant to do. I didn't deserve to hear the music. And the idea that I could do something good in this world gripped me as I fought back tears.

"They're praying for Meir and for Fluria," said Malchiah. "They are praying for all the Jewry of the town. You must be the answer to their prayers."

"But how, what will I do?" I struggled to form the words,

but we were very close to the rooftops now, and I could make out the lanes and streets of the place, and the snow covered the towers of the castle, and the roof of the cathedral that gleamed as if the starlight could shine through the drifting downfall, making all of the little town very plain.

"It's early evening in the town of Norwich," said Malchiah, his voice intimate and perfect, and undisturbed by our descent or the prayers rising in my ears. "The Christmas pageants have only just ended and a time of troubles for the Jewry has begun."

I didn't have to ask him to go on. I knew the word, "Jewry," referred to the Jewish population in Norwich and to the small area where most of them lived.

Our descent had become more rapid. Indeed I did see a river, and for a moment, I felt I saw the prayers themselves rising, but the sky was thickening, the roofs were like ghosts beneath me, and I felt again the wet brush of falling snow.

We found ourselves now passing into the town itself, and slowly I found myself standing firmly on the ground. We were surrounded by close half-timbered houses that seemed to slant inward dangerously, as if they'd tumble down on us in an instant. There were dim lights in tiny thick windows.

Only small snowflakes were swirling in the cold air.

I looked down in the dim light and saw that I was dressed as a monk, and I recognized the habit immediately. I wore the white tunic and long white scapular, and the black hooded mantle, of a Dominican. There was the familiar knotted cord of a girdle around my waist but the long scapular covered it. Over my left shoulder was a leather book bag. I was stunned.

I put up my hands anxiously and discovered that I'd been tonsured, and that I had the simple bald pate and ring of trimmed hair that monks of those times wore.

"You've made me what I always wanted to be," I said. "A Dominican friar." I felt such excitement that I couldn't contain it. I wanted to know what I carried in the leather book bag.

"Now listen," he said, and though I couldn't see him, his voice echoed off the walls. We seemed lost in the shadows. In fact, he was not visible at all. I was alone here.

I could hear angry voices in the night, not very far away. And the chorus of prayers had died away.

"I'm right beside you," he said.

For a minute I felt panic, but then I felt the press of his hand on mine.

"Listen to me," he said. "It's a mob you hear in the next street, and time is short. King Henry of Winchester sits on the English throne," he explained. "And you may reckon this to be the year 1257, but neither of these bits of information will be of interest to you here. You know the time as well perhaps as any human of your own century, and you know it as it cannot know itself. Meir and Fluria are your charges, and all the Jewry are praying because Meir and Fluria are in danger, and as you well understand, that danger may extend to the entire little Jewish population of this town. That danger could reach as far as London."

I was utterly fascinated, and wildly excited, more so than I'd ever been in my natural life. And I did know these times and the peril that had surrounded the Jews of England everywhere.

I was also getting very cold.

I looked down and saw that I wore buckled shoes. I felt woolen stockings on my legs. Thank Heaven, I wasn't a Franciscan and consigned to sandals or bare feet, I thought, and then a giddy sensation gripped me. I had to stop this nonsense and think of what I was meant to do.

"Precisely," came Malchiah's intimate voice. "But will you take pleasure in what you mean to do here? Yes, you will. There is no angel of God who does not take joy in helping humans. And you are working with us now. You are our child."

"Can these people see me?"

"Most definitely. They'll see and hear you, and you will understand them and they will understand you. You will know when you are speaking French or English or Hebrew, and when they are speaking those tongues. Such things are easy enough for us to do."

"But what about you?"

"I'll be with you always, as I told you," he said. "But only you will see and hear me. Don't try to speak to me with your lips. And don't call for me unless you have to do it.

"Now go to the mob and get into the very thick of it, because it's turning in a way that it should not. You are a traveling scholar, you've come from Italy, through France, to England, and your name is Br. Toby, which is simple enough."

I was more eager to do this than I could express.

"But what more do I need to know?"

"Trust your gifts," he said. "The gifts for which I chose you. You're well-spoken, even eloquent, and you have great confidence in playing a role for a certain purpose. Trust in The Maker and trust in me."

I could hear the voices in the nearby street growing louder. A bell was tolling.

"That must be the curfew," I said quickly. My mind was racing. What I knew of this century seemed scant suddenly and again I felt apprehension, almost fear.

"It is the curfew," said Malchiah. "And it will inflame those who are making the trouble, because they're eager for a resolution. Now go."

CHAPTER SIX

The Mystery of Lea

IT WAS AN ANGRY MOB, AND FRIGHTENING IN APPEAR-
ance because it was not all rabble by any means. Many carried
lanterns and some had torches, and a few even carried tapers,
and many were richly dressed in velvet and fur.

The houses on either side of this street were of stone, and I
remembered that the Jews had built the very first stone houses
in England, and with reason.

I could hear Malchiah's intimate voice as I approached.

"The priests in white are from the cathedral priory," he said,
as I looked to the three heavily robed men closest to the door of
the house. "The Dominicans are gathered there around Lady
Margaret, who is a niece to the Sherriff and a cousin of the
Archbishop. That's her daughter beside her, Nell, a girl of thirteen. They are the ones bringing the charge against Meir and
Fluria that they've poisoned their child and secretly buried her.
Remember, Meir and Fluria are your charges, and you are here
to help them."

There were a thousand questions I wanted to ask. I was reeling from the statement that a child might have been murdered.
And only dimly did I make the obvious connection: these people were being accused of the very crime I myself had committed habitually.

I pushed into the midst of the crowd, and Malchiah was gone and I knew it. I was on my own now.

It was Lady Margaret who pounded at the door as I approached it. She was stunningly dressed in a narrow robe with dagged leaves, all trimmed in fur, and she wore a loose hooded mantle of fur. Her face was stained with tears, and her voice was broken.

"Come out and answer!" she demanded. She seemed utterly sincere and deeply distressed. "Meir and Fluria, I demand it. Produce Lea now or answer for why she's not here. We'll have no more of your lies, I swear it."

She turned around and let her voice ring out over the crowd. "Tell us no more fanciful tales, that this child has been taken to Paris."

A great chorus of approval rose from the crowd.

I greeted the other Dominicans who moved towards me and told them under my breath that I was Br. Toby, a pilgrim, who had traveled through many lands.

"Well, you've come at the right time," said the tallest and most impressive of the friars. "I'm Fr. Antoine, the Superior here, as you no doubt know, if you've been to Paris, and these Jews have poisoned their own daughter because she dared to enter the cathedral on Christmas night."

Though he tried to keep his voice down, this brought an immediate sobbing from Lady Margaret, and her daughter Nell. And many shouts and cries of agreement from those around us.

The young girl, Nell, was as exquisitely dressed as her mother, but infinitely more distressed, shaking her head and sobbing. "It's all my fault, all my fault. I brought her to the church."

At once, the white-robed priests from the priory began to quarrel with the friar who'd spoken to me.

"That's Fr. Jerome," Malchiah whispered, "and you'll see he leads the opposition to this campaign to make another Jewish martyr and saint."

I was relieved to hear his voice, but how could I ask him for any further information?

I felt him push me forward and I suddenly found myself with my back to the door of the large stone house in which Meir and Fluria obviously lived.

"Forgive me, as I'm a stranger here," I said, my own voice sounding completely natural to me, "but why are you so certain that a murder has taken place?"

"She's nowhere to be found, that's how we know," said Lady Margaret. She was surely one of the more attractive women I've ever seen in my life, even with her eyes reddened and wet. "We took Lea with us because she wanted to see the Christ Child," she said to me bitterly, her lip trembling. "We never dreamed that her own parents would poison her and preside over her deathbed with hearts of stone. Make them come out. Make them answer."

It seemed the entire crowd started shouting at these words, and the white-clad priest, Fr. Jerome, demanded silence.

He glared at me.

"We have enough Dominicans in this town already," he said. "And we have a perfect martyr already in our own cathedral, Little St. William. Those evil Jews who murdered him are long dead, and they did not go unpunished. These Dominican brethren of yours want their own saint as ours is not good enough."

"It's Little St. Lea whom we want to celebrate now," said Lady Margaret in her hoarse and tragic voice. "And Nell and I are the cause of her downfall." She caught her breath. "All know of Little Hugh of Lincoln, and the horrors that were—."

"Lady Margaret, this isn't the town of Lincoln," insisted Fr.

Jerome. "And we have no evidence such as was found at Lincoln to believe in a murder here." He turned to me. "If you've come to pray at the shrine of Little St. William, then we welcome you," he said. "I can see you're an educated friar and no ordinary beggar." He glared at the other Dominicans. "And I can tell you right now that Little St. William is a true saint, famous throughout all England, and these people have no proof that Fluria's daughter, Lea, was ever even baptized."

"She suffered Baptism of blood," insisted the Dominican Fr. Antoine. He spoke with the confidence of a preacher. "Doesn't the martyrdom of Little Hugh tell us what these Jews will do, if allowed to do it? This young girl died for her faith, she died for entering the church on Christmas Eve. And this man and woman must answer, not merely for the unnatural crime of killing their own flesh and blood, but for the murder of a Christian, for that is what Lea became."

The crowd gave him a loud roar of approval, but I could see that many bystanders did not believe in what he'd said.

How and what was I supposed to do? I turned and knocked on the door, and said in a soft voice, "Meir and Fluria, I'm here to defend you. Please answer to me." I didn't know whether or not they could hear me.

Meantime half the town it seemed was joining the crowd, and suddenly there sounded from a nearby steeple the clang of an alarm bell. More and more people were crowding into the street of the stone houses.

Suddenly the crowd was thrown in disarray by oncoming soldiers. I saw a well-dressed man on horseback, his white hair flowing in the wind, with a sword on his hip. He brought his horse to a halt several yards from the door of the house, and there gathered behind him at least five or six horsemen.

Some people immediately ran away. Others began to shout: "Arrest them. Arrest the Jews. Arrest them." Others drew closer in as the man dismounted and came up to those who stood before the door, his eyes passing over me without any change of expression.

Lady Margaret spoke before the man could.

"My Lord Sherriff, you know these Jews are guilty," she said. "You know they were seen in the forest with a heavy burden, and no doubt buried this child right by the great oak."

The Sherriff, a big husky man with a beard as white as his hair, looked around himself disgustedly.

"Stop that alarm bell now," he shouted to one of his men.

He took my measure again, but I didn't step aside for him.

He turned to address the crowd.

"Let me remind you good people that these Jews are the property of His Highness King Henry, and if you do any damage to them or their houses or their property, you do damage to the King, and I'll place you under arrest and hold you completely accountable. These are the King's Jews. They are Serfs of the Crown. Now be gone from here. What, would we have a Jewish martyr in every town of the realm?"

This drew a storm of protest and argument.

Lady Margaret at once grabbed his arm. "Uncle," she implored him. "A terrible evil has been done here. No, it is not the dastardly thing done to Little St. William or Little St. Hugh. But it is just as evil. Because we took the child with us into the church on Christmas Eve—."

"How many times must I hear this?" he answered her. "Day in and day out, we've been friends to these Jews and now we turn on them because a young girl leaves without a farewell to Gentile friends?"

The bell had stopped, but the street was choked with people, and it seemed to me that some even came over the rooftops.

"Go back to your homes," said the Sherriff. "The curfew's

been rung. You are unlawful if you remain here!" His soldiers tried to bring their mounts a little closer in, but it wasn't easy.

Lady Margaret beckoned furiously for certain people to come forward, and at once two rather ragged individuals were produced, both of them reeking of drink. They wore the simple wool tunics and leggings of most of the men in the crowd, only their limbs were wrapped with rags, and both of them appeared dazed by the torchlight and the many people pushing and pulling at each other to see them.

"Why, these witnesses saw Meir and Fluria go into the woods with a sack," cried Lady Margaret. "They saw them by the great oak. My Lord Sherriff, and my beloved uncle, if the ground weren't frozen we would already have the child's body from where they buried it."

"But these men are drunkards," I said without thinking. "And if you don't have the body, how can you prove that there's been a murder?"

"That is exactly the case," said the Sherriff. "And here's a Dominican who isn't half mad to make a saint of someone who's beside a warm hearth right now in the city of Paris." He turned to me. "It's your brethren here who have stoked this fire. Make them come to their senses."

The Dominicans were plainly furious at this, but one other aspect of their demeanor struck me. They were sincere. They believed themselves quite obviously to be in the right.

Lady Margaret became frantic. "Uncle, don't you understand my guilt in this? I must pursue it. It was I, and Nell here, who brought the child to Mass and to see the Christmas pageants. We were the ones who explained the hymns to her, who answered her innocent questions—."

"For which her parents forgave her!" the Sherriff declared. "Who in the Jewry is more mild mannered than Meir, the scholar? Why, you, Fr. Antoine, you've studied Hebrew with him. How can you bring this charge?"

"Yes, I studied with him," said Fr. Antoine, "but I know him to be weak and under the rule of his wife. She after all was the apostate's mother—."

The crowd warmed to this loudly.

"Apostate!" cried the Sherriff. "You don't know that the young girl was an apostate! Too much is simply not known."

Clearly the crowd was beyond his control, and he realized it.

"But why are you so certain the child is dead?" I asked Fr. Antoine.

"She took sick on Christmas morn," he said. "That's why. Fr. Jerome here knows it. He's a physician as well as a priest. He attended her. They started to poison her even then. And she lay abed for a day in deepening agony, as the poison ate at her stomach, and now she's gone without a trace and these Jews have the effrontery to say her cousins took her to Paris. In this weather? Would you make such a journey?"

It seemed all who could hear had something to say on the outrage of this, but I let my voice carry as I spoke.

"Well, I've come here in this weather, haven't I?" I answered. "You cannot prove a murder with no evidence of it. That fact remains. Was not there a body of Little St. William? Was not there a victim in Little St. Hugh?"

Lady Margaret again reminded everyone that the ground around the oak was frozen.

The young girl cried bitterly, "I didn't mean any harm. She only wanted to hear the music. She loved the music. She loved the procession. She wanted to see the Babe laid in the Manger."

This brought fresh cries from the crowd all around.

"Why didn't we see her cousins who came to take her on this fanciful journey?" demanded Fr. Antoine of me, and of the Sherriff.

The Sherriff looked about himself uneasily. He raised his right hand and gave a signal to his men, and one of them rode off. He said to me under his breath, "I've sent for men to protect the entire Jewry."

"I demand," Lady Margaret interjected, "that Meir and Fluria answer. Why are all these wicked Jews locked in their houses? They know it's true."

Fr. Jerome spoke up immediately, "Wicked Jews? Meir and Fluria, and old Isaac, the doctor? These very people we've counted as our friends? And now they are all wicked?"

Fr. Antoine, the Dominican, shot back crossly, "So you owe them so much for your vestments, your chalices, your very priory," he said. "But they're not friends. They're moneylenders."

Once more the shouting started, but now the crowd was parting and an elderly man with streaming gray hair and a bent back made his way into the torchlight. His tunic and robes all but touched the snowy ground. On his shoes he wore fine gold buckles.

I saw at once the yellow taffeta patch fixed to his breast that meant he was a Jew. It was cut in the shape of the two tablets of the Ten Commandments, and I wondered, How in the world could anyone have ever seen that particular image as a "badge of shame"? But indeed they did and Jews throughout Europe had been compelled to wear it for many years. I knew and understood this.

Fr. Jerome told everyone sternly to make way for Isaac, son of Solomon, and the old man rather fearlessly took his place near to Lady Margaret and across from the door.

"How many of us," asked Fr. Jerome, "have come to Isaac for potions, for emetics? How many have been cured by his herbs and his knowledge? I've sought the man's knowledge and judgment. I know him to be a great physician. How dare you not listen to what he says now?"

The old man stood resolute and silent until all the shouting had died away. The white-robed priests of the cathedral had moved closer to him, to guard him. Finally the old man spoke in a deep and somewhat ragged voice.

"I nursed the child," he said. "True, she entered the church on the very night of Christmas, yes. True, she wanted to see the beautiful pageants. She wanted to hear the music. Yes, she did this, but she came home to her parents a Jewish child as she had left them. She was only a child, and easily forgiven! She took sick, as any child might in this inclement weather, and soon became delirious in her fever."

It seemed the shouting would break out again, but both the Sherriff and Fr. Jerome gestured for silence. The old man looked about him with a withering dignity, and then continued:

"I knew what it was. It was the iliac passion. She had sharp pain in her side. She was burning hot. But then the fever cooled, the pain went away, and before she left these parts for France, she was herself again, and I spoke with her, and so did Fr. Jerome here, your own physician, though you can hardly say that I have not been a physician to most of you."

Fr. Jerome assented to all this vigorously. "I tell you as I've told you before," he said. "I saw her before she left for her journey. She was cured."

I was beginning to realize what had happened. The child had probably suffered appendicitis, and when the appendix burst, the pain naturally lessened. But I was beginning to suspect that the journey to Paris was a desperate fabrication.

The old man was not finished. "You, Little Mistress Eleanor," he said to the young girl. "Did you not bring her flowers? Did you not see her calm and collected before her journey?"

"But I never saw her again," cried the child, "and she never told me she was making any journey."

"The whole town was busy with the continuing pageants,

busy with the plays in the square!" said the old doctor. "You know you were, all of you. And we don't attend these things. They are not part of our way of life. And so her cousins came and took her and so she went away, and you knew nothing of it."

I knew now that he wasn't telling the truth, but he seemed determined to say what he had to say to protect not only Meir and Fluria but his entire community.

A few young men who had been standing behind the Dominicans now pushed through their ranks and one of them shoved the old man and called him a "filthy Jew." The others pushed the old man to one side and then the other.

"Stop this," the Sherriff declared, and he gave a signal to his horsemen. The boys ran. The crowd parted for the riders.

"I will arrest anyone who lays a hand on these Jews," the Sherriff said. "We know what happened in Lincoln when things got out of hand! These Jews are not your property, but that of the Crown."

The old man was badly shaken. I put out my hand to steady him. He looked at me, and I saw that scorn again, that withering dignity, but also a subtle gratitude for my understanding.

More grumbling came from the crowd, soldiers or no soldiers, and the young girl began to cry again miserably.

"If only we might have a dress that belonged to Lea," she whimpered. "This would confirm what has happened, because at the mere touch of it many might be healed."

That idea was astonishingly popular, and Lady Margaret insisted they were likely to find all the child's clothes in the house because the child was dead and had never been taken away.

Fr. Antoine, the leader of the Dominicans, threw up his hands and demanded patience.

"I have a story to tell you before you proceed with this," he said, "and my Lord Sherriff, I ask that you listen as well."

I heard Malchiah's voice in my ear. "Remember you are a preacher too. Don't let him win the argument."

"Long years ago," said Fr. Antoine, "a wicked Jew in Baghdad was stunned to find that his son had become a Christian and threw the child into a roaring fire. Just when it seemed the innocent boy would be consumed, down from Heaven came the Blessed Virgin herself, and she rescued the boy, who came out of the flames unharmed. And the fire consumed that wicked Jew who had tried to do his Christian son such wicked harm."

It seemed the crowd would storm the house after this.

"That's an old tale," I shouted at once, infuriated, "and it's been told all over the world. Every time it's a different Jew and a different city, and always the same outcome, and who among you has seen anything like it with your own eyes? Why is everyone so willing to believe this?" I continued as loudly as I could, "You have here a mystery, but you don't have Our Blessed Lady and you don't have proof and you must stop."

"And who might you be, to come here and speak on behalf of these Jews!" demanded Fr. Antoine. "Who are you to challenge the Superior of our own house?"

"I mean no disrespect," I said, "but only that it proves nothing, this tale, and certainly not any guilt or innocence here." An idea came to me. I raised my voice as high as I could.

"All of you believe in your little saint," I cried. "Little St. William whose shrine is in your cathedral. Well, go to him now and pray for guidance. Let Little St. William guide you. Pray to him to discover the girl's burial place, if you're so set on it. Won't the saint be the perfect intercessor? You couldn't ask for better. Go to the cathedral, all of you, now."

"Yes, yes," cried Fr. Jerome, "this is what must be done."

Lady Margaret looked a bit stunned by this.

"Who better than Little St. William," said Fr. Jerome, flashing a quick glance at me. "Who was himself murdered by the

Jews of Norwich a hundred years ago. Yes, go into the church to the shrine."

"Everyone, go to the shrine," said the Sherriff.

"I tell you," said Fr. Antoine, "we have another saint here, and we have a right to demand of the parents that they give over to us what clothes this child has left behind. Already a miracle has been worked at the oak. Whatever clothing remains here should become as holy relics. I say, break in this door, if need be, and take the clothes."

The crowd was going wild. The horsemen drew in closer, forcing them to scatter, or back up. Some people were jeering, but Fr. Jerome stood firm with his back to the house and his arms out, crying, "The cathedral, Little St. William, we should all go now."

Fr. Antoine pushed past me and the Sherriff and he began to beat on the door.

The Sherriff was furious. He turned to the door. "Meir and Fluria, prepare yourselves. I mean to take you to the castle for safekeeping. If required, I'll take every Jew in Norwich to the castle."

The crowd was disappointed, but there was confusion on all sides, with many crying the name of Little St. William.

"And then," said the old Jewish doctor, "if you take Meir and Fluria and all of us to the tower, these people will loot our houses and burn our sacred books. Please, I beg you, take Fluria, the mother of this unfortunate, but let me talk with Meir, that perhaps some donation can be made, Fr. Antoine, to your new priory. The Jews have ever been generous in these matters."

In other words, a bribe. But the suggestion of it worked like a miracle on all who heard it.

"Yes, they should pay," someone murmured, and another, "Why not?" And the news seemed to be traveling to all those assembled.

Fr. Jerome cried out that he would now lead a procession to the cathedral, and anyone who feared for the fate of his or her immortal soul should come with him. "All you that have torches and candles, walk ahead to light the way."

As the horsemen were now putting many people in danger of being trampled, and Fr. Jerome strode off to lead the procession, many followed him, and others grumbled and began to slip away.

Lady Margaret hadn't moved, and now she approached the old doctor:

"And did he not help them?" demanded Lady Margaret, peering right into his eyes. She turned to the Sherriff with an intimate look. "Was he not, by his own words, part and party to it? Do you think Meir and Fluria are so clever as to produce a poison without his help?" She turned on the old man. "And will you remit my debts to buy me off so easily?"

"If that would calm your heart and make you amenable to the truth," said the old man. "Yes, I will remit your debts for all the worry and trouble you've suffered over this."

This silenced Lady Margaret but only tentatively. She cared very much that she not yield on this account.

The crowd was now thin, with more and more joining the procession.

At once the Sherriff motioned for two of his mounted men. "Take Isaac son of Solomon safely home," he said. "And you, all the rest of you, go with the priests to the cathedral and pray."

"None of them is to be pitied," insisted Lady Margaret, though she didn't raise her voice to address the stragglers. "They are guilty of a multitude of sins, and they read black magic in their books which they hold to be higher than the Holy Bible. Oh, this is all my doing that I had mercy on this one child. And such grief that I am in debt to the very people who murdered her."

The soldiers escorted the old man away, their horses making the last few onlookers scurry off, and I could see more clearly that many had gone on following the lanterns of the procession.

I put my hand out to Lady Margaret.

"Madam," I said. "Let me go in and talk to them. I'm not from this place. I don't belong to either side in this quarrel. Let me see if I can tell the truth of the matter. And be assured, this matter can be settled in the light of day."

She looked at me almost softly, and then wearily she nodded. She turned and with her daughter joined the end of the procession headed for the Shrine of Little St. William. Someone handed her a lighted taper as she glanced back, and gratefully she took this and went on.

The mounted soldiers drove off all the others. Only the Dominicans remained, eyeing me as if I were a traitor. Or worse, an impostor.

"Forgive me, Fr. Antoine," I said. "If I find proof that these people are guilty, I'll come to you myself."

The man did not know what to make of it.

"You school men, you think you know everything," said Fr. Antoine. "I too have studied though not at Bologna or Paris as you must have. I know sin when I see sin."

"Yes, and I promise you my full report," I responded.

At last he and the other Dominicans turned and went away. The darkness swallowed them.

The Sherriff and I remained at the door of the stone house, with what now seemed a glut of mounted men nearby.

The snow was still falling very softly, and had been all during the melee. I saw it clean and white suddenly in spite of the crowd that had just been here, and I also realized I was freezing.

The soldiers' horses were anxious in this narrow place. But more mounted men were coming, some with lanterns, and

I could hear the echo of their hooves in the nearby streets. I didn't know how big the neighborhood of the Jews was, but I was certain they did. Only now did I notice that all the windows were dark in this part of the town, except for the high windows of Meir and Fluria.

The Sherriff pounded on the door.

"Meir and Fluria, come out," he demanded. "For your own safety, you're to go with me now." He turned to me and spoke under his breath. "If it has to be so, I will take them all and keep them until this madness has stopped, or they'll burn down Norwich just to burn the Jewry."

I leaned against the heavy wooden door, and said in a voice that was soft yet loud,

"Meir and Fluria, there is help for you here. I'm a brother who believes in your innocence. Please allow us to come in."

The Sherriff merely stared at me.

But at once we heard the bar being lifted, and the door opened.

CHAPTER SEVEN

Meir and Fluria

A BRIGHT MARGIN OF LIGHT REVEALED A TALL, DARK-haired man, with deep-set eyes peering out at us from a very white face. He wore a robe of brown patterned silk, with the customary yellow badge on it. His high cheekbones appeared to be polished, so tight was his skin.

"They're gone for the moment," said the Sherriff intimately. "Let us in. And get your wife and yourself ready to go with me."

The man disappeared, and the Sherriff and I slipped into the house easily.

I followed the Sherriff up a narrow brightly lighted and carpeted stairway, and into a beautiful room, where a graceful and elegant woman sat beside a large fireplace.

Two serving women hovered in the shadows.

There were rich Turkey carpets covering the floors, and tapestries on all the walls, though the tapestries had only geometric patterns. But the ornament of the room was the woman.

She was younger than Lady Margaret. Her white wimple and headdress covered her hair entirely, and they set off her olive skin and her deep brown eyes beautifully. Her robes were a deep rose color, with rich sleeves buttoned over an undertunic of what appeared to be gold thread. She wore heavy shoes, and I saw her mantle over the back of the chair. She was dressed and ready to be taken from here.

There was a huge bookcase against one far wall, crammed with leather-bound volumes, and a large plain wooden desk heaped with what looked like ledgers and pages of parchment covered in writing. A few darkly bound volumes lay to one side. And I saw what might have been a map on another wall, but it was too far from the light of the fire for me to be certain.

The hearth itself was high and the fire luxuriantly big, and the chairs scattered about were of thick dark heavily carved wood with cushions on their seats. There were also a few benches in the shadows, in a neat row, as if students from time to time came here.

The woman stood at once, and lifted her hooded mantle from the back of the chair. She spoke softly and calmly.

"May I offer you some mulled wine before I go, my Lord Sherriff?"

The young man appeared to be paralyzed watching all the proceedings as if he couldn't think what to do and was very ashamed of this. He was handsome by anyone's standards, and had slender beautiful hands, and a soft dreamy depth to his eyes. He appeared miserable. Almost without hope. I was desperate to inspire him.

"I know what's to be done," said the woman. "You will take me to the castle for safekeeping."

She reminded me of someone I myself knew, but I couldn't think of who it was, or what it meant, and I had no time for it. She was speaking:

"We've talked with the elders, with the Magister of the synagogue. We've spoken to Isaac, and to his sons. We're all agreed. Meir will write to Paris to our cousins there. He will produce a letter from my daughter which verifies that she's alive . . ."

"That won't be enough," the Sherriff began. "It's dangerous to leave Meir here."

"Why do you say this?" she asked. "Everyone knows he will not leave Norwich without me."

"That's true," reflected the Sherriff. "Very well."

"And he will write for a thousand gold marks for the Dominican priory."

The Sherriff threw up his hands at the pity of it and nodded.

"Let me remain here," said Meir in a quiet voice. "I must write the letters and also talk further of these things with the others."

"You'll be in danger," said the Sherriff. "The sooner you raise some money, even among the Jews here, the better it will be for you. But sometimes money is not enough to stop these things. I say, send for your daughter and bring her home."

Meir shook his head. "I wouldn't have her travel again in this weather," he said, but his voice was unsteady and I knew he was saying something false, and he was ashamed of it. "One thousand gold marks and whatever debts we can remit. I don't share the tribal gift for money lending," he continued. "I'm a scholar, as you well know, and your sons know, Lord Sherriff. But I can speak again to everyone here, and certainly we can arrive at a sum. . . ."

"Very likely so," said the Sherriff. "But there's one thing I demand before I protect you further. Your sacred book, which is it?"

Meir, fair as he was, turned pale. He moved slowly to his desk, and he picked up a big leather-bound volume that lay there. There were Hebrew letters on it in deep graven gold.

"Torah," he whispered. He gazed miserably at the Sherriff.

"Put your hand on it and swear to me that you are innocent of all blame here."

The man looked as if he would lose consciousness. There was a faraway look in his eyes as if he was dreaming and the dream was a nightmare. But he didn't lose consciousness, of course.

I wanted desperately to intervene but what could I do? *Malchiah, help him.*

Finally, balancing the heavy book on his left hand, Meir laid his right upon it, and in a low quavering voice, he spoke.

"I swear that never in my life have I done harm to any human being and never would I have harmed Fluria's daughter, Lea. I swear that I have done her no harm whatsoever, in no way, but only cared for her with love, and such tenderness as befits a stepfather, and that she is . . . gone from here."

He looked at the Sherriff.

Now the Sherriff knew the girl was dead.

But the Sherriff only paused, then nodded.

"Come, Fluria," the Sherriff said. He looked at Meir. "I'll see that she's safe and has every comfort. I'll see the soldiers spread the word through the town. I'll speak to the Dominicans myself. And so can you!" He looked at me. Then went on to Meir. "Obtain the money as quickly as you can. Remit as many debts as you are able. This will cost the entire community, but it shouldn't be ruinous."

The serving women and the wife went down the stairway, and the Sherriff followed. Below I heard someone bolt the door behind them.

Now the man looked at me quietly.

"Why do you want to help me?" he asked. He seemed as deflated and dejected as a man could be.

"Because you've prayed for help," I answered, "and if I can be the answer to that prayer I'll do it."

"Do you mock me, Brother?" he asked.

"Never," I said. "But the young woman, Lea. She's dead, isn't she?"

He merely looked at me for a long moment. Then he took his chair behind the desk.

I took the dark high-backed chair that stood in front of it. We faced each other.

"I don't know where you've come from," he said under his breath. "I don't know why I trust you. You know as well as I do that it's your fellow Dominican friars who are heaping abuse on us. Campaigning for a saint, that is their mission. As if Little St. William does not haunt Norwich forever."

"I know the story of Little St. William," I said. "I've heard it often. A child crucified by Jews at Passover. A pack of lies. And a shrine to bring pilgrims to Norwich."

"Don't say such things outside this house," said Meir, "or they'll tear you limb from limb."

"I'm not here to argue with them over that. I'm here to help you solve the problem that lies before you. Tell me what happened and why you haven't fled."

"Fled?" he asked. "If we fled, we would be guilty as charged and pursued, and this madness would engulf not only Norwich but any Jewry in which we took refuge. Believe me, in this country, a riot in Oxford can spark a riot in London."

"Yes, I'm sure you're right. What happened?"

His eyes filled with tears. "She died," he whispered. "Of the iliac passion. At the end the pain stopped as it so often does. She was calm. But she was only cool to the touch because we laid cold compresses on her. And when she received her friends Lady Margaret and Nell, she only seemed to have lost her fever. Early in the morning, she died in Fluria's arms, and Fluria——. But I can't tell you all of it."

"Is she buried by the big oak?"

"Certainly not," he said, scornfully, "and those drunkards

never saw us take her from here. There was no one to see us. I carried her in both arms against my breast, as tenderly as one might carry a bride. And we walked for hours through the forest until we came to the soft banks of a stream, and there in a shallow grave we committed her to the earth, wrapped only in a sheet, and we prayed together, as we covered the grave with stones. That was all we could do for her."

"Is there someone in Paris who can write a letter that will be believed here?" I asked.

He looked up as if from a dream and seemed to be marveling at my ability to cooperate in a deception.

"Surely there's a Jewish community there——."

"Oh, indeed," he said. "We've only just come from Paris, the three of us, because I inherited this house and the loans left to me by my uncle here. Yes, there is a community in Paris, and there is one Dominican there who might very well be of help to us, not because he would scruple to write a letter pretending the girl is alive. But because he is our friend, and would be our friend in this, and would believe us, and would plead for us."

"That might very well be all that's needed. This Dominican, he's a scholar?"

"Brilliant, studying under the greatest teachers there. A doctor of the law as well as a student of theology. And much grateful to us for a very unusual favor." He stopped.

"But what if I'm wrong. What if I am completely wrong and he turns against us? There is cause for that, too, Heaven knows."

"Can you explain this to me?"

"No, I can't do it."

"How can you make up your mind whether he's to help you or turn on you?"

"Fluria would know. Fluria would know perfectly what to

do, and it's only Fluria who can make this plain to you. If Fluria said that it was right for me to write to this man . . ."

Again he paused. He had no confidence in any of his own decisions. One couldn't even call them decisions.

"But I can't write to him. I'm mad to think of it. What if he came here and pointed his finger at us?"

"What sort of man is this?" I demanded. "How is he connected to you and to Fluria?"

"Oh, you ask the very question," he said.

"What if I went to him, spoke with him, myself? How long does it take to reach Paris? Do you think you could remit enough debts, acquire enough gold, and all this with the promise of my returning with larger sums? Tell me about this man. Why did you think this man might help you?"

He bit his lip. I thought he'd draw blood. He sat back in the chair.

"But without Fluria," he murmured. "I don't have leave to do this, even though he might very well save all of us. If anyone could."

"Do you speak of the girl's paternal family?" I asked. "A grandfather? Is he your hope for the gold marks? I heard you take your vow as a stepfather."

He waved this away. "I have plenty of friends. The money is not the question. I can obtain the money. I can obtain it from London, for that matter. The mention of Paris was only to give us time, and because we claim that Lea has gone there, and that a letter from Paris would prove it. Lies. Lies!" He bowed his head. "But this man—." He stopped again.

"Meir, this doctor of the law may be the very thing. You must confide in me. If this powerful Dominican were to come, he could gain control of the small community here, and stop this mad drive for a new saint, because that is the goal that is feeding the fire, and surely a man of education and wits will understand this. Norwich is not Paris."

His face was unspeakably sad. He couldn't talk. Clearly he was torn.

"Oh, I have never been anything but a scholar," he said with a sigh. "I have no cleverness. I don't know what this man would do or not do. A thousand marks I can raise, but this man—. If only Fluria had not been taken away."

"Give me permission to talk to your wife, if that's what you want me to do," I said. "Write it out here, a note to the Sherriff permitting me to see your wife alone. They'll admit me to the castle. The man's already formed a favorable opinion of me."

"Will you keep secret whatever she tells you, whatever she asks, whatever she reveals?"

"Yes, as if I were a priest, though I'm not. Meir, trust in me. I'm here for you and for Fluria and for no other reason."

He smiled in the saddest way. "I prayed for an angel of the Lord to come," he said. "I write my poems, I pray. I implore the Lord to defeat my enemies. What a dreamer and a poet I am."

"A poet," I said, musing, and smiling. He was as elegant as his wife as he sat back against the chair, slender, and other-worldly in a manner I found so moving. And now he had attached that beautiful word to himself, and he was ashamed of it.

And people outside were plotting his death. I was certain of that.

"You're a poet and a pious man," I said. "You prayed with faith, didn't you?"

He nodded. He looked at his books. "And I swore on my sacred book."

"And you told the truth," I said. But I could see that any further talk with him would lead nowhere.

"Yes, I did, and the Sherriff knows now." He was close to breaking under the strain.

"Meir, there is no time, really, for us to ponder these matters," I said. "Write the note now, Meir. I'm not a poet or a dreamer. But I can try to be an angel of the Lord. Now do it."

CHAPTER EIGHT

The Woes of a People

I KNEW ENOUGH ABOUT THIS PERIOD OF HISTORY TO realize that people did not generally go about in the dead of night, especially in a light snowstorm, but Meir had written out for me an eloquent and urgent letter, explaining to the Sherriff and the Captain of the Guard as well, whom Meir knew by name, that I must see Fluria without delay. He had also written a letter to Fluria, which I read, urging her to speak to me and trust me.

I found I had a steep climb uphill to reach the castle, but much to my disappointment, Malchiah would only tell me that I was fulfilling my mission beautifully. No more information or advice was forthcoming.

And when I was finally admitted to Fluria's chambers in the castle, I was frozen and wet and exhausted.

But the surroundings immediately restored me. First of all, the room itself, high in the strongest tower of the castle, was palatial, and though Fluria might not have cared much for figured tapestries, they were everywhere covering the stone walls, and beautifully woven tapestries covered the floors as well.

A great many candles were burning on tall iron candelabra,

which held some five or six candles apiece, and the room was softly lighted by these as well as the roaring fire.

Only one formal chamber was allotted to Fluria, obviously, so we found ourselves in the shadow of her enormous and heavily draped bed.

The fireplace was opposite, with a round hearth of stone, and the smoke actually went up through a hole in the roof.

The bed was hung with scarlet trappings, and there were fine carved chairs for us to sit on, a luxury, surely, and a writing table that we could put between us for an intimate talk.

Fluria took her seat at the table and gestured for me to take the opposite chair.

The place was warm, almost too warm, and I set my shoes to dry by the fire with the lady's permission. She offered me mulled wine as she'd offered it to the Sherriff before, but I honestly didn't know whether I could take wine if I wanted it, and in truth I didn't want it.

Fluria read the letter written by Meir in Hebrew, asking her to confide in me and trust me. She folded the stiff parchment quickly, and she set the letter beneath a leather book on the table, much smaller than the volumes left at the house.

She wore the same wimple as before, which perfectly covered her hair, but she had taken off the more elaborate veil, and the snug-fitting silk tunic, and wore a thick wool garment with the beautiful fur-lined cape over her shoulders, the hood thrown back. A simple white veil with a circlet of gold hung down around her shoulders and her back.

Again I sensed that she reminded me of someone I had known in my life, but again there was no time to pursue the thought.

She laid down the letter.

"What I say to you, is it in perfect confidence as my husband tells me here?"

"Yes, absolutely. I'm not a priest, only a brother. But I will keep your confidence, as would any priest keep the secrets told him in confession. Believe I've come here only to help you. Think of me as the answer to a prayer."

"So he describes you," she said thoughtfully. "And so I'm glad to receive you. But do you know what our people have suffered in England over the past many years?"

"I come from far away, but I know some of it," I said.

Obviously speech came much more easily to her than it had to Meir. She reflected, but went on.

"When I was eight years old," she said, "all the Jews of London were put into the Tower for safekeeping, due to riots, on account of the King's marriage to Queen Eleanor of Provence. I was in Paris then but I knew of it, and we had troubles of our own.

"When I was ten years old, on a Saturday, when all the Jews of London were at prayer, our holy books, the Talmud, were seized by the hundreds and publicly burnt. Of course they did not take all our books. They took what they saw."

I shook my head.

"When I was fourteen, and we lived in Oxford, my father, Eli, and I, the students rioted and looted our houses on account of the debts they owed to us for their books. Had not someone . . ." She paused, then went on. "Had not someone warned us, more would have lost their precious books, and yet the students of Oxford borrow from us even now and let rooms in houses that belong to us."

I made a gesture to indicate my commiseration. I allowed her to go on.

"When I was twenty-one," she said, "Jews in England were forbidden to eat meat during Lent, or whenever Christians could not eat it." She sighed. "The laws and persecutions are really too numerous for me to tell you all of it. And now in Lincoln only two years ago, the most dreadful occurrence of all."

"You're speaking of Little St. Hugh. I heard the people in the crowd talking of him. I know something of it."

"I hope you know that all we were accused of was a perfect lie. Imagine that we would take this little Christian child, crown him with thorns, pierce his hands and feet, and mock him as the Christ. Imagine. And that Jews would come from all over England to partake of such an evil ritual, and yet this is what we were told that we had done. Had not an unfortunate member of our race been tortured, and forced to name others, the madness might not have gone so far. The King came to Lincoln and condemned the poor unfortunate Copin who had confessed these unspeakable things and had him hanged, but not before being dragged through the town behind a horse."

I winced.

"Jews were taken to London and imprisoned. Jews were put on trial. Jews died. And all for this fanciful story of a child tormented, and the child himself is now buried in a shrine perhaps more glorious than that of Little St. William who had the honor of being the subject of just such a tale many many years before. Little Hugh has all of England roused against us. The common people have made his story into songs."

"Is there no place in this world safe for you?" I asked.

"I wonder the very same thing," she answered. "I was in Paris with my father when Meir proposed marriage. Norwich has always had a good community, and long survived the tale of Little St. William, and Meir had inherited a fortune from his uncle there."

"I understand."

"In Paris, our sacred books were also burnt. And what was not burnt was given over to the Franciscans and to the Dominicans . . ."

She paused as she looked at my robes.

"Go on, please," I said. "Don't think I am in the least

against you. I know that men in both orders studied the Talmud." I wished I could remember more of what I knew.

"Tell me, what else has happened?"

"You know the great ruler, His Majesty, King Louis, detests us and persecutes us, and confiscated our property to finance his Crusade."

"Yes, I know of these things," I said. "The Crusades have cost the Jews in town after town and land after land."

"But in Paris, our learned men, including my own kindred, fought for the Talmud when it was taken away from us. They appealed to the Pope himself and the Pope agreed that the Talmud might be placed on trial. Our story is not one of endless persecutions. We have our scholars. We have our moments. At least in Paris, our teachers spoke up eloquently for our sacred books, and for their general wholesomeness and that the Talmud was no threat to the Christians who might come in contact with us. Well, the trial was in vain. How can our learned men study when their books are taken from them? Yet in these times many at Oxford and at Paris want to learn Hebrew. Your brethren want to learn Hebrew. My father has always had Christian students around him—." She broke off. Something had deeply affected her. She put her hand to her brow, and so instantly began to cry that I wasn't prepared.

"Fluria," I said quickly, restraining myself from any intimate touch that might strike her as improper. "I do know of these trials and tribulations. I know that usury was forbidden in Paris by King Louis and he drove out those who wouldn't give in to the laws. I know why your people have turned to this practice and I know they're in England now simply because of it, because they are deemed useful in lending to the barons, and to the church. You needn't plead the case of your people before me. But tell me, what must we do to solve this tragedy we face now?"

She stopped crying. She reached into her robes and brought out a silk handkerchief and gently dabbed her eyes.

"Forgive me that I've gone on so. There is no place safe for us. Paris is no different, even with so many studying our ancient tongue. Paris is perhaps an easier place to live in some respects, but Norwich seemed peaceful, or so it did to Meir."

"Meir spoke of a man in Paris who might help you," I said. "He said only you could decide if you wanted to appeal to him. And, Fluria, I must confess to you. I know that your daughter, Lea, is dead."

She broke down again and turned away from me, her handkerchief covering her face.

I waited. I sat still listening to the crackle of the fire, and letting her get over the worst of it, and then I said,

"Long years ago, I lost my brother and sister." I paused. "Yet I cannot imagine the pain of a mother losing a child."

"Br. Toby, you don't know the half of it." She turned towards me again, and clenched her handkerchief tightly in her hand. Her eyes were soft and wide now. And she took a deep breath. "I have lost two children. And as for the man in Paris, I believe he would cross the sea to defend me. But I cannot say what he would do when he finds out Lea is dead."

"Can't you let me help you make this decision? If you decide you want me to go to Paris to this man, I will."

She studied me for a long moment.

"Don't doubt me," I said. "I am a wanderer, but I do believe it's the will of the Lord that I'm here. I do believe I have been sent to help you. And I will risk anything to do just that."

She continued to ponder and rightly so. Why should she accept me?

"You say you've lost two children. Tell me what happened. And tell me about this man. Whatever you say to me can't be used to hurt anyone, but only to help you think the matter through."

"Very well," she said. "I will tell you the whole tale, and maybe in the telling we'll find the decision, because this is no ordinary tragedy we face, and this is no ordinary tale."

CHAPTER NINE

Fluria's Confession

FOURTEEN YEARS AGO, I WAS VERY YOUNG AND VERY rash and a traitor to my faith, and to all I hold dear. We were in Oxford then where my father was studying with several scholars. We went to Oxford often, because he had pupils there, students who wanted to learn Hebrew and paid him well as a teacher.

Scholars for the first time, it seems, in those days wanted to learn the ancient tongue. And more and more documents from olden days were coming to light. My father was in great demand as a teacher, and much admired by Jews and Gentiles alike.

He thought it a good thing for Christians to learn Hebrew. He disputed with them in matters of faith, but all this was friendly.

What he could not know was that I'd given my heart entirely to one young man who was just finishing the Arts at Oxford.

He was almost twenty-one, and I only fourteen. I conceived a great passion for him, enough to give up my faith, and my father's love, and any wealth that was to come to me. And this young man loved me as well, so much so that he vowed he would give up his faith, if that's what was required of him.

It was this young man who came to warn us before the Oxford riots, and we warned as many other Jews as we could to escape. If it hadn't been for this young man, we might have lost a great deal more of our library than we did, and many valuable possessions as well. My father was devoted to this young man on account of that, but also in general because he loved this young's man inquiring mind.

My father had no sons. My mother had died giving birth to twin boys, neither of whom survived.

This young man's name was Godwin, and all you need know of his father is that he was a powerful earl, rich, and furious when he discovered that his son had become enamored of a Jewess, furious when he learned that his studies had put him in the company of a Jewish girl for whom he was ready to give up everything.

There had been a deep bond between the Earl and Godwin. Godwin was not the eldest, but he was his father's favorite, and Godwin's uncle, dying childless, had left to Godwin a fortune in France all but equal to that which his older brother, Nigel, was to inherit from their father.

Now his father took vengeance on Godwin for this disappointment.

He sent him to Rome to remove him from me and be educated there in the Church. He threatened to expose the seduction, as he called it, unless I never spoke the name of Godwin again and unless Godwin left immediately, and never spoke my name again aloud either. In truth, the Earl feared the disgrace that would come on him if it was known that Godwin had a great passion for me, or if we were to attempt marriage in secret.

You can imagine the disaster that might have followed for

all had Godwin really come over into our community. There have been converts to our faith, yes, but Godwin was the son of a proud and powerful father. Talk of riots! There have been riots for less than a nobleman's son converting to our faith, and in these restless times when we are constantly persecuted.

As for my father, he did not know what we would be accused of, but he was as wary as he was enraged. That I might convert was unthinkable to him, and soon he made it quite unthinkable for me.

He felt that Godwin had betrayed him. Godwin had come under his roof, to study Hebrew, to talk philosophy, to sit at my father's feet, and yet he had done this dastardly thing of seducing the great teacher's daughter.

He was a man with a tender heart for me, as I was all that he had, but he was in a rage against Godwin.

Godwin and I soon realized our love was hopeless. We would bring riot and ruin no matter what we did. If I became Christian, I would be excommunicated, and my inheritance from my mother confiscated, and my father deserted in his old age, which was a thought I couldn't bear. Godwin's disgrace would not be much less than if he had converted to become a Jew.

So it was set and determined that Godwin would go to Rome.

His father let it be known that he still had dreams of greatness for his son, a bishop's miter, certainly, if not a cardinal's hat.

Godwin had kindred among the powerful clergy in Paris and in Rome. Nevertheless this was a severe punishment, this forcing of vows on Godwin, because Godwin had no faith in any Lord whatsoever and had been a very worldly young man.

Whereas I loved his wit and humor and his passion, others admired the amount of wine he could take in an evening and his skill with the sword, on horseback, and in the dance. In fact, his gaiety and charm, which so seduced me, were wound up with great eloquence, and love of poetry and song. He had written much music for the lute, and he had often played this instrument as he sang to me when my father had gone to bed and did not hear us in the rooms below.

A life in the church was something utterly unappetizing to Godwin. In fact, he would have preferred to take the cross and go crusading to the Holy Land, and find adventure there and along the way.

But his father would not equip him for that, and arranged to send him to the strictest and most ambitious of his clerical relations in the Holy City and told him to succeed in Holy Orders or be disowned.

Godwin and I met one last time, and Godwin told me then that we must never see each other again. He didn't give two farthings for a great life in the church. He said his uncle in Rome, the Cardinal, had two mistresses. His other cousins he also regarded as blatant hypocrites, with appropriate contempt. "There are wicked and licentious priests aplenty in Rome," he said, "and bad bishops and I'll become another one. And with any luck I will someday join the Crusaders, and will in the end have all. But I won't have you. I won't have my beloved Fluria."

As for me, I had come to realize that I could not leave my father, and I was filled with misery. My love for Godwin did not seem to be something I could exist without.

The more we vowed we could not have each other, the more incensed we became. And I think that night we were in the nearest danger of running off together, but we did not.

Godwin came to a plan.

We would write to each other. Yes, this was disobedience on my part to my father, no doubt of it, and certainly disobedience for Godwin, but we saw our letters as a means by which we might obey our parents with greater strength. Our letters, unbeknownst to our elders, would help us to accept their demands.

"If I thought we could not have that," Godwin said, "the outpourings of our hearts in letters, I would not have the courage to leave here now."

Godwin went to Rome. His father had made something of a peace with him, as he couldn't bear to be angry with him. And so Godwin left one day quite early, without any further farewell.

Now my father, fine scholar that he was, and is, was nearly blind, which might account for how well educated I am, though I think I would be, even if he were not.

My point is that it was simple for me to keep our letters secret, but in truth, I thought Godwin would quickly forget me altogether, and be swept up into the licentious atmosphere into which he would surely be plunged.

In the meantime, my father surprised me. He told me that he knew Godwin would write to me, and he said, "I won't forbid you these letters, but I don't think there will be very many of them and you only mortgage your heart."

Both of us were completely wrong. Godwin wrote letters from every town along his journey. Sometimes twice a day, the letters would arrive, by messengers both Gentile and Jewish, and I kept to my room whenever I could and poured out my heart with ink. In fact, it seemed we grew in our love through these letters and became two new beings, deeply bound to each other, and nothing, absolutely nothing, could drive us apart.

No matter. I soon had a greater worry than I'd ever anticipated. Within two months, the measure of my love for Godwin was perfectly plain to me and I had to tell my father. I was with child.

Another man might have abandoned me or worse. But my

father has always doted on me. I alone survived of all his children. And I think there was a frank desire in him to have a grandson though he never spoke the words. After all, what did it matter to him that the father was Gentile if the mother was Jewish? And my father hit upon a plan.

He packed up our household and off we went to a small city in the Rhineland where there were scholars who knew of my father, but no kindred we could call our own.

There an elderly rabbi, who had much admired my father's writing about the great Jewish teacher Rashi, agreed to marry me and to give out that the child born to me was his. He did this really from great generosity. He said, "I have seen so much suffering in this world. I will be father to this child, if you want it, and never claim a husband's privileges as I am far too old for that."

There I bore not one child by Godwin, but twins, two beautiful girls, both of exactly the same stamp, so alike that even I could not always tell one from the other, but had to tie a blue ribbon on the ankle of Rosa so that I could know her from Lea.

Now I know you would interrupt me if you could, and I know what you are thinking, but let me go on.

The old rabbi died before the children were a year old. As for my father, he loved these two baby girls, and he thanked Heaven that he still had some sight left to see their beautiful faces before he became completely blind.

Only as we returned to Oxford did he confess to me that he had hoped to place the babies with an aged matron in the Rhineland and had had to disappoint her because of his love for me and for the baby girls.

Now all the while I had been in the Rhineland, I had written to Godwin, but I had told him not one word about these baby girls. Indeed, I had given him vague reasons for the trip— that it had to do with the acquisition of books which were now hard to come by in France and England, and that my father was dictating quite a lot to me, and needed these books for the treatises that occupied his every thought.

The treatises, his every thought, and the books—all that was simple and true.

We settled into our old house in the Jewry of Oxford in the parish of St. Aldate, and my father commenced taking pupils again.

Since the secret of my love for Godwin had been crucial to all parties, no one knew of it, and they believed my elderly husband to have died abroad.

Now while I was traveling I hadn't received Godwin's letters, so there were many of them waiting for me when I came home. I set about opening them and reading them when the nurses had the children, and I argued with myself frantically as to whether I should tell Godwin about his daughters or not.

Was I to tell a Christian man that he had two daughters who would be brought up as Jewesses? What might his response have been? Of course he could have bastards aplenty in the Rome he described to me and among his worldly companions for whom he had nothing but undisguised contempt.

In truth, I didn't want to cause him misery, and I did not want to confess to him the sufferings I had endured myself. Our letters were filled with poetry, and the depths of our thoughts, undetached perhaps from realities, and I wanted to keep things this way because, in truth, this way was more real to me than day-to-day life itself. Even the miracle of these baby girls did not diminish my belief in the world we sustained in our letters. Nothing could.

But just as I weighed my decision to keep quiet with the greatest scrupulosity, there came a very surprising letter from Godwin, which I want to relate to you from memory as best I can. I have the letter here, in fact, but securely hidden among my things, and Meir has never seen it, and I cannot bear to take it out and read it so let me give you the substance of it in my own words.

I think my own words now are Godwin's words, anyway. So let me explain.

He began again with his usual excursions of life in the Holy City.

"If I had converted to your faith," he wrote, "and we were righteous man and wife, poor and happy, surely, that would be better in the eyes of the Lord—if the Lord exists—than a life such as these men live here, for whom the church is nothing but a source of power and greed."

But then he went on to explain the strange occurrence.

He'd been drawn, it seemed, to one quiet little church over and over, where he sat upon the stone floor, his back to the cold stone wall, as he talked to the Lord contemptuously of the dismal prospects he saw for himself as a wenching and drinking priest or bishop. "How can you have sent me here?" he demanded of God, "to be among seminarians who make my former drunken friends in Oxford seem positively saintly?" He gnashed his teeth as he uttered his prayers, even insulting The Maker of All Things by reminding Him that he, Godwin, did not believe in Him and considered His church an edifice of the filthiest lies.

He went on with his heartless mockery of The Almighty. "Why should I wear the garments of Your church when I have nothing but contempt for all I see, and no desire to serve You? Why have You denied me the love of Fluria, which was the one pure and selfless impulse of my eager heart?"

You can imagine, I shuddered to read this blasphemy and he had written it down, all of it, before he described what then came to pass.

On a certain evening, as he was saying these very prayers to the Lord, in hatred and rage, brooding and repeating himself, and even demanding of the Lord why He had taken from Godwin not only my love but the love of his father as well, a young man appeared before him, and without preamble began to speak to him.

At first Godwin thought this young man was mad, or some sort of tall child, as he was very beautiful, as beautiful as angels painted on the walls, and also he spoke with a directness that was completely arresting.

In fact, for a moment Godwin considered that this might be a woman in male disguise, which was not so uncommon, apparently, as I might think, Godwin said, but he soon realized that this was no woman at all, but an angelic being in his midst.

And how did Godwin know? He knew on account of the fact that the creature knew Godwin's prayers and spoke directly to him now of his deepest hurt and his deepest and most destructive intentions.

"All around you," said the angel or creature or whatever it was, "you see corruption. You see how easy it is to advance in the Church, how simple to study words for the sake of words, and covet for the sake of coveting. You already have a mistress, and are thinking of taking another. You write letters to the lover you've forsworn with little regard for how this might affect her and her father, who loves her. You blame your fate on your love for Fluria and your disappointments, and you seek to bind her to you still, whether it is good or bad for her. Will you live an empty and bitter life, a selfish and profane life, because something precious was denied you? Will you waste every chance for honor and happiness given you in this world simply because you have been thwarted?"

In that instant, Godwin saw the folly of it. That he was constructing a life upon anger and hate. And amazed that this man would speak this way to him, he said,

"What can I do?"

"Give yourself to God," said the strange man. "Give him your whole heart and your whole soul and your whole life. Outsmart all of those others—your selfish companions who love your gold as much as you, and your angry father who has sent you here to be corrupt and unhappy. Outsmart the world that would make of you a common thing when you can yet be exceptional. Be a *good* priest, be a *good* bishop, and before you become either one, give away all you possess down to the last of your many gold rings, and become a humble friar."

Godwin was even more amazed.

"Become a friar, and to be good will become much easier for you," said the stranger. "Strive to be a saint. What greater thing could you achieve? And the choice is yours. No one can rob you of such a choice. Only you can throw it away and continue forever in your debauchery and your misery, crawling from your lover's bed to write to pure and holy Fluria, so that these letters to her are the only good thing in your life."

And then as quietly as he had come, the strange man went away, all but melting into the semidarkness of the little church.

He was there and then he was not there.

And Godwin was alone in the cold stone corner of the church staring at the distant candles.

He wrote to me that at that moment the light of the candles seemed to him to be the light of the dimming sun or the rising sun, a thing precious and eternal and a miracle wrought by God, a miracle meant for his eyes at that moment so that he would understand the magnitude of all that God had done in making him and in making the world around him.

"I will seek to be a saint," he vowed then and there. "Dear Lord, I give You my life. I give You all that I am and all that I can be and all that I can do. I forswear every instrument of wickedness."

That's what he wrote. And you can see that I've read the letter so many times that I know it by memory.

The letter went on to tell me that that very day he had gone to the Friary of the Dominicans and asked to be taken among them.

They took him with open arms.

They were very pleased that he was educated, and knew the ancient Hebrew language, and they were even more pleased that he had a fortune in jewels and rich fabrics to give them to be sold for the poor.

In the manner of Francis, he stripped off all the luxuriant clothing he wore, gave them his gold walking stick as well, and his fine gold-studded boots. And he took from them a patched and worn black habit.

He even said he would leave behind his learning and pray on his knees for the rest of his life, if that is what they wanted. He would bathe lepers. He would work with the dying. He would do whatever the Prior told him to do.

The Prior laughed at this. "Godwin," he said, "a preacher must be educated if he is to preach well, whether to the rich or to the poor. And we are the Order of Preachers, first and above all.

"Your education is to us a treasure. Too many want to study theology who have no knowledge of the arts and sciences, but you possess all this already, and we can send you now to the University of Paris, to study with our great teacher Albert, who is already there. Nothing would give us greater happiness than to see you there in our Paris friary and delving deep into the works of Aristotle, and the works of your fellow students, to sharpen your obvious eloquence in the finest spiritual light."

That was not all that Godwin had to tell me.

He went on with a ruthless self-examination such as I'd never read from him before.

"You know perfectly well, my beloved Fluria," he wrote, "this has been the most vicious vengeance upon my father that I could conceivably work, to have become a mendicant friar. In fact, my father at once wrote to my relations here to take me captive, and force women upon me until I had come to my senses and given up the fancy to be a beggar and a wayside preacher, dressed in rags.

"Be assured, my blessed one," he wrote, "that nothing so simple has happened. I am on my way to Paris. My father has disowned me. I am as penniless as I might have been had you and I married. But I have taken to myself Holy Poverty, to use the words of Francis, who is esteemed by us as highly as our founder, Dominic, and I will serve only my Lord and King now as the Prior orders me to do."

He went on to write, "I have asked of my superiors only two things: one, that I be allowed to keep my name Godwin, indeed to receive it anew as my new name, as the Lord would call us by a new name when we enter upon this life, and secondly, that I be allowed to write to you. I must confess, to obtain the last indulgence, I revealed some of your letters to my superiors and they marveled at the elevation and loveliness of your sentiments as much as I do myself. Permission for both has been granted, but I am Brother Godwin now to you, my blessed sister, and I love you as one of God's tenderest and dearest creatures, and with only the purest thoughts."

Well, I was astonished by this letter. And I soon learned that others had been astonished by Godwin as well. Happily, he wrote to me, his cousins had given him up as hopeless, seeing in him a saint or an imbecile, neither of which any of them thought to be useful, and they had reported to his father that no blandishment on earth could make Godwin leave the life of the Friars Minor to which he'd given himself.

I received a constant flow of letters from Godwin, as I had

before. These became the chronicle of his spiritual life. And in his newfound faith, he had more in common with my people than ever before. The pleasure-loving youth who had so enchanted me was now a serious scholar as my father was a serious scholar, and something immense and wholly indescribable now made the two men in my mind very much alike.

Godwin wrote to me of the many lectures he attended, but also much about his life in prayer—how he had come to imitate the ways of St. Dominic, the founder of the Black Friars, and how he had come to experience what he felt was the love of God in a wholly wondrous way. All judgment dropped from Godwin's letters. The young man who had gone to Rome so long ago had had only harsh words for himself as well as everyone around him. Now this Godwin, who was still my Godwin, wrote to me of the wonders he beheld everywhere he looked.

But, I ask you, how could I tell this Godwin, this wondrous and saintly person who had blossomed from the young shoot I had earlier loved, that he had two children living in England, both being brought up to be exemplary Jewish girls?

What good would such a confession have done? And how might his zeal have affected him, loving as he was, had he known that he had daughters living in the Jewry of Oxford, far from any exposure to the Christian faith?

Now, I have told you that my father did not forbid these letters. He had thought in the early years that they would not go on. But as they did go on, I made them known to him for more reasons than one.

My father is a scholar, as I've told you, and he not only studied the Talmud commentary by the great Rashi, but had translated much of it into French to aid those students who wanted to know it, but did not know the Hebrew in which it was written. As he became blind, he dictated more of his work to me, and it was his desire to translate much of the great Jewish scholar Maimonides into Latin if not French.

It came as no surprise to me that Godwin began to write to me on these very subjects, of how the great teacher Thomas of his order had read some of Maimonides in Latin, and how he, Godwin, wanted to study this work. Godwin knew Hebrew. He had been my father's best pupil.

So as the years passed, I revealed Godwin's letters to my father, and frequently commentary of my father on Maimonides, and even on Christian theology, made its way into the letters I wrote to Godwin.

My father himself would never dictate an actual letter to Godwin, but I think he came to know better and to love better the man whom he believed had once betrayed him and his hospitality and so a form of forgiveness was granted there. It was granted to me at least. And every day, after I was finished listening to my father's lectures to his students, or copying out his meditations for him, or aiding his students to do it, I would retire to my room and write to Godwin, telling him all about life in Oxford, and discussing all these many things.

Naturally in time, Godwin put the question to me: why had I not married? I gave him vague answers, that the care of my father consumed all my time, and sometimes I said simply that I had not met the man who was meant to be my husband.

All this while, Lea and Rosa were growing into beautiful little girls. But you must give me a moment here because if I don't weep for both my daughters I simply cannot go on.

◦‿◦

At this point, she did begin to cry, and I knew there was nothing I could do to comfort her. She was a married woman, and a pious Jewish woman, and I couldn't dare put my arms around her. It was not expected. In fact, it was likely forbidden for me to take such a liberty.

But when she looked up and saw the tears in my eyes, too, tears I couldn't quite explain because they had as much to do with all she'd told me about Godwin, as about herself, she was comforted by that, and seemed to be comforted by my silence as well, and she went on.

CHAPTER TEN

Fluria Continues Her Story

BROTHER TOBY, IF YOU EVER MEET MY GODWIN, HE will love you. If Godwin is not a saint, perhaps there are no saints. And who is the Almighty, Blessed Be He, that he would send me a man so like Godwin just now, and so like Meir, for you are that as well.

Now, I was saying to you that the girls were flowering, and each year grew more lovely, and more devoted to their grandfather, and more a joy to him in his blindness than possibly children are to many a man who can see.

But let me make mention here of Godwin's father, only to say that the man died despising Godwin for his decision to become a Dominican friar, and leaving all his fortune, of course, to his eldest son, Nigel. On his deathbed, the old man exacted a promise from Nigel that he would never set eyes on his brother, Godwin, and Nigel, who was a worldly and clever man, gave in to this with a shrug.

Or so Godwin told me in his letters, because Nigel immediately left the grave of their father in the church and went to France to see the brother he both missed and loved. Ah, when I think of his letters, they were like cool drinking water to me, all of those years, even though I couldn't share with him the joy I had in Lea and Rosa. Even though I kept that secret fastened in my heart.

I became a woman of three great pleasures, a woman who listened to three great songs. The first song was the daily teaching of my beautiful daughters. The second song was my reading and writing for my beloved father who depended upon me often for this, though he had students aplenty to read to him, and the third song was the letters of Godwin, and these three songs became a small choir that soothed and educated and improved my soul.

Don't think me evil that I kept the secret of the children from their father. Remember what was at stake. For even with Nigel and Godwin reconciled and writing regularly to each other, I couldn't envisage anything coming of my revelation except disaster all around.

Let me tell you more of Godwin. He told me all about his classes and his disputations. He would not be able to teach theology until he was thirty-five, but he was preaching regularly to large crowds in Paris and had quite a following. He was happier than he had ever been in his life, and he said over and over again, he wanted me to be happy, and asked why I had not married.

He said the winters were cold in Paris, just as they were in England, and the friary was cold. But he'd never known such joy, when he had had pockets of money to buy all the firewood he would want, or all the food. All he wanted in the world was to know how it went with me, and had I too found happiness.

When he wrote of this, the untold truth pressed in on me painfully, because I was so happy with our two daughters at my knee.

Gradually, I realized that I wanted Godwin to know. I wanted him to know that these two fine flowers of our love had bloomed safely and gave forth their beauty now in innocence and with protection.

And what made the secret all the more painful was this, that Godwin continued so ardently with his Hebrew studies, that he often disputed with the learned Jews in Paris, and would go to their houses to study with them and talk with them, just as he had long ago done when he went back and forth between London and Oxford. Godwin was as much now as ever a lover of our people. Of course he wanted to convert those with whom he disputed, but he had a great love for their keen minds, and above all for the devout lives that they lived, which he said often taught him more about love than the conduct of some of the theology students at the university.

Many a time I wanted to confess the whole state of affairs, but these considerations stopped me, as I've told you. One, that Godwin would be deeply unhappy if he knew that I had been left with child. And secondly, that he might, as any Gentile father might, be alarmed that two daughters born to him were being brought up as Jews, not so much because he would judge me for what I had done, or fear for their souls, but because he knew the persecutions and violence to which our people are often subjected.

Two years ago, he knew what had happened in the matter of Little St. Hugh of Lincoln. And we had written to each other candidly about our fears for the Jewry of London at that time. When we are accused in one place, the violence can break out in another. The hatred of us and the lies about us can spread like a plague.

But such horrors as that pressured me to keep the secret. For what if Godwin knew he had daughters in danger of riot and murder? What would he do?

What finally caused me to put the whole question before him was Meir.

Meir had come into our house just as Godwin had years ago, to study with my father. As I've indicated, my father's blindness did not stop the flow of students. The Torah is written on his heart, as we say it, and after all his years of commentary on the Talmud he knows it by heart as well. And all of Rashi's commentary on Talmud, that he knows too.

The Masters of the Oxford synagogues came to our house regularly to consult with my father. People even brought him their disputes. And Christian friends he had aplenty who sought his advice on simple matters, and now and then, when they needed money, with the laws now against our lending, they came for him to find some way to borrow without the interest being recorded or known. But I don't want to talk of those things. I have never managed my own property.

And very soon after Meir began to come to my father, he managed my affairs for me, and so I didn't have to think of material things.

You see me here dressed richly and in this white wimple and veil and you see nothing to mar the image of a rich woman except this taffeta badge affixed to my breast which brands me as a Jewess, but believe me when I say I seldom think of material things.

You know why we are moneylenders for the King and for those of his realm. You know all of this. And you know probably that since the King outlawed our money lending at interest, ways have been found around it, and we still hold in the name of the King a great deal of parchment on many a debt.

Well, my life being devoted to my father and my girls, I didn't consider that Meir might ask for my hand, though I couldn't help but notice what any woman would, and I'm sure

even you have noted, that Meir is a fine-looking man of considerable gentleness and keen mind.

When he very respectfully asked for my hand, he put it
to my father in the most generous terms—how he hoped,
not to deprive him of me and my love, but rather to invite
all of us to move with him to the house he'd only just inherited in Norwich. He had many connections there, and relations, and was a friend to the richest of the Jews in Norwich
of whom there are many, as I think you know simply from the
sight of the many stone houses that stand out so remarkably.
You know why we build our houses of stone. I don't have to
tell you.

Now my father had almost no sight left to him. He could
tell when the sun had risen and he knew when it was night, but
as for me and my daughters he knew us by the touch of his gentle hands, and if there was anything that he loved almost as
much as he loved us, it was instructing Meir, and guiding
Meir's reading. For Meir is not only a student of Torah and Talmud, and of Astrology and Medicine, and all those other subjects which have interested my father in passing, but Meir is a
poet, and he has a poet's view of things, and he sees beauty
everywhere that he looks.

If Godwin had been born a Jew, he would have been a twin
to Meir. But I'm talking nonsensically, for Godwin is the sum
of many amazing currents as I've explained. Godwin enters a
room as if a collection of people have just taken it by storm.
Meir appears quietly and with a silken manner. They are alike
and not alike at all.

My father consented at once that I might marry Meir,
and that, yes, he would go to Norwich, where we knew the
Jewish community was very prosperous and where there had
been peace for some time. After all, the horrid accusations
that Jews had killed Little St. William were almost a hundred

years old. And yes, people went to the shrine, and looked on us with fear in their fervor, but we had many friends among the Gentiles and old injuries and slights sometimes do lose their sting.

But was I to enter into marriage with Meir and not tell him the truth? Was I to let such a secret lie between us, that my daughters had a living father?

We could not seek the advice of anyone, or so my father thought, and he brooded over the matter, not wanting me to proceed unless somehow this problem could be solved.

So what do you think I did? Without telling my father, I turned for counsel to the one man in all the world whom I most trusted and loved, and that was Godwin. To Godwin, who had become a living saint amongst his brothers in Paris, and a great scholar of the science of God, I wrote and put the question.

And writing the letter in Hebrew as I did so often, I told him the whole story.

"Your daughters are beautiful in mind and heart and body," I told him, "but they believe themselves to be the children of a dead father, and the secret has been so well kept that Meir, who has proposed marriage to me, does not dream of the truth.

"Now I put it to you, you who are now well beyond the point where the birth of these children would cause you misery or worry, just as I assure you that these precious girls receive every blessing that they can, what should I do as to Meir's proposal? Can I become this man's wife without giving him a full account?

"How can one keep such a secret from a man who brings to the marriage nothing but tenderness and kindness? And now that you know, what is it that you, in your heart of hearts, want for your daughters? And accuse me now if you will, of failing to tell you that these peerless young women are your girls. Accuse me now before I enter into marriage with this man.

"I have told you the truth, and feel some great selfish relief in it, I must confess, but also a selfless joy. Should I tell my daughters the truth when they are of age, and what do I do with this good man, Meir, now?"

I implored him that this not be a shock to him, but that he give me his most pious advice on what I should do. "It is to Br. Godwin that I write," I told him, "the brother who has given himself to God. It is on him that I depend for an answer that is both loving and wise." I also told him that I had meant to deceive him, but could never resolve whether I had protected him or done him wrong.

I don't remember what else I wrote. Perhaps I told him how quick of wit were the two girls, and how well they had progressed in their own studies. I certainly told him that Lea was the quieter one, and Rosa had always something clever and amusing to say. I told him that Lea disdained all things of the world as not important, whereas Rosa could not have too many dresses, or too many veils.

I told him Lea was devoted to me, and clung to me, whereas Rosa peered out the window at the goings-on in Oxford or London whenever she was confined at home.

I told him that he was represented in all ways in both his daughters, in Lea's piety and discipline, and in Rosa's irrepressible gaiety and ready laugh. I told him that the girls had much property from their legal father, and that they would inherit from my father as well.

Now as I sent the letter off I feared that if I had angered or disappointed Godwin, I might have lost him forever. Though I no longer loved him as I had in my youth, as I no longer dreamed of him as a man, I loved him with all my heart and my heart was in every letter I wrote to him.

Well, what do you think happened?

I had to confess I had no idea what had happened, and there was so much running through my mind that it was with a great effort that I let Fluria go on. She had spoken of losing both her children. She was filled with emotion as she talked with me. And a great deal of this emotion had taken hold of me as well.

CHAPTER ELEVEN

Fluria Continues Her Story

IN TWO WEEKS, GODWIN CAME TO OXFORD AND APPEARED at the door of our house.

He wasn't the Godwin, naturally enough, I had once known. He had lost the sharp edge of youth, the inveterate recklessness, and something infinitely more radiant had replaced it. He was the man I knew from our letters. He was mild when he spoke and gentle, yet filled with an inner passion that was difficult for him to restrain.

I admitted him, without telling my father, and at once brought in the two girls.

It seemed I had no choice now but to let them know that this man was in fact their father, and gently, kindly, this is what Godwin begged me to do.

"You've done no wrong, Fluria," he said to me. "You've borne a burden all these years that I should have shared. I left you with child. I didn't even think on the matter. And now let me see my daughters, I beg you. You have nothing to fear from me."

I brought the girls in to meet him. This was less than a year ago, and the girls were thirteen.

I felt an immense and joyful pride when I presented them,

because they had become beauties without question, and they had inherited the radiant and happy expression of their father.

In a quavering voice, I explained to them that this man was in fact their father, and that he was the Br. Godwin to whom I wrote so regularly, and that up until these past two weeks, he had not known of their existence, but wanted only to lay eyes on them now.

Lea was shocked, but Rosa smiled immediately at Godwin. And in her usual irrepressible manner, declared that she had always known some secret surrounded their birth, and she was happy to lay eyes on the man who was her father. "Mother," she said. "This is a joyful time."

Godwin was stricken with tears.

He approached his daughters with loving hands, which he laid on both their heads. And then he sat weeping, overwhelmed, looking again and again at both of his daughters as they stood there, and giving way over and over to soundless sobs.

When my father realized he was in the house, when the elder servants told him that Godwin knew now about his daughters and they knew about him, my father came down and into the room and threatened to kill Godwin with his bare hands.

"Oh, but you are blessed that I'm blind, and can't find you! Lea and Rosa, I charge you, take me directly to this man."

Neither of the girls knew what to do, and I stepped at once between my father and Godwin, and begged my father to be calm.

"How dare you come here on this errand!" my father demanded. "Your letters I've tolerated and even from time to time I've written to you. But now, knowing the extent of your betrayal, I ask how dare you be so bold as to come under my roof?"

As for me, he had equally harsh language. "You told this man these things without my consent. And what have you told Lea and Rosa? What do these children actually know?"

At once Rosa tried to calm him. "Grandfather," she said, "we have always sensed that some mystery surrounded us. We've asked in vain many times for the writings of our supposed father, or some keepsake by which we could remember him, but nothing ever came of this, except our mother's obvious confusion and pain. Now we know that this man is our father, and we can't help but be happy on account of it. He's a great scholar, Grandfather, and we have heard mention of his name all our lives."

She tried to embrace my father, but he pushed her away.

Oh, it was dreadful to see him this way, staring blindly before him, clutching his walking stick, yet without his bearings, feeling now that he was alone amongst enemies of his own flesh and blood.

I began to cry and couldn't think of what to say.

"These are daughters of a Jewish mother," my father said, "and these are Jewish women who will be someday the mothers of sons who are Jews, and you will have nothing to do with them. They are not of your faith. And you must leave here. Don't tell me stories of your high sanctity and fame in Paris. I have heard enough of this many a time. I know who you really are, the man who betrayed my trust and my house. Go preach to the Gentiles who accept you as the reformed sinner. I accept no confession of guilt from you. If you don't visit a woman every night of your life in Paris, I stand to be surprised. Get out!"

You don't know my father. You can't know the heat of his wrath. I barely touch on the eloquence he used to flog Godwin. And all this in the presence of the girls who were staring from me to their grandfather, and then to the Black Friar who went down on his knees and said:

"What can I do but beg your forgiveness?"

"Come close enough," said my father, "and I will beat you with all my strength for what you've done in my house."

Godwin merely stood up, bowed to my father, and giving me a tender glance, and looking back on his daughters sorrowfully, made to leave the house.

Rosa stopped him, and indeed threw her arms around him, and he held her with his eyes closed for a long moment—things my father couldn't see or know. Lea stood stock-still, weeping, and then ran from the room.

"Get out of my house," roared my father. And Godwin obeyed at once.

I was in dreadful fear as to what he was doing or where he had gone, and now there seemed to me to be nothing to do but to confess to Meir the whole tale.

Meir came that night. He was agitated. He'd been told there had been a quarrel under our roof and that a Black Friar had been seen leaving and the man had been in great distress.

I shut myself up with Meir in my father's study and told him the truth. I told him I didn't know what was to happen. Had Godwin gone back to Paris, or was he still in Oxford or London? I had no idea.

Meir looked at me for a long time with his soft and loving eyes. Then he surprised me completely. "Beautiful Fluria," he said, "I've always known the girls were your daughters by a young lover. Do you think there are those in the Jewry who do not remember your affection for Godwin, and the tale of his break with your father many years ago? They don't say anything outright, but everyone knows. Calm yourself on this account, insofar as it concerns me. What faces you now is not my defection, surely, for I love you as much today as I did yesterday and the day before that. What faces us all is what Godwin means to do."

He went on speaking to me in the calmest manner.

"Grave consequences can await a priest or brother accused of having children by a Jewish woman. You know this. And grave consequences can await a Jewess who confesses that her children are daughters of a Christian man. The law forbids such things. The Crown is anxious for the property of those who violate it. It is impossible to see how anything can be done here, except that the secret be kept."

Indeed, he was right. It was the old stalemate, which I had faced when Godwin and I had first loved each other, and Godwin had been sent away. Both sides had reason to keep the secret. And surely, my girls, clever as they were, understood this very well.

Immediately Meir had produced a calm in me that wasn't too different from the serenity I often felt when I read Godwin's letters, and in this moment of remarkable intimacy, because it was very truly that, I saw the meekness and innate kindness of Meir more clearly than before.

"We must wait to see what Godwin will do," he repeated. "In truth, Fluria, I saw this friar leave your house, and he seemed a humble and gentle man. I was watching, because I didn't want to come in if your father was in this study with him. And so I happened to see him very clearly as he came out. His face was white and drawn, and he seemed to carry an immense burden on his soul."

"Now you carry it too, Meir," I said.

"No, I carry no burden. I only hope and pray that Godwin will not seek to take his daughters from you, for that would be a horrid and terrible thing."

"How can a friar take his daughters from me?" I asked.

But just as I asked this question, there came a loud knocking, and the maidservant, my beloved Amelot, came to tell me that Earl Nigel, son of Arthur, was here with his brother the friar, Br. Godwin, and that she had shown them in and made them comfortable in the best room of the house.

I rose to go, but before I could, Meir rose beside me and took my hand. "I love you, Fluria, and want you for my wife. Remember this, and I knew this secret without anyone having to tell me. I even knew that the old Earl's youngest son was the likely man. Believe in me, Fluria, that I can love you unstintingly, and if you do not want to give me your answer now as to my proposal, things being as they are, be assured that I wait patiently for you to decide whether we will be married or not."

Well, I had never heard Meir put that many words together in my presence, or even in my father's. And I felt greatly comforted by this, but in total terror of what awaited me in the front rooms.

Forgive me that I cry. Forgive me that I can't help it. Forgive me that I can't forget Lea, not now as I recount these things.

Forgive me that I weep for Rosa as well.

> *O Lord, hear my prayer,*
> *listen to my cry for mercy;*
> *in your faithfulness and righteousness*
> *come to my relief.*

> *Do not bring your servant into judgment*
> *for no one living is righteous before you.*

You know this psalm as well as I do. It is my constant prayer.

I went in to greet the young Earl who had inherited the title from his father. Nigel, too, I had known as one of my father's students. He looked troubled but not angry. And when I turned my gaze on Godwin I was once again astonished by the gentleness and quiet that seemed to surround him, as though he were present, yes, and vibrantly so, but in another world as well.

Both men greeted me with all the respect they might have shown a Gentile woman, and I urged them to be seated and take some wine.

My soul was quaking. What could the presence of the young Earl mean?

My father entered and demanded to know who was in his house. I begged the maid to go to Meir and ask him to come in with us, and then, my voice unsteady, I told my father that the Earl was here with his brother, Godwin, and that I had invited them to take some wine.

As Meir came in and stood beside my father, I told all the servants, and the whole body of them had come in to wait on the Earl, to please go out.

"Very well, Godwin," I said. "What have you to say to me?" I tried not to cry.

If the people of Oxford knew that two Gentile children had been brought up as Jews, might they not try to harm us? Might there not be some law under which we could in fact be executed? I didn't know.

There were so many laws against us, but then these children were not the legal children of their Christian father.

And would a friar such as Godwin want the disgrace of having his paternity known to everyone? Godwin, so beloved by his students, could not possibly wish for such a thing.

But the power of the Earl was considerable. He was one of the richest in the realm, and had the most power in resisting the Archbishop of Canterbury whenever he chose, and also the King. Something terrible might be done now in whispers and without a public display.

As I considered these things, I tried not to look at Godwin, because I felt only a pure and elevated love when I looked at him, and the worried expression on the face of his brother caused me fear and pain.

I felt again that this was a stalemate. I was gazing at a chessboard on which two figures faced each other, and neither had an opening for a good move.

Don't think me hard at such a moment for calculating. I saw myself as to blame for everything that was now taking place. Even the quiet and pensive Meir was now on my conscience as he had asked for my hand.

Yet I calculated as if I were doing sums. *If exposed we will be condemned. But claim them and Godwin faces disgrace.*

What if my girls were taken from me, and theirs was to be a life of unendurable captivity in the Earl's castle? This is what I dreaded above all else.

All my deception had been through silence, and now I knew that the chess pieces faced each other and I waited for the reach of the hand.

My father, though offered a chair, remained standing, and he asked Meir if he would take the lamp and light the face of both the men who stood opposite him. Meir was loath to do this, and I knew it, and so I did it, begging the Earl's pardon, and the man only gestured his acceptance and looked directly beyond the flame.

My father sighed and gestured for a chair and then sat down. He put his hands on top of his walking stick.

"I don't care who you are," he said. "I despise you. Trouble my house, and you inherit the wind."

Godwin drew himself up and came forward. My father, hearing his footsteps, raised his walking stick as if to push him back, and Godwin stopped in the center of the room.

Oh, this was agony, but then Godwin, the preacher, the man who moved crowds in the squares of Paris, and in the lecture halls, began to speak. His Norman French was perfect, and of course so was my father's and so is mine as you can hear.

"The fruit of my sins," he said, "is now before me. I see what my selfish acts have wrought. I see now that what I so thoughtlessly did has had grave consequences for others, and that they have accepted these consequences with generosity and grace."

I was deeply moved by this, but my father indicated his impatience.

"Take these children from us, and I will condemn you before the King. We are, if you have even for a moment forgotten it, the King's Jews, and you will not do such a thing."

"No," said Godwin in the same meek and eloquent manner. "I would do nothing without your consent, Magister Eli. I haven't come into your house with the pretense of any demand. I come with a request."

"And what could that be? Mind you," said my father, "I am prepared to take this stick and beat you to death."

"Father, please," I begged him to stop and listen.

Godwin accepted this as though he had the patience to be stoned in public without lifting a finger. Then he made his intentions clear.

"Are there not two of these beautiful children?" he said. "Has not God sent two because of our two faiths? Look at the gift he's given to Fluria and to me. I, who never expected to have the devotion or love of a child, am now possessed of two, and Fluria lives daily, without disgrace in the loving company of her offspring, which might have been torn from her by someone cruel.

"Fluria, I beg you: give one of these beautiful girls to me. Magister Eli, I beg you, let me take one of these beautiful girls from this house.

"Let me take her to Paris to be educated. Let me watch her

grow up, Christian, and with the loving guidance of a devoted father and uncle.

"You keep close to your heart always the other. And which you choose to come with me, I will accept, for you know their hearts and you know which one is most likely to be happy in Paris, and happy with a new life, and which is more timid, perhaps, or more devoted to her mother. That both love you, I have no doubt.

"But Fluria, I beg you, realize what it means to me as a believer in Jesus Christ, that my children cannot be with their own, and that they know nothing of those most important resolves their father has made: to serve his Lord Jesus Christ in thought, word, and deed forever. How can I return to Paris without begging you: give one of the girls to me. Let me raise her as my Christian daughter. Let us divide between us the fruit of our wicked fall, and our great good fortune that these beautiful girls have life."

My father went into a fury. He rose to his feet, clutching his walking stick.

"You disgraced my daughter," he shouted, "and now you come wanting to divide her children? Divide? You think you are King Solomon? If I had my sight I'd kill you. Nothing would stop me from it. I would kill you with my bare hands, and bury you beneath the backyard of this house to keep it from your Christian brethren. Thank your God that I'm blind and sick and old and can't tear your heart out. As it is, I order you out of my house, and insist that you never return, and do not seek to see your daughters. The door is barred against you. And allow me to put your mind at ease on this account: these children are legally ours. How will you prove otherwise to anyone, and think what scandal you bring upon yourself if you do not leave here in silence and give up this brash and cruel request!"

I did everything in my power to restrain my father, but with a sharp elbow he pushed me to the side. He swung his walking stick, his blind eyes searching the room before him.

The Earl was stricken with sorrow, but nothing could touch the look of misery and heartbreak in Godwin. As for Meir, I couldn't tell you how he was taking this argument because it was all I could do to put my arms around my father and beg him to be quiet, to let the men speak.

I was in terror, not of Godwin, but of Nigel. Nigel was the one after all with the power to seize my two daughters, if he chose, and to subject us to the harshest judgment. Nigel was the one with money enough and men enough to seize the girls and lock them up in his castle miles from London and deny me that I would ever see them again.

But I saw only gentleness in the faces of both men. Godwin was again weeping.

"Oh, that I have caused you pain, I am so sorry," he said to my father.

"Caused me pain, you dog!" my father said. With difficulty he recovered his chair and sat down again, trembling violently. "You have sinned against my house. You sin now against it. Get out of it. Go."

But what surprised everyone at this moment of passion was that Rosa came into the room and in a clear voice asked her grandfather to please say nothing more.

Now with twins, even identical twins often are not doublets in heart and soul. As I've already hinted to you, one can be more inclined to directness and to command than the other. So it was with my daughters, as I've said. Lea behaved always as if she were younger than Rosa; Rosa it was who often decided what they would do or not do. In this she resembled me as much as she resembled Godwin. She resembled my father as well, as he was always a man who spoke with force.

Well, forcefully, Rosa spoke now. She said to me in the gentlest yet firm manner that she wanted to go to Paris with her father.

At this Godwin and Nigel were both deeply moved, but my father was speechless and bowed his head.

Rosa went to him, and wrapped her arms around him, and kissed him. But he would not open his eyes, and he dropped his walking stick and balled his fists on his knees, ignoring her as if he did not feel her touch.

I tried to give him back his walking stick as he was never without it, but he had turned away from all of us, as if coiled into himself.

"Grandfather," said Rosa, "Lea cannot bear to be separated from our mother. You know this, and you know that she would be afraid to go to a place such as Paris. She's fearful now of going with Meir and Mother to Norwich. I am the one who should go with Br. Godwin. Surely you can see the wisdom of this and that it is the only way for all of us to be at peace."

She turned and looked at Godwin, who was regarding her with such loving-kindness I could scarcely bear to see it.

Rosa went on, "I knew this man was my father before I ever saw him. I knew that the Br. Godwin of Paris to whom my mother wrote with such devotion was in fact the man who had given me life.

"But Lea never suspected, and now wants only to be with Mother and with Meir. Lea believes what she would believe, not on the strength of what she sees, but what she feels."

She came to me now and put her arms around me. She said to me gently, "I want to go to Paris." She frowned and seemed to be struggling to form her words, but then she said simply, "Mother, I want to be with this man who is my father." She kept her eyes on me. "This man is not like other men. This man is like the saintly ones." Here she referred to those strictest of Jews who try to live entirely for God, who keep Torah and Talmud so totally that they have acquired with us the name Chasidim.

My father sighed and stared upwards, and I could see his lips moving in prayer. He bowed his head. He stood up and made his way to the wall, turning his back to all of us, and he began bowing from the waist as he prayed.

I could see that Godwin was overjoyed at this decision on the part of Rosa. And so was his brother, Nigel.

And it was Nigel who spoke now, explaining in a low respecting voice that he would see that Rosa had all the clothing and all the luxuries that she could possibly need, and that she would be educated in the finest convent in Paris. He had already written to the nuns. He went to Rosa and kissed her and said, "You've made your father very happy."

Godwin appeared to be praying, and then he said under his breath, "Dear Lord, you have placed a treasure in my hands. I promise you that I will safeguard forever this child, and that hers will be a life rich in earthly blessings. Please, Lord, grant her a life of spiritual blessings."

At this I thought my father would lose his mind. Of course Nigel was an Earl, you understand, and had more than one estate, and was used to being obeyed not only by his household but by all his serfs and everyone who encountered him. He didn't realize how deeply his assumptions would offend my father.

Godwin saw the picture, however, and again, as he had before, he went down on his knees to my father. He did it with utter simplicity as though it were nothing for him, and what a picture he made there in his black habit and sandals, kneeling before my father and pleading with him to forgive everything and trust that Rosa would be loved and cherished.

My father was unmoved. Finally with a deep sigh he gestured for everyone to be silent, because by this time Rosa was pleading with him, and even the proud but gentle Nigel was begging him to see the fairness of it.

"The fairness of it?" my father said, "that the Jewish daughter of a Jewish woman should be baptized and become a Christian? Is that what you think is fair? I should see her dead before such a thing should be allowed to happen."

But Rosa, in her boldness, pressed close to him and wouldn't let him take his hand from hers. "Grandfather," she said, "*you* must be King Solomon now. You must see that Lea and I are to be divided, because we are two, not one, and we have two parents, a father and a mother."

"It's you who have made the decision," my father said. He was speaking wrathfully. I never saw him so angry, so bitter. Not even when I had first told him years ago that I was with child had he shown such anger.

"You are dead to me," he said to Rosa. "You go with your mad and simpleminded father, this devil who worked his way into my confidences, listening to my tales and legends and would-be instruction, all the while he had his wicked eye on your mother. You go ahead, and you are dead to me and I will mourn for you. Now leave my house. Leave it and go with this Earl who has come here to take a child from a mother and grandfather."

He left the room, easily finding his way out, and slammed the door behind him.

In that moment I thought my heart would break, that I would never know peace or happiness or love again.

But something occurred then, which affected me more deeply than any spoken words.

As Godwin stood and turned to Rosa, she slipped into his arms. Irresistibly she was drawn to him, and lavished her childlike kisses on him, and laid her head on his shoulder, and he closed his eyes and cried.

I saw myself in that moment, as I had loved him years ago. Only I saw the purity of it, that it was our daughter he held close to him. And I knew then that there was nothing I could or should do to oppose this plan.

Only to you, Br. Toby, do I admit this, but I felt a complete release. And in my heart I said my silent farewell to Rosa, and my silent confirmation of love for Godwin, and I took my place at Meir's side.

Ah, you see how it is. You see. Was I wrong? Was I right?

The Lord in Heaven has taken Lea from me, my child who remained with me, my faithful, timid, and loving Lea.

He has taken her, as my father in Oxford refuses even to speak to me, and mourns for Rosa who is yet alive.

Has the Lord passed judgment on me?

Surely my father has learned of the death of Lea. Surely he knows what we face here in Norwich and how the town has made of Lea's death a great cause for our condemnation and possible execution, how the evil hatred of our Gentile neighbors may break out against all of us once again.

It is a judgment on me, that I let Rosa become the ward of the Earl and go with him and Godwin to Paris. It is a judgment, I can't help but believe it. And my father, my father has not spoken a word to me, nor written a word since that very hour. Nor will he even now.

He would have left our house that very day, if Meir hadn't taken me away immediately, and if Rosa had not gone that very night. And poor Lea, my tender Lea, she struggled to understand why her sister was leaving her for Paris, and why her grandfather sat silent as one made of granite, refusing to speak even to her.

And now my tender darling, brought to this strange city of

Norwich, and beloved of all who laid eyes upon her, has died, helplessly, of the iliac passion as we stood by unable to save her, and God has placed me here, imprisoned, until such time as the town breaks out in riots and we are all to be destroyed.

I wonder if my father is not laughing at us, bitterly, for we are surely undone.

CHAPTER TWELVE

The End of Fluria's Story

FLURIA WAS IN TEARS AS SHE FINISHED. AGAIN I WANTED to put my arms around her but I knew this wasn't proper, and wouldn't be tolerated.

I told her once more in a low whisper that I couldn't imagine her pain in losing Lea, and I could only do quiet homage to her heart.

"I don't believe the Lord would take a child to punish anyone for anything," I said. "But what do I know of the ways of the Lord? I think you did what you thought right when you let Rosa go to Paris. And Lea died in the course of things as a child might die."

She softened a little when I said this. She was tired and perhaps her exhaustion calmed her as much as anything else.

She rose from the table and went to the narrow slit of a window and appeared to be looking out at the falling snow.

I stood behind her.

"We have many things to decide now, Fluria, but the chief thing is this. If I go to Paris and persuade Rosa to come here, to act the part of Lea . . ."

"Oh, do you think I haven't thought of this?" she asked. She turned to me. "It's much too dangerous," she continued. "And

Godwin would never allow such a deception. How could such a deception be right?"

"Wasn't it Jacob who deceived Isaac?" I said. "And became Israel and the father of his tribe?"

"Yes, that's so, and Rosa is the clever one, the one with the greatest gift for words. No, it's too dangerous. What if Rosa cannot answer Lady Margaret's questions, or recognize in Little Eleanor a close friend? No, it can't be done."

"Rosa can refuse to speak to those who've abused you," I said. "Everyone would understand this. She need only appear."

This hadn't occurred to Fluria obviously.

She began to pace the floor and to wring her hands. All my life, I'd heard that expression: to wring one's hands. But I'd never seen anyone do it until now.

It struck me that I knew this woman better now than I knew anyone in the world. It was an odd and chilling thought, not because I loved her any less, but because I couldn't bear to think of my own life.

"But if it could be done, for Rosa to come here," I asked, "how many in the Jewry know that you had twins? How many know your father, and knew you in Oxford?"

"Too many, but none will speak of it," she insisted. "Remember, to my people, a child who converts is dead and gone, and no one even mentions her name. We never made mention of it when we came here. And no one spoke of Rosa to us. And I would say it is the best-kept secret in the Jewry right now."

She went on speaking as if she needed to reason through it.

"Under the law, Rosa might have lost all her own property, inherited from her first stepfather, simply for converting. No, there are those who know here, but they know in silence and our physician and our elders can see that they remain quiet."

"And what of your father? Have you written to tell him that Lea is dead?"

"No, and even if I did he would burn the letter unopened. He promised me that he would do this if ever I wrote to him.

"And as for Meir, in his sorrow and misery, he blames himself for Lea's taking sick because he brought us here. He imagines that, snug and safe in Oxford, she might never have taken ill. He has not written to my father. But that does not mean that my father does not know. He has too many friends here for him not to know."

She began to cry again.

"He will see it as God's punishment," she whispered through her tears, "of that I'm sure."

"What do you want me to do?" I asked. I wasn't at all sure we would be in agreement, but she was obviously clever and reflective and the hour was late.

"Go to Godwin," she said, and her face softened as she spoke his name. "Go to him and ask him to come here and calm the Dominican brethren. Have him insist upon our innocence. Godwin is greatly admired within the order. He studied with Thomas and Albert before they left to begin their preaching and teaching in Italy. Surely Godwin's writings on Maimonides and Aristotle are known even here. Godwin will come on my account, I know that he will, and because . . . because Lea was his child."

Again her tears flowed. She looked frail standing there in the candlelight with her back to the cold window, and I could hardly bear it.

For a moment I thought I heard voices in the distance and some other errant sound in the wind. But as she did not appear to hear it, I didn't say anything about it. I wanted so to hold her as my sister, if only I could.

"Maybe Godwin can reveal the entire truth and be done with it," she said, "and make the Black Friars understand that we did not kill our daughter. He is a witness to my character and my soul."

This obviously gave her hope. It gave me hope too.

"Oh, would it be a great thing to be rid of this terrible lie," she said. "And as we speak, you and I, Meir is writing for sums of money to be donated. Debts will be remitted. Why, I would face utter ruin, all my property gone, if only I could take Meir with me away from this terrible place. If only I knew I had brought no harm to the Jews of Norwich, who have in other times suffered so much."

"That would be the best solution, no doubt of it," I said, "because an imposture would carry dreadful risks. Even your Jewish friends might say or do something to undo it. But what if the town won't accept the truth? Not even from Godwin? It will be too late to insist upon the old deception. The opportunity for an imposture would be lost."

Again I heard those noises in the night. Soft shapeless sounds, and others more piercing. But the falling snow seemed to muffle all.

"Br. Toby," she said, "go to Paris and put the entire case before Godwin. To him you may tell everything, and let Godwin decide."

"Yes, I will do this, Fluria," I said, but again I heard those noises and what sounded like the distant clanging of a bell.

I gestured for her to let me approach the window. She stepped aside.

"That's the alarm," she said in terror.

"Perhaps not," I said. Suddenly another bell began to ring.

"Are they burning the Jewry?" she said, her voice dying in her throat.

Before I could answer her, the wooden door to the chamber opened and the Sherriff appeared, fully armed, his hair wet with snow. He stepped aside as two serving boys dragged several trunks into the room, and then in came Meir.

His eyes fixed on Fluria, and he threw back his snow-covered hood.

Fluria fell into his open arms.

The Sherriff was in dreadful humor, which was to be expected.

"Br. Toby," he said, "your advice to the faithful to pray to Little St. William produced a stunning result. The crowd stormed the house of Meir and Fluria for relics of Lea and have made off with all her clothes. Fluria, my dearest, it might have been wise of you to pack up all those dresses and bring them up here when you came." He sighed again and looked around as if he wanted something on which he might bang his fist. "Miracles are being claimed already in the name of your daughter. Lady Margaret's guilt has driven her on a little crusade."

"Why didn't I foresee this!" I said miserably. "I only thought to direct them away."

Meir wrapped his arms all the more tightly around Fluria as if he could shield her from all these words. The man's face was a marvel of resignation.

The Sherriff waited until the serving boys were gone, and the door was closed, and then he addressed the couple directly.

"The Jewry is under heavy guard and the small fires started have been put out," he said. "Thank Heaven for your stone houses. And thank Heaven that Meir's letters requesting donations have already been sent. And thank Heaven that the elders have given large gifts of gold marks to the friars and to the priory."

He stopped and sighed. He glanced at me helplessly for an instant, then returned his attention to them.

"But I will tell you right now," he said, "that nothing is going to stave off a massacre here except that your daughter, herself, should return and put an end to this mad rush to make her a saint."

"Well, that is what will be done," I said before either of them could speak up. "I'm on my way to Paris now. I assume I will find Br. Godwin your advocate in the Dominican Chapter House near the University? I'll begin my journey tonight."

The Sherriff was unsure. He looked at Fluria.

"Your daughter can return here?"

"Yes," I answered. "And surely Br. Godwin, a worthy advocate, will come with her. You have to hold on until then."

Meir and Fluria were speechless. They looked at me as if they were entirely dependent upon me.

"And until then," I said, "will you let the elders come here to the castle to consult with Meir and Fluria?"

"Isaac, son of Solomon, the physician, is already here for safekeeping," said the Sherriff. "And more will be brought here if need be." He ran a gloved hand back through his wet white hair. "Fluria and Meir, if your daughter cannot be brought back, I ask that you tell me now."

"She'll come," I said. "You have my word on it. And both of you, pray for my safe journey. I'll travel as fast as I'm able."

I went to the couple and I placed my hands on their shoulders.

"Trust in Heaven, and trust in Godwin. I'll be with him as soon as I can."

CHAPTER THIRTEEN

Paris

By the time we reached Paris, I had had enough of thirteenth-century travel to last me easily the rest of four lifetimes, and though I'd been dazzled repeatedly by a thousand unusual sights, from the dizzying, tightly packed half-timbered houses of London, to the spectacle of Norman castles on varying hilltops, and the never-ending snow falling upon village and town through which I passed, we were intent only on reaching Godwin and laying the case before him.

I say "we" because Malchiah was visible to me off and on through the journey and even went part of the way by wagon with me to the capital, but he would give me no advice except to remind me that Fluria's and Meir's lives depended on what I might do.

When he appeared, it was in the garb of a fellow Dominican, and whenever it seemed that my transportation had fatally broken down, he would manifest himself to remind me I had gold in my pockets, that I was strong and capable of doing what was required of me, and then a cart would appear, or a wagon, with a gentle driver willing to let us ride with the bundles, or the firewood, or whatever was being transported, and in many different vehicles I slept.

If there was any one part that was an agony, it was crossing the Channel in weather that kept me perpetually sick on board the small ship. There were times when I thought we would all be drowned, so stormy was the winter ocean, and I asked Malchiah more than once, and in vain, if in the midst of this assignment it was possible for me to die.

I wanted to talk with him about all that was happening, but that he wouldn't allow, reminding me that he wasn't visible to other people and I would look like a madman talking out loud to everyone. As for my talking to him only in my mind, he insisted this was too imprecise.

I took this to be an evasion. I knew he wanted me to complete this mission on my own.

At last we passed through the gates of Paris, without mishap, and reminding me that I would find Godwin in the University quarter, Malchiah left me with the stern reminder that I had not come here to gaze idly at the great Cathedral of Notre Dame or to wander the precincts of the Palace of the Louvre but to find Godwin without delay.

It was as fiercely cold in Paris as it had been in England, but the sheer press of human beings who swarmed the capital provided some meager warmth. Also there were little fires burning everywhere round which people warmed themselves and many spoke of the dreadful weather and how unusual it was.

I knew from my earlier reading that Europe at this time had been entering into a period of spectacularly cold weather that would last for centuries, and once again I was grateful that Dominicans were allowed to wear wool stockings and leather shoes.

No matter what Malchiah had told me, I went immediately to the Place de Grève and stood for a long moment before the recently complete facade of Notre Dame. I was stunned, as I always had been in my own time, by the sheer magnitude and magnificence of it, and could not get over the fact that it was, here before me, just beginning its adventure in time as one of the greatest cathedrals anyone could ever behold.

I could see scaffolding and workmen surrounding a distant corner of the building, but the edifice was very nearly complete.

I went inside, finding it thronged with people in the shadows, some on their knees, others drifting from shrine to shrine, and I knelt on the bare stones, near one of the towering columns, and I prayed for courage and I prayed for strength. I had the strangest feeling when I did this, however, that I was somehow going over Malchiah's head.

I reminded myself that that was nonsense, that we were both working for the same Lord and Master, and there came to my lips again the prayer that had come earlier, much earlier: "Dear God, forgive me that I ever separated myself from You."

I cleared my mind of all words, listening only for the guidance of God. That I was kneeling in this massive and magnificent monument to faith during the very age when it had been built lulled me into a wordless gratitude. But above all I did what this immense cathedral meant for me to do: I laid myself open to the voice of The Maker and bowed my head.

An awareness came over me, all of a sudden, that though I was in dread of failing in what I had to do, and though I was in pain for Fluria and Meir and all the Jewry of Norwich, I was myself happier than I had ever been. I felt strongly that I had been given such a priceless gift in this mission that I could never give thanks enough to God for what was happening to me, for what had been placed in my hands.

This didn't engender pride in me. Rather I felt wonder. And, as I pondered, I felt myself talking to God without words.

The longer I remained there, the deeper came my realization that I was now living in a way that I had never lived in my own time. I had so thoroughly turned my back on life in my own time that I didn't know a single person as I knew Meir and Fluria, and had no devotion to anyone as I now had a deep devotion to Fluria. And the folly of this, the deliberate despair and resentful emptiness of my own life, struck me with full force.

I looked through the dusty gloom to the faraway choir of the great cathedral, and I begged for forgiveness. What a miserable instrument I was. But if my ruthlessness and my craftiness could be eclipsed now in this mission, if my cruel tools and talents could be useful here, I could only marvel at the majesty of God.

A deeper thought nudged at me, but I could not quite grasp it. It had something to do with the binding fabric of good and evil, with the way in which the Lord might extract the glorious from the seeming disasters of human beings. But the thought was too complex for me. I felt I was not meant to complete this realization—only God knew how the dark and the light were mingled or separated—and I could only give voice to my contrition again and pray for courage, pray to succeed. Indeed, I sensed a danger in pondering why God allowed evil, and how He might use it. I felt He alone understood this, and we were never meant to justify evil or to do it out of any misguided notion that evil had in every day and age, its certain role. I was content not to understand the mystery of the workings of the world. And I felt something surprising suddenly: whatever was happening that was evil had nothing to do with the great goodness of Fluria and Meir that I'd experienced firsthand.

Finally, I said a small prayer to the Mother of God to intercede for me, and then I rose, and walking as slowly as I could to savor the sweet candle-lighted darkness, I went out into the cold winter light.

It is pointless to describe in detail the filth of the Paris streets, with their slops in the central gutters, or the jumble of the many three- and four-story houses, or the reek of the dead from the massive cemetery Les Innocents in which people transacted all manner of business in the snowfall right amongst the many tombs. It's pointless to try to capture the feeling of a city in which people—crippled, humpbacked, dwarfed, or tall and gangly, advancing on crutches, carrying huge bundles on their bent shoulders, or hurrying upright and with purpose— were going every which way at once, some selling, some buy- ing, some carrying, some scurrying, some rich and carried in litters or marching bravely through the mud in their bejeweled boots, and most rushing about in simple jerkins with hooded tunics; a populace wrapped to the teeth in wool or velvet or fur of all different quality, to defend themselves against the cold.

Over and over beggars beseeched me for help, and out of my pockets I put coins in their hands, nodding to their prayer- ful gratitude, as it seemed my pockets contained an endless supply of silver and gold.

A thousand times I was seduced by what I saw but had to resist it. I hadn't come, as Malchiah had told me, to seek out the royal palace, no, nor to watch puppeteers bravely putting on their little shows at the little crossroads, or to marvel at how life went on in the bitterest of weather, with tavern doors open, or how life was lived in this most remote and yet familiar of times.

It took me less than an hour to push my way through the crowded and winding streets, and into the student quarter where I was suddenly surrounded by men and boys of all ages dressed as clerics, wearing robes or gowns.

Nearly everyone was wearing a hood due to the abysmal winter, and some sort of heavy mantle, and one could tell the rich from the poor by the amount of visible fur lining their gar- ments and even trimming their boots.

Men and boys were coming and going from many small

churches and cloisters, the streets were tantalizingly narrow and crooked, and lanterns were hung out to fight the dismal gloom.

Yet I was easily directed to the priory of the Dominicans, with its small church and open gates, and found Godwin, whom the students quickly identified for me as a tall, hooded brother, with sharp blue eyes and pale skin, atop a bench, obviously lecturing in the open cloister court itself to a huge and attentive crowd.

He was speaking with effortless energy, in a beautiful and fluid Latin, and it was a pure delight to hear someone speaking—and the students replying and questioning—in this tongue with such ease.

The snow had slackened. Fires had been built here and there to warm the students, but the cold was miserable and I soon learned from a few whispered remarks to me by those on the fringes that Godwin was so popular now, in the absence of Thomas and Albert who had gone on to teach in Italy, that his students simply couldn't be contained indoors.

Godwin gestured colorfully as he addressed this sea of eager figures, some of whom sat on benches, writing frantically as he spoke, and others sitting on cushions of leather or soiled wool, or even on the very stone ground.

That Godwin was an impressive man didn't surprise me, yet I couldn't help but be amazed at how very impressive he truly was.

His height alone was striking, but he had the very radiance that Fluria had tried so meaningfully to describe. His cheeks were ruddy from the weather, and his eyes were ablaze with a deep passion for the concepts and ideas he was expressing. He seemed utterly invested in what he was saying, what he was doing. A genial laughter punctuated his sentences, and he turned from right to left gracefully to include all his listeners in the points being made.

His hands appeared to be wrapped in rags except for his

fingertips. As for the students almost all wore gloves. My hands were freezing but I too wore leather gloves and had since I'd left Norwich. I felt sad that Godwin did not have such fine gloves.

He had his students laughing riotously at some witticism when I found a place beneath the arches of the cloister, and against a stone pillar, and then he demanded of them that they remember some very crucial quotation from St. Augustine, which any number called out eagerly, and after that, it seemed he was going to launch on a new subject, but our eyes connected, and he stopped in mid-sentence.

I couldn't tell if anyone knew why he'd stopped. But I knew. Some silent communication passed between us and I dared to nod my head.

Then, with a few preoccupied words, he dismissed the entire class.

He would have been surrounded forever by those asking him questions, except that he told them with careful patience and gentleness that he had important business now, and besides that he was frozen, and then he came to me, took me by the hand, and drew me after him, through the long low-ceilinged cloister, past many an archway, and past many interior doors, until we reached his own cell.

The room, thank Heaven, was spacious and warm. It was no more luxurious than the cell of Junípero Serra at the Carmel Mission of the early twenty-first century, but it was cluttered with wonderful things.

Coals heaped generously in a brazier gave off the delicious heat, and quickly he lighted several thick candles, placing them on his desk, and on his lectern, both of which stood very near his narrow bed, and then he gestured for me to have a seat on one of several benches to the right side of the room.

I could see that he often lectured here, or had done so before the demand for his words had reached such heights.

A crucifix hung on the wall, and I thought I spied several

small votive pictures, but in the shadows, I couldn't make out what they were. There was a very hard thin cushion there before the crucifix and what was obviously a picture of the Madonna, and I surmised that that was where he knelt when he prayed.

"Oh, but forgive me," he said to me in the most generous and affable manner. "Come, warm yourself by the fire. You're white from the cold and your head is damp."

Quickly, he removed my dappled hood and mantle, and then he removed his own. These he hung on pegs on the wall, where I knew that the heat of the brazier would soon make them dry.

He then produced a small towel and wiped my head and face with it, and then his own.

Only then did he unwrap his hands and stretch his fingers over the coals. I realized for the first time that his white cassock and scapular were thin and patched. His was a lean frame, and the simplicity of his short cut ring of hair made his face all the more vital and striking.

"How do you know me?" I asked.

"Because Fluria wrote to me and told me that I would know you when I saw you. The letter preceded you by only two days. One of the Jewish scholars teaching Hebrew here brought it to me. And I've been worried ever since, not by what she wrote, but by what she failed to write. And then there is another matter, and she's told me to open my heart entirely to you."

He said this with ready trust and again I had a sense of his graceful demeanor and his generosity when he brought one of the short benches up to the brazier and sat down.

There was a firmness and a simplicity to his smallest gestures, as if the time for him was long past when any artifice needed to affect anything that he did.

He reached into one of his voluminous and hidden pockets,

beneath his white scapular, and drew out the letter, a folded sheet of stiff parchment, and put it in my hand.

The letter was in Hebrew, but as Malchiah had promised I was able to read it plainly:

My life is in the hands of this man, Br. Toby. Welcome him and tell him all, and he will tell you all, as there is nothing he does not know about my past and present circumstances, and no more than this do I dare to put down here.

Fluria had signed herself with only the first letter of her first name.

I realized no one would know her hand better than Godwin.

"I've known something was wrong for some time," he said, his brows knitting in distress. "You know everything. I know that you do. So let me tell you before I attack you with questions, that my daughter Rosa was seriously ill for some days, insisting that her sister Lea was in great pain.

"It was during the most beautiful days of Christmas when the pageants and the plays before the cathedral are more lovely than any time of the year.

"I thought perhaps, our Christian ways being new to her, she was simply frightened. But she insisted that her misery was on account of Lea.

"These two, you know, are twins, and so it is that Rosa can feel those things that are happening to Lea, and only two weeks ago, she told me that Lea was no longer in this world.

"I've tried to comfort her, to tell her this can't be so. I've assured her that Fluria and Meir would have written to me if anything had befallen Lea, but Rosa can't be persuaded that Lea is alive."

"Your daughter is right," I said sadly. "That's the heart of the entire dilemma. Lea died of the iliac passion. Nothing could be done to prevent it. You know what this is, as well as I do, a disease of the stomach and the insides that causes great pain. Surely people almost always die of it. And so Lea, in the arms of her mother, has died."

He dropped his face in his hands. For a moment I thought he'd break into sobs. And I felt just a tinge of fear. But he murmured over and over the name of Fluria, and in Latin, he begged the Lord to console her for the loss of her child.

Finally he sat back and looked at me. He whispered, "And so this beautiful one whom she kept has been taken from her. And my daughter remains here, ruddy and strong, with me. Oh, this is bitter, bitter." The tears stood in his eyes.

I could see agony in his face. His genial manner had completely collapsed in this misery. And his expression had a childlike sincerity as he slowly shook his head.

"I am so deeply sorry," I whispered as he looked at me. But he didn't answer.

We kept a long silence for Lea. He had a faraway look in his eyes for a while. And once or twice he warmed his hands, but then he simply let them fall on his knees.

Then gradually I saw the same warmth and openness in him as before.

He whispered: "You know this child was my daughter, of course, I've told you as much already in my own words."

"I do," I said. "But it's the child's very natural death which is bringing ruin to Fluria and to Meir now."

"How can this be?" he asked. He seemed innocent when he asked me, as if his learning had given him an innocence. Perhaps "humility" would have been a better word.

I also could not avoid noticing that he was a handsome man, not merely because of his regular features and near shining face, but because of this humility and the muted power that it conveyed. A humble man can conquer anyone, and this man seemed to hold nothing back out of the usual masculine pride that suppresses emotions and expression.

"Tell me everything, Br. Toby," he said. "What is happening to my beloved Fluria?"

A film of tears appeared in his eyes. "But before you start, let me tell you something straight-out. I love God and I love Fluria. That is how I characterize myself in my heart, and God understands."

"I understand too," I said. "I know of your long correspondence."

"She has been my guiding lamp many a time," he answered. "And though I gave up all the world to come into the Dominicans, I did not give up my exchange with Fluria, because it has never meant anything to me but the highest good."

He brooded for a moment, and then added, "The piety and goodness of a woman like Fluria are things one doesn't find so often among Gentile women, but then I know little of them now. It seems a certain gravity is common to Jewish women like Fluria, and she has never written to me a single word that I couldn't share with others, or should not have shared with others for their benefit—until this note came to me two days ago."

This had a strange effect on me because I think I was half in love with Fluria for the same reasons, and I realized for the first time how very serious Fluria had been, and the name for this is "gravitas."

Once again, Fluria in memory reminded me of someone, someone I had known, but I couldn't think who this person was. Some sadness and fear were connected with this. But I had no time to think on it now. It seemed a perfect sin to think about my "other life."

I looked around the little chamber. I looked at the many

books on the shelves and the parchment pages scattered on the desk. I looked at the face of Godwin who was waiting on me intently, and then I told him all.

I talked for perhaps half an hour explaining everything that had happened, and how the Dominicans of Norwich were in the grip of a delusion about Lea, and how Meir and Fluria could not share with anyone except their fellow Jews the awful truth of the matter that they had lost their beloved child.

"Imagine the grief of Fluria," I said, "when there is no time for grief because fabrications have to be made." I stressed this. "And it is a time for fabrications, just as it was for Jacob when he deceived his father, Isaac, and later when he deceived Laban to increase his own flock. It's a time for dissimulation because the lives of these people are at stake."

He smiled and nodded to this reasoning. He gave no objection to it.

He rose and began to pace back and forth in a tight little circle because that was all that the room allowed.

Finally, he sat down at the desk, and oblivious to my presence began a letter at once.

I sat for quite some time merely watching him as he wrote, blotted, and wrote some more. Finally he signed the letter, blotted for the last time, then folded the parchment and sealed it with wax, and looked up at me.

"This will go now to my fellow Dominicans at Norwich, to Fr. Antoine, whom I know personally, and it is full of my strong advice that they are on the wrong path. I vouch for Fluria and Meir, and give here a frank admission that Eli, Fluria's father, was once my teacher at Oxford. I think it will make a difference but not enough of a difference. I cannot write to Lady Margaret of Norwich and if I did, she would no doubt commit the letter to the flames."

"There's a danger in this letter," I said.

"How so?"

"You admit a knowledge of Fluria to which other Dominicans may be privy. When you visited Fluria in Oxford, when you went away with your own daughter, didn't your friars in Oxford know of these things?"

"O Lord help me," he sighed. "My brother and I did everything to keep it a secret. Only my confessor knows that I have a daughter. But you're right. The Dominicans of Oxford were most familiar with Eli, the Magister of the synagogue, and their sometime teacher. And they know that Fluria had two daughters."

"Exactly," I said. "If you write a letter, drawing the attention of the world to your connection, then an imposture which might save Fluria and Meir cannot be attempted at all."

He threw the letter on the brazier and watched it go up in flames.

"I don't know how to solve this," he said. "I've never faced anything more bleak and ugly in my life. Dare we attempt an imposture when Dominicans from Oxford might well tell those in Norwich that Rosa is impersonating her sister? I can't bring my daughter into this danger. No, she cannot make the journey."

"Too many people know too much. But something has to happen to stop this scandal. Do you dare to go, and to defend the couple before the Bishop and the Sherriff?"

I explained to him that the Sherriff already suspected the truth that Lea was dead.

"What are we to do?"

"Attempt the imposture, but do it with more cunning and more lies," I said. "That is the only way I see to do it."

"Explain," he said.

"If Rosa is willing to impersonate her sister, we take her to Norwich now. She will insist that she is Lea and that she has been with her twin sister, Rosa, in Paris, and she can show great indignation that anyone has so maligned her loving parents. And she can express an eagerness to return to her twin sister at once. By admitting the existence of the twin, converted to the church, you provide a reason for her sudden trip to Paris in the middle of winter. It was to be with her sister, from whom she'd been separated only a short time. As for your being the father, why should any mention be made?"

"You know what the gossips say," he offered suddenly. "That Rosa is in fact the love child of my brother Nigel. Because Nigel was with me every step of the journey. As I told you, only my confessor knows the truth."

"All the better. Write to your brother at once, if you dare, and tell him what has happened, and that he must proceed to Norwich at once. This man loves you, Fluria told me so."

"Oh, indeed, and he always has, no matter what my father sought to make him think or do."

"Well, then, let him go, and vow that the twins are together in Paris, and we will journey there as quickly as we can with Rosa, who will then claim to be Lea, indignant and bereft over the state of her parents, and she will be eager to return to Paris with her uncle Godwin at once."

"Ah, I see the wisdom in this," he said. "It will mean disgrace for Fluria."

"Nigel need not say outright that he is the father. Let them think it, but he need not say it. The girls have a legal father. Nigel need only claim the interest of a friend to the child who has converted to Christianity, as he was a guardian to her sister before her, her sister who waits in Paris for Lea, the new convert, to return."

He was deeply absorbed in what I was saying. I knew he was thinking of the many aspects. The girls, as converts, might be excommunicated and thereby lose their fortune. Fluria had spoken of this. But I could still see a passionate Rosa, pretending to be an indignant Lea, and pushing back the forces that threatened the Jewry, and no one in Norwich surely would have the gall to demand that the other twin come there as well.

"Don't you see?" I said. "It's a tale that accommodates everything."

"Yes, very elegant," he answered, but he was still thinking.

"It explains why Lea left. Lady Margaret's influence did make her accept the Christian faith. And so she sought to be with her Christian sister. Lord knows, everyone in England and France wants to convert the Jewish tribe to Christianity. And it is a simple matter to explain that Meir and Fluria have been most mysterious about all this because to them it is a double disgrace. As for you and your brother, you are the patrons of the newly converted twins. It's all very plain in my mind."

"I see it all," he said slowly.

"Do you believe that Rosa can impersonate her sister, Lea?" I asked. "Do you believe that she can do such a thing? Will your brother lend a hand? As for Rosa's willingness to try it, do you have any idea?"

He thought on this for a long moment, and then he said simply that we had to go to Rosa now this very evening, though it was late and obviously getting dark.

When I looked through the little window of the cell, I saw only darkness, but that might have been the thickness of the snow.

Again, he sat down and applied himself to writing a letter. And he read it aloud to me as he wrote.

"Beloved Nigel, I am in great need of you, for Fluria and Meir, my beloved friends, and the friends of my daughters, are in grave danger, due to recent events, which I cannot explain here but will confide in you as soon as we meet. I ask that you go at once to wait for me in the town of Norwich, where I am now heading this very night. And that you present yourself there to the Lord Sherriff, who holds many Jews in the castle tower for their protection, and you make known to the Lord Sherriff that you are well acquainted with the Jews in question, and that you are the guardian of their two daughters—Lea and Rosa—who have become Christian and now live in Paris, under the guidance of Br. Godwin, their godfather, and their devoted friend. Please understand that the inhabitants of Norwich are not aware that Meir and Fluria had two children, and they are very much perplexed as to why the one child whom they knew has left the town.

"Insist to the Lord Sherriff that he keep this matter secret until I can meet you and explain further why these actions must be undertaken now."

"Splendid," I said. "Do you think your brother will do it?"

"My brother will do anything for me," he said. "He's a kindly and loving man. I would say more if I thought that such a letter might not fall into the wrong hands."

Once again he blotted his many sentences, and his signature, folded the letter, sealed it with wax, and then he rose, bidding me to wait, and went out of the room.

He was gone for some time.

It struck me as I looked around the little room, with its scent of ink and old paper, its scent of leather book binding and burning coals, that I could spend my whole life here happily, and that, in fact, I was living a life now so superior to anything that I'd ever lived before that I almost wanted to cry.

But this was no time to think of myself.

When he returned, he was out of breath and somewhat relieved.

"The letter will go out tomorrow morning, and make much greater progress than we will make, on its way to England, as I've sent it care of the Bishop who presides over St. Aldate's, and the manor house of my brother, and he will deliver the letter into Nigel's hands."

He looked at me and once again the tears came up in his eyes. "I could not have done this alone," he said gratefully.

He removed his mantle from the peg, and mine as well, and we dressed for the snow outside. He started to wrap his hands again with the rags that he'd laid to the side, but I reached into my pockets whispering a prayer and drew out two pairs of gloves.

"Thank you, Malchiah!"

He looked at the gloves, but then, with a nod, took the pair I offered and put them on. I could see he didn't like the fine leather or the fur trim, but he knew that we had work that we had to do.

"Now, we go to see Rosa," he said, "and tell her what she already knows, and ask her what she wishes to do. If she refuses this task, or feels she cannot do it, we will go to testify in Norwich on our own."

He paused. He whispered, "Testify," and I knew he was troubled now by the amount of lies involved.

"Never mind it," I said. "There will be bloodshed if we don't do this. And these good people, who have done nothing, will die."

He nodded and out we went.

A boy with a lantern, who looked very much like a heap of wool garments, waited for us outside, and Godwin said we would go to the convent where Rosa lived.

We were soon hurrying through the darkened streets, passing an occasional noisy tavern door, but generally groping our way behind the boy who held the lantern, and a heavy snow had begun to fall.

CHAPTER FOURTEEN

Rosa

THE CONVENT OF OUR LADY OF THE ANGELS WAS VAST, solid, and lavishly appointed. The immense room in which we greeted Rosa was more expensively and beautifully furnished than any room I'd yet seen. The fire was immediately fed and raked for us, and two young nuns, heavily covered in linen and wool, set out bread and wine on the long table. There were numerous tufted stools, and the most spectacular tapestries everywhere that I'd yet observed. Tapestries had been laid down over the polished pavers of the floor.

Candles blazed in many sconces, and large diamond-paned windows caught the reflection of the lights beautifully in their thick glass.

The Abbess, an impressive woman of obvious and easy authority, was clearly devoted to Godwin, and left us at once to whatever it was we had to say.

As for Rosa, clad in a white robe and beneath it a thick white tunic which might have been her nightgown, she was the image of her mother, except for her startling blue eyes.

For a moment it was shocking to me to see the coloring of the mother with the vibrancy of the father in her face. Indeed her eyes were so like Godwin's as to be continually unnerving.

Her thick curling black hair was loose over her shoulders, and down her back.

She was a woman already at fourteen, quite obviously, and she had a woman's shape and bearing.

That all the gifts of her parents were mingled in her was plain.

"You've come to tell me that Lea is dead, haven't you?" she said immediately to her father, after he'd kissed her on both cheeks and on the top of her head.

He began to weep. They sat down opposite each other in front of the fire.

She held both his hands in hers, and nodded more than once as though talking to herself about it. And then she spoke up again.

"If I told you that Lea has come to me in a dream, I would be lying to you. But when I woke this morning, I knew not only for certain that she was dead, but that my mother needed me. Now you come with this friar and I know you wouldn't be here at this hour if something wasn't required of me at once."

Godwin at once brought up a stool for me and asked me to outline the plan.

As briefly as possible I told her what had happened, and she began to gasp when she realized the danger to her mother, and to all the Jews of this town of Norwich where she had never been.

She told me quickly that she'd been in London when many Jews from Lincoln had been tried and executed for the murder of Little St. Hugh, just such a supposed crime.

"But do you think you can play the part of your sister?"

"I long to do it!" she said. "I long to stand up to these people who dare to say my mother killed her daughter. I long to upbraid them for these wild accusations. I can do it. I can insist that I am Lea, for in my heart I am Lea as much as I am Rosa, and Rosa as much as Lea. And it will be no lie to say that I'm eager to leave Norwich and return to Rosa, my very self, in Paris at once."

"You mustn't overplay it," said Godwin. "Remember, no matter what your anger or your disgust with these accusers, you must talk softly as Lea talked softly, and you must insist softly as Lea would have done."

She nodded. "My anger and my determination are for you and Br. Toby," she said. "Have confidence in me that I will know what to say."

"You realize if this goes wrong, you will be in danger," said Godwin, "just as we are. What sort of father is it that would let his own daughter go so near to a blazing fire?"

"A father who knows that a daughter must do her duty by her mother," she answered at once. "Has she not already lost my sister? Has she not lost the love of her father? I have no hesitation, and I think the frank admission that we are twins is a great advantage and without it the imposture would surely be undone."

She left us then, telling us she would prepare for the journey.

Godwin and I went off to arrange for a wagon to take us to Dieppe, from which we'd sail to England over the treacherous Channel once more, and this time in a hired boat.

As we left Paris, the sun was just rising, and I was filled with misgivings, perhaps because Rosa was so angry and so confident, and Godwin so seemingly innocent, even in the way he lavished upon every servant his brother's money as we set out.

Nothing material meant anything to Godwin. He burned with zeal to endure anything that nature or the Lord or circumstance forced upon him. And something in me thought that a healthy desire to survive what lay before us might have served him a little better than the guileless manner in which he moved headlong to what fate had in store.

He was absolutely committed to the deception. But it was unnatural to him in the extreme.

He had been himself in all his debaucheries, he told me when his daughter was sleeping apart from us, and he had in his conversion and commitment to God been nothing but himself.

"I don't know how to dissemble," he said, "and I'm afraid I'll fail at it." But I thought, more than once, that he wasn't afraid enough. It was almost as if he had become, in his inveterate goodness, a little bit of a simpleton as is bound to happen, I think, if and when one gives oneself absolutely to God. Again and again, he said that he trusted God would make everything right.

It is impossible to relate here all the other things we spoke of during that long ride to the coast; or how we talked together constantly even as the boat tossed on the rough waters of the Channel, and as our newly hired cart made its way to Norwich over the muddy frozen roads from London.

The most important thing for me to note is that I came to know both Rosa and Godwin better than I had known Fluria, and tempted though I was to ply Godwin with questions about Thomas Aquinas and Albertus Magnus (who was already being called by this great title), we talked more about Godwin's life among the Dominicans, his delight in his brilliant students, and how committed he was to his Hebrew study of Maimonides and Rashi.

"I am no great scholar when it comes to writing," he said, "except perhaps in my informal letters to Fluria, but I hope that what I am and what I do will survive in the minds of my students."

As for Rosa, she had guiltily enjoyed her life among the

Gentiles, and no small part of it had been her extreme pleasure at seeing the Christmas pageants before the cathedral, until she had felt that Lea, so many miles from her, was suffering grievous pain.

"I keep this ever before my mind," she said to me once while Godwin slept in the cart beside us, "that I did not give up my ancestral faith out of fear or because some wicked person tormented me into it, but because of my father, and because of the zeal I saw in him. Surely he worships the same Lord of the Universe that I worship. And how could a faith be wrong, which has brought such simplicity and happiness to him? I think his eyes and his manner did more to convert me than anything that was said to me. And I find him always a shining example of what I mean to be. As for the past, it weighs on me. I can't bear to think of it, and now that my mother has lost Lea, I can only pray with all my heart that, young as she is, she'll be the mother of many children by Meir, and for this, their life together, I make this journey, giving in perhaps too easily to what has to be done."

She seemed aware of a thousand difficulties of which I hadn't even thought.

First and foremost, where would we stay when we reached Norwich? Would we go at once to the castle, and how would she play the part of Lea before the Sherriff, not knowing whether Lea ever knew the man face-to-face?

Indeed, how could we even approach the Jewry and seek shelter with the Magister of the synagogue, for with one thousand Jews in Norwich, there was bound to be more than one synagogue, and should Lea not have known a Magister by likeness and by name?

I sank into silent prayer when I thought of these things. *Malchiah, you have to guide us!* I insisted. But the danger of presumption struck me as very real.

Because Malchiah had brought me here did not mean there was no suffering ahead. I thought again of what had so struck me about the mix of good and evil in the cathedral. Only the Lord Himself knew what was really good and evil, and we could only strive to follow every Word He'd revealed as to the good.

In sum, that meant anything might happen. And the number of people involved in our plot worried me more than I allowed my companions to know.

It was midday, under a lowering and snowy sky, when we approached the town, and I was visited by exhilaration much as I was before I took a life, only this time I knew a spectacular new aspect of it. The fate of many people depended on what I might bungle or accomplish, and that had never actually been the case before.

When I'd murdered Alonso's enemies, I'd been brash almost as Rosa was brash now. And I had not done it for Alonso. This I now knew. I had done it to strike back at God Himself for what He had allowed to happen to my mother and my brother and sister, and the monstrous arrogance of this gripped me and wouldn't give me any peace.

At last as our wagon with its double team of horses rolled into Norwich, we hit upon this plan.

Rosa would sleep, feverishly in her father's arms, her eyes closed, as she was ill from the journey, and I, who didn't know anyone in the Jewry, would ask of the soldiers whether or not we might take Lea into her own house, or must we go to the Magister of Meir's synagogue, if the soldier knew whom that man might be.

I could naturally claim utter innocence of any knowledge of the community, and so could Godwin, and we all knew that our plan would be immeasurably helped if Lord Nigel had arrived and was at the castle awaiting his brother.

Perhaps the guards of the Jewry would be prepared for this.

As to what happened, none of us was prepared at all.

The sun was a dim glimmer beyond the gray clouds as we entered the street before Meir's house, and all of us were surprised to see lights in the windows.

We could think only that Meir and Fluria had been released, and I climbed out of the cart and immediately knocked on the door.

Guards appeared out of shadows almost immediately, and one very belligerent man, large enough to crush me between his hands, demanded that I not harry the inhabitants of the house.

"But I come as a friend," I whispered, not wanting to wake the ailing daughter. I gestured to her. "Lea, the daughter of Meir and Fluria. Can't I take her into her parents' house there to rest until she is strong enough to see her parents in the castle?"

"Go in then," said the guard, and he pounded on the door abruptly with the outside of his right fist.

Godwin stepped down out of the cart, and then received Rosa into his arms. She lay against his shoulder as he hooked his right arm beneath her knees.

At once the door opened, and I saw there a gaunt individual with thin white hair and a high forehead. He wore a heavy black shawl over his long tunic. His hands were bony and white and he appeared to stare dully at Godwin and the girl.

Godwin gasped, and immediately stopped in his tracks.

"Magister Eli," Godwin said in a whisper.

The old man stood back and, glancing meaningfully at the guard, he gestured for us to enter the house.

"You may tell the Earl, his brother is come," said the old man to the guard, and then he shut the door.

It was now clear to me that the man was blind.

Godwin planted Rosa on her feet gently. She too was white with shock at the realization that her grandfather was here.

"I didn't expect to see you here, Grandfather," she said at once, in the kindest voice, and she moved towards him, but he, staring forward, gestured for her to stay where she was.

He looked cold and remote, and then he took a deep breath, as if he were savoring her faint perfume.

Then he turned disdainfully away.

"Am I to believe you are your pious sister?" he asked. "Do you think I don't know what you mean to do? Oh, you are her very double, how well I remember, and was it not your wicked letters to her from Paris that prompted her to go with these Gentiles into the church? But I know who you are. I know your scent. I know your voice!"

I thought Rosa would give way to tears. She bowed her head. I could feel her trembling though I wasn't touching her. The thought that she had killed her sister must have already occurred to her, but now it seemed to hit her full force.

"Lea," she whispered. "My beloved Lea. I am incomplete for the rest of my days."

Out of the shadows, another figure came towards us, a young and robust man, with dark hair and heavy brows, who also wore a heavy shawl over his shoulders against the chill in the room. He too wore the yellow taffeta badge of the Ten Commandments.

He stood with his back to the firelight.

"Yes," said the stranger. "I do believe you are her very double. I could not have told the two of you apart. It is possible that this will work."

Godwin and I nodded to him gratefully for this little enthusiasm.

The old man turned his back to us and moved slowly to the chair by the fire.

As for the younger man, he looked about himself and at the old man, and then he went to him and whispered something to him under his breath.

The old man made a despairing gesture.

The young man turned to us.

"Be swift and wise," he said to Rosa and to Godwin. He didn't seem to know what to make of me. "The cart outside, is it big enough to hold your father and mother, and your grandfather? For as soon as you work your little spell, you should all leave here at once."

"Yes, it's quite big enough," said Godwin. "And I agree with you that haste is most important. As soon as we know that our plan has worked."

"I'll see to it that it's taken around the back," said the man. "An alleyway leads to the other street." He eyed me thoughtfully, then went on: "All of Meir's books have gone to Oxford," he said, "and every other precious thing has been moved out of this house in the quiet of the night. It took some bribing of the guards, of course, but it's been done. You should be ready to leave as soon as your little play has been performed."

"We will be," I said.

Then bowing to us, the man went out the front door of the house.

Godwin glanced at me helplessly and then at the old man.

Rosa wasted no time.

"You know why I've come here, Grandfather. I've come to work any deception required of me to remove suspicion from my mother that she poisoned my sister."

"Don't talk to me," said the old man, staring forward. "I'm not here on account of a daughter who would give up her own child to Christians." He turned as if he could see the brightness of the fire. "I am not here on behalf of children who have given up their faith for fathers who are no better than thieves in the night."

"Grandfather, I beg you, don't judge me," said Rosa. She knelt down beside the chair and kissed his left hand.

He didn't move or turn to her.

"I'm here," the old man said, "to provide the money that is needed to save the Jewry from the madness of these people, spawned by your sister's foolishly entering their very church. And that much, I've already done. I'm here to save the priceless books that belong to Meir which might have been carelessly lost. As for you and your mother—."

"My sister paid for entering the church," said Rosa, "did she not? And my mother, how she has paid for everything. Won't you come with us and won't you vouch for me that I am who I will say I am?"

"Yes, your sister paid for what she did," said the old man. "And now it seems that innocent people would pay for it, and so I've come. I should have suspected your little plot even if Meir had not confessed it to me, and why I still love Meir after his having been fool enough to love your mother, I can't say."

He suddenly turned to her as she knelt there. It was as if he were struggling to see her.

"Having no sons, I love him," he said. "I once thought my daughter and my granddaughters the greatest treasure I could possess."

"You will go along with what we mean to do," said Rosa, "for Meir's sake then and the sake of all the others here. It is agreed?"

"They know that Lea has a twin sister," he said coldly. "Too many people in the Jewry knew it for it to remain secret. You take a great risk. I wish you had left it to us to buy our way free of this."

"I don't mean to contradict the fact of us being twins," Rosa answered. "Only to claim that Rosa is waiting for me in Paris, which in its own way is true."

"You disgust me," he said under his breath. "I wish I had

never set eyes on you as a babe in your mother's arms. We're persecuted. Men and women die for their faith. But you leave your faith for nothing but the pleasure of a man who has no right to call you his daughter. Do what you will and be done with it. I want to leave this place and never speak to you or your mother again. And that I will do as soon as I know the Jews of Norwich are safe."

Godwin approached the old man at this point, and he bowed before him, whispering his name again, Magister Eli, and waited before his chair as if for permission to speak.

"You've taken everything from me," said the old man in a low hard voice as he stared in the direction of Godwin. "What more do you want now? Your brother awaits you at the castle. He dines with the Lord Sherriff and with this zealous Lady Margaret, and he reminds her that we are valuable property. Ah, such power." He turned to the fire. "Would that money had been enough—."

"Then plainly it is not," said Godwin very softly. "Beloved Rabbi, please speak some words to give Rosa courage for what she has to do. If money would have done it, then it would be done, is that not so?"

The old man didn't answer him.

"Don't blame her for my sins," said Godwin. "I was bad enough in my youth to harm others in my recklessness and carelessness. I thought life was like the songs I used to sing when I played my lute. I know now that it isn't. And I've pledged my life to the same Lord that you worship. In His name, and for the sake of Meir and Fluria, please forgive me for all the things I've done."

"Don't preach to me, Br. Godwin!" said the old man with bitter sarcasm. "I'm not one of your addle-brained students in Paris. I will never forgive you for taking Rosa from me. And now that Lea is dead, what is there for me but my loneliness and my misery?"

"Not so," said Godwin. "Surely Fluria and Meir will raise up sons of Israel, and daughters. They're newly married. If Meir can forgive Fluria, how can you not?"

The old man at once flushed with rage.

He turned and pushed Rosa away from him with the very hand that she held and tried to kiss again.

She fell back with a start and Godwin caught her and helped her to her feet.

"I've given one thousand marks of gold to your miserable Black Friars," said the old man looking toward them, his voice now trembling with his anger. "What more can I do but remain quiet? Take the child with you to the castle. Work your blandishments on Lady Margaret, but don't overplay your hand. Lea was meek and sweet by nature. This daughter of yours is a Jezebel. Keep that uppermost in your mind."

I stepped forward. "My Lord Rabbi," I said, "you don't know me, but my name is Toby. I too am a Black Friar, and I will take Rosa and Br. Godwin with me to the castle. The Lord Sherriff knows me and we will make swift work of what we have to do. But please, the cart out back, see that you are ready to go in it, just as soon as the Jews in the castle are safely released."

"No," he said shortly, "that you should leave this town after the little pageant is imperative. But I will remain to make sure the Jews are safe. Now get away from me. I know you're the one who dreamt up this deception. Carry it out."

"Yes, I was," I confessed. "And if anything goes wrong with it, I'm to blame for it. Please, please be ready to leave."

"I might give you the same caution," said the old man. "Your friars are disgusted with you that you went off to Paris to seek 'Lea.' They want to make a saint out of a foolish girl. Mind, if this fails you'll suffer with the rest of us. You'll suffer as much for what you're attempting here."

"No," Godwin said. "No one will be harmed here, especially not one so devoted to helping us. Come, Toby, we have to go up to the castle now. There's no time for me to speak to my brother alone. Rosa, are you ready for what we must do? Remember, you're ill from your journey. You weren't up to this long ordeal, and speak only when Lady Margaret speaks to you, and keep in mind your sister's quiet ways."

"Will you give me your blessing, Grandfather?" Rosa pressed. I wished she hadn't. "If not that, will you give me your prayers?"

"I'll give you nothing," he said. "I am here for others who would give up their lives rather than do what you did."

He turned his shoulder against her. He looked as sincere and miserable in his rejection of her as any man could.

I couldn't fully grasp it, because she appeared so fragile and gentle to me. She had her fiery purpose, yes, but she was still a girl of fourteen, and a great challenge lay before her. I wondered now if I had proposed the right thing. I wondered if I hadn't made a terrible blunder.

"Very well, then," I said. I looked at Godwin. He put his arm gently around Rosa. "Let's go."

A heavy knock on the door startled all of us.

I could hear the voice of the Sherriff announcing his presence, and that of the Earl. Suddenly there were shouts from outside, and the sound of people beating on the walls.

CHAPTER FIFTEEN

Judgment

THERE WAS NOTHING TO BE DONE BUT TO OPEN THE door, and at once we saw the Sherriff still on his mount, surrounded by soldiers, and a man who could be none other than the Earl, on foot beside his mount, and with what appeared to be his own guard of several mounted men.

Godwin went directly into his brother's arms, and holding his brother's face in his hand spoke to him intently under his breath.

The Sherriff waited on this.

A crowd began to gather of rather rough-looking individuals, some with clubs in their hands, and the Sherriff immediately ordered his men to drive them back in a harsh voice.

Two of the Dominicans were there and several of the white-robed cathedral priests. And it seemed the crowd was gaining size by the moment.

A gasp went up from the whole assemblage as Rosa stepped out of the house and threw back the hood on her mantle.

Her grandfather had also come out, and so had the stocky Jewish man, whose name I never learned. He stood close to Rosa as if to guard her and so did I.

Conversations broke out everywhere, and I could hear the name "Lea" repeated over and over.

Then one of the Dominicans, a young man, said in an iron voice, "Is it Lea, or is it her sister, Rosa?"

The Sherriff, obviously feeling that he had waited as long as he could, said:

"My Lord," to the Earl, "we should go up now to the castle and settle this matter. The Bishop is waiting for us in the great hall."

A groan of disappointment rose from the crowd. But at once the Earl kissed Rosa on both cheeks, and demanding one of his soldiers dismount, placed her on the horse, and proceeded to lead the gathering towards the castle.

Godwin and I remained close throughout the long walk to the castle mound and then up the winding road until we all passed through the archway and into the castle courtyard.

As the men dismounted, I gained the Earl's attention by tugging on his sleeve.

"Have one of your men go for the cart that's behind Meir's house. It's wise to have it ready here at the gates when Meir and Fluria are released."

He nodded to this, motioned for one of his soldiers, and sent the man out on the errand.

"You can be sure," the Earl said to me, "they will travel out of here with me and my guard surrounding them."

I was relieved at this, as he had some eight soldiers with him, all with beautiful caparisoned mounts, and he himself did not seem in the least anxious or afraid. He received Rosa in his arms, and put his arm around her as we proceeded under the archway and into the great hall of the castle.

I hadn't seen this vast room on my earlier visit, and at once I saw that a court had been convened.

At the elevated table that commanded the room stood the

Bishop and on either side of him the cathedral priests and more of the Dominicans including Fr. Antoine. I saw Fr. Jerome of the cathedral was there, and he looked miserable over the proceedings.

More gasps of amazement went up as Rosa was led forward to face the Bishop to whom she bowed humbly as did everyone present, including the Earl.

The Bishop, a younger man than I might have expected, and fully dressed in his miter and taffeta robes, at once gave the order for Meir and Fluria, and the Jew, Isaac, and his family, to be brought down at once from their rooms in the tower.

"All the Jews are to be brought down," he finally said.

Many of the rougher men were now inside, as well as some women and children. And tougher men who hadn't been allowed admittance were making their voices heard, until the Bishop ordered one of his men to go silence them.

That's when I realized that a row of armed guards behind the Bishop were obviously his own soldiers.

I was shaking and I did my best to conceal it.

Out of one of the anterooms came Lady Margaret, obviously dressed for the occasion in impressive silks, and, with her, Little Eleanor, who was crying.

In fact, Lady Margaret was near to tears herself.

And when Rosa now threw back her hood and bowed to the Bishop, voices rose all around us.

"Silence," the Bishop declared.

I was terrified. I had never seen anything quite as impressive as this court, with so many assembled, and I could only hope and pray that the various contingents of soldiers might keep order.

The Bishop was clearly angry.

Rosa stood before him with Godwin to one side and Earl Nigel to the other.

"You see now, My Lord," said Earl Nigel, "that the child is hale and hearty and has returned, with great difficulty given her recent illness, to make her presence known to you."

The Bishop sat down, in his great backed chair, but he was the only one to do so.

We were pressed forward by the increasing crowd as many worked their way into the audience.

Lady Margaret and Nell stared at the figure of Rosa. And then Rosa dissolved into tears and laid her head on Godwin's shoulder.

Lady Margaret drew closer and then gently took the shoulder of the girl, and she said,

"Are you indeed the child I so tenderly loved? Or are you her twin sister?"

"My lady," said Rosa, "I've come back, leaving my twin sister in Paris, only to prove to you that I am alive." She began to sob. "I am so distressed that my defection has caused misery to my mother and father. Can't you understand why I left in the quiet of the night? I was bound to join my sister, not only in Paris, but in her Christian faith, and would not bring disgrace openly upon my father and mother."

This she said in the most deeply affecting manner, and it silenced Lady Margaret entirely.

"Then you do solemnly swear," declared the Bishop, his voice ringing out, "that you are the child whom these people knew, and not the twin of that child, come here to mask the fact of your sister's murder?"

A great murmur went up from those assembled.

"My Lord Bishop," said the Earl, "do I not know the two children who are under my guardianship? This is Lea, and she is ill once more for having made this difficult journey."

But suddenly everyone was distracted by the appearance of the Jews who'd been kept prisoner. Meir and Fluria came first into the room, and after them Isaac, the physician, and the several other Jews, easily recognized for their badges but nothing else, who clustered together.

Rosa at once broke from the Earl and ran to her mother. She embraced her tearfully and said loud enough to hear:

"I have caused you disgrace and unspeakable pain and I'm sorry for it. My sister and I have nothing but love for you, no matter that we've been baptized into the Christian faith, and how can you and Meir forgive me?"

She didn't wait for an answer, but embraced Meir, who kissed her in return, though he was pale with fear and clearly repelled by these proceedings.

Lady Margaret now stared at Rosa with the hardest eye and, turning to her daughter, whispered something to her.

At once the young girl went up to Rosa, even as Rosa hung on her mother's shoulder, and said,

"But Lea, why did you send no message to us that you were to be baptized?"

"How could I?" asked Rosa through a continuing flood of tears. "What could I tell you? Surely you understand the heartbreak I brought to these my beloved parents by my decision? What could they do but send for the Earl's soldiers to take me to Paris, which they did, and there I joined my sister. But I would not have had it trumpeted about the Jewry that I had so betrayed my loving parents."

She went on in this same manner, crying so bitterly that the absence of familiar names wasn't noticed, and begging for all those to understand how she felt.

"Had not I seen the beautiful Christmas pageant," she said suddenly, treading a little close to danger when she did so, "I would not have understood why my sister, Rosa, converted. But I did see it, and I did come to understand, and as soon as I was well enough, I went to join her. Do you think

I knew that anyone would accuse my mother and father of harming me?"

The young girl was now on the defensive.

"We thought you were dead, you must believe that," she said.

But before she could go on, Rosa demanded to know, "How could you have doubted the goodness of my mother and father? You who have been in our house, how could you think they would do harm to me?"

Lady Margaret and the young girl were both now shaking their heads, murmuring that they only did what they thought was right and mustn't be blamed for it.

So far so good. But Fr. Antoine now let his voice be heard loud enough to echo off the walls.

"This is a very grand show," he said, "but as we know full well, Fluria; daughter of Eli, who has come here this day, had twins, and twins have not come here together to exonerate her. How do we know that you are not Lea but in fact Rosa?"

Voices everywhere rose to emphasize his question.

Rosa didn't hesitate.

"Father," she said to the priest, "would my sister, a baptized Christian, come here to defend my parents if the life of her sister had been taken by them? Surely you must believe me. I am Lea. And I want only to return to my sister in Paris, along with my guardian, Earl Nigel."

"But how are we to know?" demanded the Bishop. "Were these twins not identical?" He motioned to Rosa to come closer.

The hall was filled with angry and contrary voices.

But nothing alarmed me as much as the way that Lady Margaret had stepped forward and was staring with narrow eyes at Rosa.

Rosa again told the Bishop that she would swear on the

Bible that she was Lea. And now she wished that her sister had come, but she had never thought that her friends here would not believe her.

Lady Margaret suddenly cried out, "No! This is not the same child. This is her double, but with a different heart and a different spirit."

I thought the crowd would riot. Angry cries came from all sides. The Bishop at once demanded, "Silence."

"Bring the Bible for this child to swear," said the Bishop, "and bring the sacred book of the Jews for the mother to swear that this is her daughter Lea."

At once, there were panicked glances exchanged between Rosa and her mother. And Rosa began to cry again and ran into her mother's arms. As for Fluria, she seemed exhausted from her imprisonment and weak and incapable of saying or doing anything.

The books were produced, though what the "sacred book of the Jews" was I couldn't have said.

And Meir and Fluria murmured the lies required of them.

As for Rosa, she took the huge leather-bound volume of the Bible, and immediately laid her hand on it. "I swear to you," she said, her voice muted and breaking with emotion, "by all I believe as a Christian, that I am Lea, born to Fluria, and the ward of Earl Nigel, come here to clear the name of my mother. And I want only to be allowed to leave this place, knowing that my Jewish parents are safe, and will pay no penalty for my defection."

"No," cried Lady Margaret. "Lea never spoke with such ease as that, never in her life. She was a mute compared to this one. I tell you, this child is deceiving us. She is party to the murder of her sister."

At this the Earl lost his temper. He shouted louder than anyone present except the Bishop.

"How dare you contradict my word?" he demanded. He glared at the Bishop. "And you, how dare you challenge me when I tell you that I am Christian guardian to both these girls who are being educated by my brother?"

Godwin stepped forward. "My Lord Bishop, please, do not let this go on any further. Restore these good Jews to their homes. Can you not imagine the pain of these parents who have seen their daughters take up the Christian faith? Much as I am honored to be their teacher, and to love them with a true Christian love, I cannot but feel compassion for the parents they've left behind."

A moment of silence fell except for the feverish murmurings of the crowd that seemed to move hither and thither through those assembled as if a game of whispering were being played.

It seemed everything hung now on Lady Margaret and what she might say.

But just as she was about to protest, throwing her finger out at Rosa, old Eli, Fluria's father, stepped forward and cried,

"I demand to be heard."

I thought Godwin would perish with apprehension. And Fluria collapsed on the breast of Meir.

But the old man commanded the silence of all. Indeed, he stepped up, with Rosa's guidance, until he stood facing Lady Margaret blindly with Rosa between them.

"Lady Margaret, latent friend of my daughter Fluria and her good husband, Meir, how dare you challenge a grandfather's wits and reason? This is my grandchild, and I would know her no matter how many doubles of her roamed this world. Do I want to embrace an apostate child? No, never, but she is Lea, and I would know her were there a thousand Rosas to fill this room and say otherwise. I know her voice. I know her as no one with sight could possibly know her. Are you to

challenge my gray hairs, my wisdom, my honesty, my honor!"
He at once reached out for Rosa, who went into his arms. He
crushed Rosa to his shoulder. "Lea," he whispered. "Lea, my
own."

"But I only wanted—," began Lady Margaret.

"Silence, I say," said Eli with an immense deep voice, as if
he wanted everyone in the great room to hear it. "This is Lea. I,
who have ruled the synagogues of the Jews all my life, avow it.
I avow it. Yes, these daughters are apostates and must eventu-
ally be excommunicated from their fellow Jews and this is bitter, bitter to me, but even more bitter is the obstinacy of a
Christian woman who is the very cause of this child's defection. Were it not for you she would never have left her pious
parents!"

"I only did what—."

"You tore at the heart of a home and hearth," he declared.
"And now you deny her when she comes all this way to save her
mother? You are heartless, My Lady. And your daughter, what
part does she have in this? I defy you to prove that this is not
the girl you knew. I defy you to put forth one shred of evidence
that this child is not Lea, daughter of Fluria!"

The crowd roared with applause. All around people were
murmuring, "The old Jew tells the truth," and "Yes, how can
they prove it?" and "He knows her by her voice," and a hundred other variations of the same theme.

Lady Margaret burst into a flood of tears. But they were
silent compared to the tears shed by Rosa.

"I meant no harm to anyone!" wailed Lady Margaret suddenly. She threw up her arms to the Bishop. "I truly thought
the child was dead and thought myself the cause of it."

Rosa turned. "Lady, be comforted, I beg you," she said in a
halting and timid voice.

The crowd went quiet as she went on. And the Bishop

motioned furiously for order as the priests began to quarrel with one another, and Fr. Antoine stood staring in disbelief.

Rosa continued, "Lady Margaret, if it were not for your kindness to me," she said, her voice frail and tender, "I would never have gone to join my sister in her new faith. What you cannot know is that it was her letters to me that laid the ground for my going with you that night to Christmas Mass, but it was you who sealed my conviction. Forgive me, forgive me with all your heart, please, that I did not write to you and tell you of my gratitude. Again, my love for my mother . . . Oh, do you not understand? I beg you."

Lady Margaret could resist no longer. She took Rosa in her arms, and again and again protested how sorry she was that she'd caused such misery.

"My Lord Bishop," declared Eli, turning his blind eyes towards the tribunal. "Will you not let us return to our homes? Fluria and Meir will leave the Jewry after this disturbance, as you are sure to understand, but no one has committed any crime here whatsoever. And we will deal with the apostasy of these children in time as they are yet . . . children."

Lady Margaret and Rosa were now tangled in each other's arms, sobbing, whispering, and Little Eleanor had put her arms around them.

Fluria and Meir stood mute, staring, as did Isaac the physician and the other Jews, his family perhaps, who had been prisoners in the tower.

The Bishop sat down. He threw out his hands in an expression of frustration.

"Very well, then. It is done. You recognize this child as Lea."

Lady Margaret nodded vigorously. "Only tell me," she said to Rosa, "that you forgive me, forgive me for the pain I've brought to your mother."

"I do with all my heart," Rosa said, and she said a great deal more, but the entire room was in motion.

The Bishop declared the proceedings closed. The Dominicans stared hard at all involved. The Earl at once gave his soldiers the order to mount up, and without waiting for any further word from anyone he motioned for Meir and Fluria to come with him.

I stood stock-still, watching. I could see the Dominicans held back, and regarded everyone with a cold eye.

But Meir and Fluria were led from the hall, the old man with them, and now Rosa went out, her arms around Lady Margaret and Little Eleanor, all three of them weeping.

I glanced out through the archway, and saw the entire family, including Magister Eli, mounting into the cart, and Rosa giving one last embrace to Lady Margaret.

The other Jews had begun their march down the hill. The soldiers were on their horses.

It was as if I woke from a dream when Godwin pulled on my arm. "Come now, before anything changes."

I shook my head. "Go," I said. "I'll stay here. If there is any further trouble, I must be here."

He wanted to protest but I reminded him of how urgent it was that he climb into that cart and go.

The Bishop rose from the table and he and the white-robed priests of the cathedral disappeared into one of the anterooms.

The crowd was fragmented, and powerless, and watched as the cart made its way down the hill, flanked on both sides by the Earl's soldiers. As for the Earl he rode behind the cart, with a straight back, and his left elbow out as if his hand were on the hilt of his sword.

I turned around and started out of the yard.

Stragglers eyed me and eyed the Dominicans who came after me.

I began to walk faster and faster down the hill. I could see the Jews walking safely ahead, and the cart was gaining speed. Suddenly the horses began to trot and all the entourage picked up the pace. They would be free of the town in minutes.

I picked up my own pace. I could see the cathedral and some instinct pushed me to go to it. But I could hear the footsteps of men right behind me.

"And where do you think you will go now, Br. Toby!" demanded Fr. Antoine in an angry voice.

I continued to walk though he put a hard hand on my shoulder.

"To the cathedral, to give thanks, where else?"

I walked as fast as I could without running. But suddenly the Dominican friars were on both sides of me, and a good many of the toughs of the town were on either side of them, looking on with curiosity and suspicion.

"You think you will seek sanctuary there!" demanded Fr. Antoine. "I think not."

We were at the foot of the hill, when he pushed me around, and jabbed his finger in my face.

"Just who are you, Br. Toby? You who came here to challenge us, you who brought from Paris a child who may not be the child she claims to be."

"You've heard the decision of the Bishop," I said.

"Yes, and it will stand, and all will be well, but who are you and where do you come from?"

I could see the great facade of the cathedral now and I made my way through the streets towards it.

Suddenly he spun me around, but I pulled loose of him.

"No one has heard of you," said one of the brothers, "no one from our house in Paris, no one from our house in Rome, no one from our house in London, and we have written back and forth enough from here to London and to Rome to know that you are not one of us."

"Not one of us," declared Fr. Antoine, "knows anything of you, traveling scholar!"

I walked on and on, hearing the thunder of their steps behind me, thinking, *I am leading them away from Fluria and Meir as surely as if I were the Pied Piper.*

At last I gained the square before the cathedral, when suddenly two of the priests took hold of me.

"You will not enter that church until you answer us. You're not one of us. Who sent you here to pretend you were! Who sent you to Paris to bring back this girl who claims to be her own sister!"

All around I could see the tough young men and, again, women and children in the crowd, and torches began to appear, to fight the gloom of the late winter afternoon.

I struggled to be free, and this only incited others to lay hold of me. Someone ripped the leather bag from my shoulder. "Let's see what letters of introduction you carry," demanded one of the priests, and then he emptied out the bag and all that fell from it was silver and gold coins rolling everywhere.

The crowd gave a loud roar.

"No answer?" demanded Fr. Antoine. "You admit that you are nothing but an impostor? We have been worried about the wrong impostor all this time? Is that what we are given to know now? You are no Dominican friar!"

I furiously kicked at him, and pushed him back, and I turned around to face the doors of the cathedral. I made a dash for it, when suddenly one of the young men caught me in his grip and slammed me back against the stone wall of the church so that everything went black for me for an instant.

Oh, that it had been forever. But I couldn't wish for that. I opened my eyes to see the priests trying to hold back the furious crowd. Fr. Antoine cried out that this was *their matter* and they would settle it. But the crowd was having none of it.

People were pulling at my mantle, at last tearing it off. Someone else yanked my right arm and I felt a riot of pain move through my shoulder. Once again I was slammed against the wall.

In flickers, I saw the crowd as if the light of consciousness in me were going on and off, on and off, and slowly a dreadful sight materialized.

The priests had all been pushed to the rear. Only the tough young men of the town and the rougher women now surrounded me. "Not a priest, not a friar, not a brother, impostor!" came the cries.

And as they struck me and kicked me and tore at my robes, it seemed that all through the shifting mass, I made out other figures. These figures were all known to me. These figures were the men I'd murdered.

And there very near me, wrapped in silence, as though he was not part of the melee at all, but invisible to the ruffians who worked their fury on me, stood the man I'd lately killed at the Mission Inn, and right beside him the young blond-haired girl I'd shot so many long years ago in Alonso's brothel. All looked on, and in their faces I saw not judgment, not glee, but only something faintly sad and wondering.

Someone had ahold of my head. They were beating my head against the stones, and I could feel the blood running down my neck and down my back. For a moment I saw nothing.

I thought in the strangest most detached way of my question to Malchiah, which he had never answered. "Could I die in this time? Was that possible?" But I didn't call out for him now.

As I went down in a torrent of blows, as I felt the leather shoes kicking at my ribs and at my stomach, as the breath went out of me, as the sight left my eyes, as the pain shot through my head and limbs, I said only one prayer.

Dear Lord, forgive me that I ever separated myself from You.

CHAPTER SIXTEEN

World Enough and Time

DREAMING. HEARING THAT SINGING AGAIN THAT SOUNDED like the reverberation of a gong. But it was slipping away as I came to myself. The stars were slipping away, and the vast dark sky was fading.

I slowly opened my eyes.

No pain anywhere.

I was lying in the half tester bed at the Mission Inn. All the familiar furnishings of the suite were around me.

For a long moment I stared up at the checkered silk tester, and I realized, made myself realize, that I was back, in my own time, and there was no pain anywhere in my body.

Slowly I sat up.

"Malchiah?" I called out.

No answer.

"Malchiah, where are you?"

Silence.

I felt something in me was about to break loose and I was terrified of it. I whispered his name once more but it didn't surprise me that there was no answer.

One thing I did know, however. I knew that Meir, Fluria, Eli, Rosa, Godwin, and the Earl had all safely left Norwich. I knew it. Somewhere deep inside my clouded mind was a vision of that cart, surrounded by soldiers, safely away, on the road to London.

That seemed as real as anything in this room, and this room seemed completely real, and reliably solid.

I looked down at myself. I was a bit of a wrinkled mess.

But I was wearing one of my own suits, a khaki jacket and pants with a khaki vest, and a white shirt open at the neck. Just usual clothes for me.

I reached into my pocket and discovered I had the identification that I used when I came here, as myself. Not Toby O'Dare, of course, but the name I used for walking around without a disguise.

I shoved the driver's license back in my pocket and I climbed off the bed and went into the bathroom and stared into the mirror. No bruises, no marks.

But I think I actually looked at my own face for the first time in years. I saw Toby O'Dare, aged twenty-eight, staring back at me.

Why did I think there would be any bruises and marks?

The fact was, I couldn't believe I was still alive, couldn't believe I'd survived what had surely seemed to be the death I'd deserved outside the cathedral.

And if this world had not seemed as vivid as that world, I would have thought I was dreaming.

I walked around the room in a daze. I saw my usual leather bag there, and realized how much it resembled the bag I'd been toting all through the thirteenth century. My computer was there, too, the laptop I used only for research.

How did these things get here? How did I get here? The computer, a Macintosh laptop, was open and plugged in, just the way I might have left it after using it.

For the first time, it occurred to me that everything that had happened was a dream, was something that I'd imagined. Only trouble was I could never have imagined it. I could never have imagined Fluria or Godwin, or the old man, Eli, and the way he had turned the trial at the pivotal moment.

I opened the door and I went out onto the tiled veranda. The sky was clear blue and the sun was warm on my skin, and after the muddy snowy skies I'd known for the last few weeks, it felt absolutely caressing.

I sat down at the iron table, and I felt the breeze passing over me, keeping the heat of the sun from building up on me—that old familiar coolness that always seems at work in the air of southern California.

I put my elbows on the table and bowed my head, resting it on my hands. And I cried. I cried so hard that I was sobbing.

The pain I felt was so awful that I couldn't describe it even to myself.

I knew people were passing me, and I didn't care what they saw or what they felt. At one point, a woman came up to me and put her hand on my shoulder.

"Can I do anything?" she whispered.

"No," I said. "Nobody can. It's all over."

I thanked her, and took her hand in mine and told her she was kind. She smiled and nodded and she went on with her party of tourists. They disappeared down the steps of the rotunda.

I checked my pocket, found a valet ticket for my car, and I went downstairs, out through the lobby, and under the campanario, and gave the ticket to the valet along with a twenty-dollar bill and stood there, dazed, looking at everything as if I'd never seen it before—the campanario with its many bells, the zinnias blooming along the garden path, and those great slender palms rising upwards as though to point to the flawless blue sky.

The valet came up to me.

"You okay, sir?" he asked.

I wiped at my nose. I realized I was still crying. I pulled a linen handkerchief out of my pocket and blew my nose.

"Yeah, I'm okay," I said. "I just lost a whole bunch of close friends," I said. "But I didn't deserve to have them."

He didn't know what to say, and I didn't blame him.

I climbed behind the wheel of the car and drove as fast as it was safe to drive to San Juan Capistrano.

All that had happened was passing through my mind like a great ribbon, and I noticed nothing of the hills or the highway, or the signs. I was in the past in my heart, while I guided the car by instinct in the present.

When I entered the Mission grounds, I looked around hopelessly, and once again, I whispered, "Malchiah."

There was no answer, and no one who even faintly resembled him. Just the usual families making their way among the beds of flowers.

I went straight to the Serra Chapel.

Thankfully, there weren't very many people in it, and the few that were there were praying.

I walked up the aisle, staring at the tabernacle with the sanctuary light on the left, and I wanted with all my heart to lie down on the floor of the chapel with my arms out and pray, but I knew that others would come up to me if I did that.

It was all I could do to kneel in the first pew, and say again the prayer I'd said when the mob attacked me.

"Lord God," I prayed. "I don't know whether it was a dream or it was real. I only know I'm Yours now. I never want to be anything else but Yours."

I sat back in the pew finally and cried quietly for what must have been an hour. I didn't make enough noise to disturb people. And when anyone did come close, I looked down and closed my eyes, and they just moved on past to do their praying or light their candles.

I looked at the tabernacle and I emptied my mind, and many thoughts came to me. The most crushing thought was that I was alone. All those I'd known and loved with all my heart were utterly removed from me.

I would never see Godwin and Rosa again. I would never see Fluria or Meir again. I knew this.

And I knew that never, never in my life would I ever see the only people I'd ever really known and loved. They were gone from me; we were separated by centuries, and there was nothing I could do about it, and the more I thought of it all the more I wondered if I'd ever see Malchiah again.

I don't know how long I stayed there.

At one point, I knew it was getting near evening.

I had told the Lord over and over how sorry I was for every evil thing I'd ever done, and whether the angels had done this thing with illusions, to show me the error of my ways, or whether I had really been in Norwich and Paris, whether I had really been there or not, I didn't deserve the mercy that had been shown me.

Finally, I went out, and drove back to the Mission Inn.

It was dark by that time, as it was springtime, and the darkness came early. I let myself into the Amistad Suite and I went to work on the computer.

It wasn't difficult at all to find pictures of Norwich, pictures of the castle and the cathedral, but pictures of the castle were radically different from the old Norman place that I had seen. As for the cathedral, it had been greatly expanded since my visit.

I keyed in "Jews of Norwich," and read with a vague sense of dread the whole horrible story of the martyrdom of Little St. William.

Suddenly, with my hands trembling, I keyed in Meir of

Norwich. To my utter amazement there popped up more than one article on him. Meir, the poet of Norwich, was a real person.

I sat back, simply overcome. And for a long time I couldn't do anything. Then I read the brief articles to the effect that this man was known only by a manuscript of poems in Hebrew in which he had identified himself, a manuscript that was in the Vatican Museum.

After that I keyed in many different names, but came up essentially with nothing I could relate to what had happened. No story of any massacre over another child.

But the sad history of the Jews in England in the Middle Ages soon came to an abrupt finish in 1290 when all Jews were expelled from the island.

I sat back.

I had done enough research, and what I had come to know was that Little St. William had the distinction of being the first case of a ritual murder attributed to Jews, a charge that would reoccur over and over again throughout the Middle Ages and after. And England was the first country to expel the Jews entirely. There had been expulsions from cities and territories before, but England was the first country.

I knew the rest. The Jews had been welcomed back centuries later by Oliver Cromwell because Oliver Cromwell thought the world was about to end and the conversion of the Jews had to play a role in it.

I got up from the computer with my eyes hurting and I fell on the bed and slept for hours.

Sometime early in the morning, I woke up. It was three a.m. by the bedside clock. That meant it was six a.m. in New York, and The Right Man would be at his desk.

I opened my cell phone, observed it was a prepaid phone, such as I always used, and punched in his number.

As soon as I heard his voice, I said,

"Look, I'm never going to kill again. I'm never going to harm anyone if I can possibly help it. I'm not your needle sniper now. It's finished."

"I want you to come here, Son," he said.

"Why, so you can kill me?"

"Lucky, how could you think something like that?" he said. He sounded perfectly sincere and a little hurt. "Son, I'm worried about what you might do to yourself. I've always been worried about that."

"Well, you don't have to worry about that anymore," I said. "I have something to do now."

"What's that?"

"Write a book about something that happened to me. Oh, don't worry, it has nothing to do with you or anything you've ever asked me to do. All that will remain secret as it always has. You might say I'm taking the advice of Hamlet's father. I'm leaving you to Heaven."

"Lucky, you're not right in your head."

"Yes, I am," I said.

"Son, how many times have I tried to tell you that you were working for The Good Guys all along? Do I have to spell it out? You've been working for your country."

"Doesn't change a thing," I said. "I wish you luck. And speaking of luck, I want to tell you my real name. It's Toby O'Dare and I was born in New Orleans."

"What's happened to you, Son?"

"Did you know that was my name?"

"No. We were never able to trace you back before your New York friends. You don't have to be telling me these things. I won't pass them on. This is an organization you can quit, Son. You can walk away. I just want to know that you know where you're going."

I laughed.

For the first time since my return, I laughed.

"I love you, Son," he said.

"Yeah, I know, Boss. And in a way, I love you. That's the mystery of it. But I'm no good for what you want now. I'm going to do something worthwhile with my life, if it's only the writing of a book."

"Will you call me from time to time?"

"I don't think so, but you can always keep your eye on the bookstores, Boss. Who knows? Maybe you'll find my name on one of the covers someday. I gotta go now. I want to say . . . well, it wasn't your fault what I became. It was all my doing. In a way, you saved me, Boss. Somebody much worse might have crossed my path, and that could have been worse than what actually happened. Good luck, Boss."

I closed the phone before he could say anything.

For the next two weeks I lived at the Mission Inn. I typed on my laptop the entire story of what had happened.

I wrote about Malchiah's coming to me, and I wrote the version of my life that he had told me.

I wrote all about what I'd done, as best I could remember it. It hurt so bad to describe Fluria and Godwin that I could hardly endure it, but writing seemed the only thing that I could do and so I continued.

Finally, I included the notes on the true things I knew about the Jews of Norwich, the books that dealt with them, and that tantalizing fact that Meir, the poet of Norwich, had really existed.

Lastly, I wrote the title of the book, and that was *Angel Time*.

It was four in the morning when I finally finished.

I went out on the veranda, found it completely dark and deserted, and sat at the iron table, merely thinking, waiting for the sky to get light, for the birds to start their inevitable singing.

I could have cried again, but it seemed for a moment I had no more tears.

What was real to me was this: I didn't know whether or not it had all happened. I didn't know whether it was a dream I'd made up, or someone else had made up to surround me. I only knew that I was completely altered and that I would do anything, anything, to see Malchiah again, to hear his voice, to just look into his eyes. To just know that it had all been real, or to lose the feeling that it had been undeniably real, which was driving me crazy.

I was on the verge of another thought, but I'll never remember what it was. I just started to pray. I prayed to God again to forgive me for all I'd done. I thought of the figures I'd seen in the crowd and I made a deep heartfelt Act of Contrition for every single one of them. That I could remember them all, even the men I'd first murdered so long ago, amazed me.

Then I prayed out loud:

"Malchiah, don't leave me. Come back, if it's just to give me some guidance as to what I should do now. I know I don't deserve for you to come back, any more than I deserved for you to come the first time. But I'm praying now: don't leave me. Angel of God, my guardian dear, I need you."

There was no one to hear me on the still, dark veranda. There was only the faint morning breeze, and the last sprinkling of stars in the misty sky above me.

"I'm longing for all those people I left," I went on talking to him, though he wasn't there. "I'm longing for the love I felt from you, and the love I felt for all of them, and the happiness, the sheer happiness I felt when I knelt in Notre Dame and thanked Heaven for what was given me. Malchiah, if it was real, or if it wasn't real, come back to me."

I closed my eyes. I listened for the songs of the Seraphim. I tried to imagine them before the throne of God, to see that glorious blaze of light, and hear that glorious unending song of praise.

Maybe in the love I had felt for those people in that distant time I had heard something of that music. Maybe I'd heard it when Meir and Fluria and all the family had left Norwich safely.

It was a long time before I opened my eyes.

The daylight had come, and all the colors of the veranda were visible. I was staring at the purple geraniums that surrounded the orange trees in the Tuscan pots, and thinking how gloriously beautiful they were, when I realized that Malchiah was sitting at the table opposite me.

He was smiling at me. He looked exactly as he had the first time I ever saw him. Delicate build, soft mussed black hair, and blue eyes. He sat with his legs to one side, leaning on his elbow, merely looking at me, as if he'd been doing that for a long time.

I began to shake all over. I put my hands up, as if in prayer, to cover the gasp coming out of my mouth, and I whispered in a tremulous voice,

"Thank Heaven."

He laughed softly. "You did a marvelous job of it," he said.

I dissolved into tears. I cried the way I had cried when I first came back.

A quote from Dickens came to my mind, and I said it out loud, because I'd long ago memorized it:

"Heaven knows we need never be ashamed of our tears, for they are rain upon the blinding dust of earth, overlying our hard hearts."

He smiled at this, and he nodded.

"If I were human, I would cry too," he whispered. "That's more or less a quote from Shakespeare."

"Why are you here? Why did you come back?"

"Why do you think?" he asked. "We have another assignment and not much time to lose, but there's something you have to do before we start, and you should do it immediately. I've been waiting all these days for you to do it. But you've been writing a story you had to write, and what you have to do now isn't clear to you."

"What can it possibly be? Let me do it, and let us be gone on our next assignment!" I was too excited to even remain in the chair, but I did, staring eagerly at him.

"Did you learn nothing practical from Godwin's treatment of Fluria?" he asked.

"I don't know what you mean."

"Call your old girlfriend in New Orleans, Toby O'Dare. You have a ten-year-old son. And he needs to hear from his father."

The End.
1:40 p.m.
July 21, 2008

Author's Note

THIS BOOK IS A WORK OF FICTION. HOWEVER, REAL events and real persons inspired some of the events and persons in the novel.

Meir of Norwich was a real person, and a manuscript of his poems in Hebrew is in the Vatican Museum. But little or nothing is known about this real person, except that he did live in Norwich and he did leave us a manuscript of poems. He is described by V. D. Lipman in *The Jews of Medieval Norwich,* published by the Jewish Historical Society of London, and this book also includes Meir's poems in their original Hebrew. As far as I know, there is no translation of Meir's work into English.

Let me emphasize again that my version of Meir in this novel is fictional, and it is meant to be a tribute to a person about whom nothing is known.

Names in the novel, particularly Meir, Fluria, Lea, and Rosa, were names that were used by Jews in Norwich and are taken from V. D. Lipman's book and other source materials. Again my characters are fictional. There definitely was an Isaac in Norwich who was a great Jewish physician, but my portrayal of this man is fictional.

Norwich at this time did have a real sherriff who can, no doubt, be historically identified, and also a bishop, but I did not want to use their names or involve any details concerning them, as they are fictional characters in a fictional tale.

Little St. William of Norwich did indeed exist, and the tragic story of Jews accused of killing him is told in Lipman's book, and also by Cecil Roth in *A History of the Jews in England,* published by the Clarendon Press. The same holds true for Little St. Hugh of Lincoln, and for the riot in Oxford by the students against the Jews. Roth and Lipman were immense resources for me.

Many other books were of invaluable help to me in writing this book, including *The Jews of Medieval Western Christendom, 1000–1500,* by Robert Chazan, published by the Cambridge University Press, and *The Jew in the Medieval World: A Source Book, 315–1791* by Jacob Rader Marcus, published by the Hebrew Union College Press in Cincinnati. Two other valuable resources were *Jewish Life in the Middle Ages* by Israel Abrahams, published by the Jewish Publication Society of America, and *Medieval Jewish Civilization: An Encyclopedia* edited by Norman Roth and published by Routledge. I consulted many other books which are too numerous to mention here.

Readers interested in the Middle Ages have abundant resources, including books on everyday life in the Middle Ages, and even large picture books on medieval life intended for young people but illuminating for everyone. There are numerous books on medieval universities, cities, cathedrals, and the like.

I am especially grateful to the Jewish Publication Society of America for its many publications on Jewish history and life.

In this book, I have been inspired by Lew Wallace, the author of *Ben-Hur,* who created a great and seminal classic which both Christians and Jews can enjoy. It is my hope that this book will appeal equally to Christians and Jews, and to readers of all faiths, or no faith at all. I have endeavored to paint an accurate picture of the complex interaction between Jews and Christians even during times of danger and persecution for the Jews.

As one scholar has observed, one cannot think of the Jews of the Middle Ages only in terms of their suffering. Jewish scholarship included many great thinkers and writers, such as Maimonides and Rashi, who are mentioned more than once in this novel. Jewish communication, community organization, and other aspects of Jewish life are all richly documented today by many scholars, and information is still being vigorously collected as to Jewish life during earlier times.

On the subject of angels and their role in human affairs, I would like to refer the reader to the book mentioned in the novel—*The Angels* by Fr. Pascal Parente, published by TAN Books and Publishers, Inc., which has become a little bible for me in this work. Also of great interest is Peter Kreeft's *Angels (and Demons),* published by Ignatius Press. A great and venerable source of information on angels and Christian beliefs about them is St. Thomas Aquinas's *Summa Theologica.*

I want to thank Wikipedia, the online encyclopedia, for quick reference to Norwich, Norwich Castle, Norwich Cathedral, Maimonides, Rashi, and St. Thomas. Other Internet sites were also helpful, and again they are too numerous to mention here.

I should also thank the Mission Inn and the Mission of San Juan Capistrano for being real places, which obviously and greatly inspired me in this book.

This novel was written to provide enjoyment, but if it inspires further research on the part of readers, I hope these notes will be of help.

Lastly, let me include my fervent prayer:

Angel of God, my guardian dear,
to whom God's love commits me here,
always and forever, I thank you.

Anne Rice

*Bless the LORD, ye his angels, that excel in strength, that
do his commandments, hearkening unto the voice of his
word.*

*Bless ye the LORD, all ye his hosts; ye ministers of his,
that do his pleasure.*

*Bless the LORD, all his works in all places of his
dominion: bless the LORD, O my soul.*

—Psalm 103
King James Version

A NOTE ON THE TYPE

THIS BOOK was set in Adobe Garamond. Designed for
the Adobe Corporation by Robert Slimbach, the fonts are
based on types first cut by Claude Garamond (c. 1480–1561).
Garamond was a pupil of Geoffroy Tory and is believed to
have followed the Venetian models, although he introduced
a number of important differences, and it is to him that we
owe the letter we now know as "old style." He gave to his
letters a certain elegance and feeling of movement that won
their creator an immediate reputation and the patronage of
Francis I of France.

Composed by Creative Graphics,
Allentown, Pennsylvania
Printed and bound by R. R. Donnelley,
Harrisonburg, Virginia
Designed by Virginia Tan